THE FAIREST OF THEM ALL

THE FAIREST OF THEM ALL

SNOW WHITE AND 21 TALES OF MOTHERS AND DAUGHTERS

MARIA TATAR

The Belknap Press of
Harvard University Press
Cambridge, Massachusetts
London, England
2020

Printed in the United States of America

First printing

Library of Congress Cataloging-in-Publication Data

Names: Tatar, Maria, 1945- author.
Title: The fairest of them all : Snow White and 21 tales of mothers and daughters / Maria Tatar.
Description: Cambridge, Massachusetts : The Belknap Press of Harvard University Press, 2020. | Includes bibliographical references.
Identifiers: LCCN 2019041841 | ISBN 9780674238602 (hardcover)
Subjects: LCSH: Snow White (Tale) | Mothers and daughters in literature. | Mothers and daughters—Fiction. | LCGFT: Fairy tales.
Classification: LCC GR75.S6 T37 2020 | DDC 398.2 [Fic]—dc23
LC record available at https://lccn.loc.gov/2019041841

FOR BOOKER, ISABEL, AND ROXY

CONTENTS

PREFACE

There is a moment in the biopic *Tolkien* (2019) when a professor of philology at Oxford explains how words work their magic. "A child points, and he's taught a word." Over time, that word—"oak," in this case—comes to be invested with meaning. The boy stands beneath its branches for shelter; he sleeps under it; he passes it on his way to war; a spirit may have dwelt in its trunk; its wood may have been used to build boats; its leaves are carved on monuments. "All this," we are told, "the general and the specific, the national and the personal, all this, he knows and feels and summons somehow, however faintly." Words live, breathe, and resonate.

The same holds true for fairy tales, which work their magic as they evolve, layer upon layer, giving us both story and history. The narrative we know by the name of "Snow White" has a long, complex, stratified history, and this volume is something of an archaeological dig, unearthing different layers from our own culture and from places around the world, each forming part of the history for what we tell today.

"The fairest of them all"—that phrase takes us back to ancient times, when Aphrodite, Hera, and Athena all lost their dignity competing for a golden apple inscribed with the words, "For the most beautiful." It was the Judgment of Paris, his decision to award the fruit to Aphrodite in exchange for the most beautiful mortal that led, eventually, to the Trojan War. A conflict pitting Greek men against Trojans, in other words, is attributed to the petty jealousies that divide women. All the more reason, I thought, as I contemplated writing a book about "the fairest," to take a closer look at stories about mother-daughter conflict fueled by the need to win beauty contests judged by men.

Few languages have a word like "fair," which can shade into so many meanings ranging from beautiful to pale-skinned to equitable and just. Stories about beautiful girls and their mothers have done cultural work in all of the different linguistic registers evoked by "fairest," but today we risk losing those narratives because of the cultural associations of fairness with "skin white as snow." But it was not always so. Snow White can be found in nearly every place that stories are told, and she rarely has white skin. Her one constant attribute is her beauty, and Disney's "skin white as snow" is an exception in the fairy-tale universe rather than the rule.

"European standards of beauty are something that plague the entire world: The idea that darker skin is not beautiful, that light skin is the key to success and love," Lupita Nyong'o once declared in an interview. Today we have an opportunity to consider "the fairest of them all" in other ways, to make stories about beautiful girls new by thinking more and thinking harder about what is at stake in fairness and how it takes us to a complex and challenging site where beauty, race, and social justice might intersect. How do we take symbolic stories from times past and use them as our ancestors did: to make sense of the world, to work out cultural contradictions and social dilemmas, and to make it easier to talk about the vulnerabilities and challenges we face as humans?

This volume came about through conversations and debates about a story that many of my interlocutors wanted to banish while others could not stop talking about it. My students at Harvard University, as is so often the case, enabled me to identify the fault lines in the stories we read together and to imagine how they could become something new and relevant. Colleagues at Harvard's Society of Fellows, the Department of Germanic Languages and Literatures, and the Program in Folklore and Mythology provided countless tips, fresh angles, and new examples of old stories, challenging me to think in global rather than merely local terms.

At Harvard University Press, Sharmila Sen made me feel right at home with her expansive vision of story worlds and their cultural value. With a passion for everything from the creative genius of storytellers to the devilish details of the production process, she guided the book through its many stages. I am also grateful to Kathleen Drummy, Heather Hughes, and Stephanie Vyce at Harvard University Press for their valuable assistance in the final phases of the project. Doris Sperber, with her usual good cheer and lightning speed, retrieved books from the Harvard College Library, tracked down sources, and battled the gremlins that occasionally crept into drafts and the final manuscript.

Commerce uses the term "friends and family" so loosely these days that I would recoil from invoking that category were it not for the endless reservoirs of love, support, companionship, encouragement, and sustenance of true friends and caring family members. I would love to acknowledge them all, but because they each deserve a paragraph of their own, I will instead thank them collectively and dedicate this volume to the fairest ones of all in the next generation.

THE FAIREST OF THEM ALL

INTRODUCTION

Sno . . . is not Snow White. . . . Bits and pieces change around depending on the time and the other people involved in *their* stories. If you read enough of the so-called folk and fairy tales, you'll see it happened in them too—partly because the original reports of these events became confused with time and telling. . . . When things are told from person to person they're much more fluid. Set down on paper, it appears that if one version is right, that no others can be.

ELIZABETH ANN SCARBOROUGH, *The Godmother*

WHO DOES NOT envy Snow White, the fairest of them all? She is the heroine of a fairy tale that has become our cultural story about an innocent girl, her evil stepmother, the rivalry that divides them, and a romantic rescue from domestic drudgery and maternal persecution. "Snow White" is a close cousin to "Cinderella," the makeover fable par excellence, with its narrative arc that moves the heroine from proverbial rags to storied riches. Like Cinderella, Snow White lives happily ever after, but not without first enduring panic, helplessness, and several brushes with death. Her story, an exercise in extreme emotion, repeatedly describes her as the fairest of them all, but her fairy-tale life itself is defined by a series of deeply traumatic events.[1]

Death in childbirth, maternal malice, and child abandonment: it's all part of the daily rhythm in the fairy-tale universe. Add death and resurrection (just another day at the office), and you have the story we know as "Snow White," with its heroine who remains as attractive and enchanting today as in her other, earlier incarnations as the Greek Chione, the Nordic Snæfriðr, the Armenian Nourie Hadig, or the Indian Sodewa Bai. Almost every culture has a story to tell about an innocent persecuted by her cruel stepmother, and the tale, like its heroine, will not die. "Snow White" has endured, in large part because fairy tales, despite their humble origins in the domestic arena, have a mythic energy that rivals anything told by the Ancients.

The horrors of fairy tales, like those of myth, are often all in the family. We repeat these stories and pass them on in large part because they hit home, as it were, compelling us to sit up, listen, and take notice. In real life, every unhappy family may be unhappy in its own way, but in fairy tales, unhappy families are all very much alike. Nearly every sibling is a rival, and at least one parent is at best a selfish monster, at worst a bloodthirsty ogre. The younger generation may at times do battle with dragons, giants, and other cannibalistic creatures, but more often they are the victims of abusive family members. Cinderella suffers at the hands of her cruel stepmother and vain stepsisters. Beauty is tormented and duped by her sisters. Tom Thumb's parents conspire to abandon their boys, all seven of them, in the woods. Rapunzel lives in a tower with an enchantress because of her parents' reckless appetites and actions. Catskin has to flee home to escape a father who demands her hand in marriage. Time and again an accident during childbirth or an event following hard upon a birth accounts for the misfortunes chronicled in the tale. Mothers die, leaving their children weak and vulnerable; parents are so desperate for offspring that they declare themselves prepared to accept a pig, a hedgehog, or any living creature as a son; a slighted tutelary spirit makes a sinister prophecy at a christening. Sometimes the dark, unforgiving magic of a curse or plain, dumb bad luck conspires to torment the young, but usually parents—or their proxies—are responsible for the misfortunes that beset them.

Why do we ritually repeat the story of Snow White all over the world, telling it time and again, recycling it, modifying it, remixing it, rescripting it, and mashing it up with other stories? Is this one of those narratives that no one in the world seems to get right? Why the fixation on a vindictive woman and a terrified child? What happens to the story as it is told and retold, passed down from one generation to the next, its ragged edges fraying even as its fabric remains intact? And why has the story of a girl with the name Snow White become our master narrative when so many other versions of the story are available?

The tale of the rivalry between a beautiful, innocent girl and her (almost) equally beautiful, but vain and cruel, mother has a tight discipline that is endlessly repeated and remade in cultures all over the world. Go to Greece and you will hear the story of Maroula, a girl despised by Venus and rescued from a catatonic trance by her brothers. In the southern part of the United States, King Peacock finds a girl floating on the waters in a gold coffin and brings her back to life by removing a seed from her mouth. If you travel to Switzerland, you might hear a story about seven dwarfs who offer shelter to a girl and are then murdered by robbers, all because the girl refused to help an old woman. Nourie Hadig's Armenian mother orders her husband to slay his daughter because the moon has declared the girl to be "the most beautiful of all." It is something of a challenge not to conclude that these ominous collisions, driven by jealousy, reflect some kind of recurring psychological complications in the mother-daughter relationship, culturally specific in the details but with nearly universal features at its core. As noted, fairy tales seem to be all in the family—their plots unfold at home—and they also display, even in their rich cultural variation, distinctive family resemblances. "Snow White," "King Peacock," and "Nourie Hadig": these are all different names for a story so capacious as to accommodate all kinds of different cultural ingredients.

In many ways, the same old story is told again and again, but it stays alive and relevant because each generation of tellers adds a new spin, giving it an unexpected twist designed to take us by surprise. Unlike sacred narratives, the fairy tale—worldly and wise—is malleable, elastic, and at its liveliest when refashioned. "The Story of the Beautiful Girl," as the tale about mother-daughter rivalry is often called, belongs to that great Cauldron of Story that J. R. R. Tolkien once described as always boiling with "new bits, dainty and undainty," constantly added.[2] Like soups and stews, stories are at their best when allowed to simmer, with fresh ingredients adding flavor and zest. Every culture concocts its own version of "The Beautiful Girl," reaching out to the long ago and far away of ancestral wisdom but always also in the presence of listeners with lively imaginations seeking, and often demanding, something bearing on their own life experiences.

Myths and fairy tales are larger than life and often twice as unnatural, a potent mix of mischief and malice, along with altruism and enchantment. They are renowned for their exquisite beauty but also denounced for displays of monstrosity in its most perverse forms. Is it the mix of the sublime and the grotesque that creates the magic? Fairy tales amplify and exaggerate, using the counterfactual to capture our attention. A father's curse transforms all seven of his boys into ravens. A door opens, and a woman finds a room, its floor covered in blood, with multiple corpses hanging from the walls. A fisherman is granted wishes by a shimmering flounder he catches and releases. Fairy tales challenge us to decode their mysteries. After all, why the weirdness? At times they mystify and mislead us, though often only because they coyly decline to offer a hotline to correct cultural values, preferring instead to work by unsettling us, starting conversations rather than shutting them down.

Winston Churchill once referred to Russia as a "riddle, wrapped in a mystery, inside an enigma," and we could say the same about fairy tales. They challenge us to make sense of them, and for precisely that reason, many collectors of fairy tales felt obliged to help their readers by pinning morals to the stories they put between the covers of books. "Don't stray from the path!" is the lesson attached to the story of "Little Red Riding Hood," as if that would have helped the girl avoid the jaws of the wolf. "If you make a promise, you must keep it!" a king tells his daughter when an erotically ambitious frog insists on sharing her bed. "Don't be curious about what is behind a locked door!" is the lesson we are to learn from a story about a serial killer who murders his wives. Perhaps because these stories, once told by adults to multigenerational audiences, were reoriented to an implied audience of children, we feel compelled to add some etiquette and instruction, even if they are irrelevant to the story, entirely incongruent with its premises.

Fairy tales do more than offer simple solutions to complex problems. They not only activate our sense of curiosity about what's next but also lead us to think big about questions fundamental to the human condition. The Snow White story, for example, can make our hearts beat faster, but it also challenges us to ask questions about mothers and daughters, trust and deceit, compassion and revulsion, nature and nurture, and beauty and monstrosity. Each new engagement with the story reveals a different element in its narrative matrix and adds a new twist to conversations about the social, cultural, and emotional stakes in the story.

Do myths and fairy tales "state and enforce culture's sentences," as some critics have declared?[3] Do stories about beautiful girls, like the Greek myth about goddesses quarreling over who will earn the golden apple inscribed with the words, "For the Fairest," perpetuate the notion that women are constantly competing with each other to win beauty contests? Many readers, listeners, and viewers will respond with an emphatic "no," for, much as fairy tales are encoded with cultural values conforming to social norms, we invariably come to these stories with a healthy combination of curiosity and skepticism. Every fairy-tale fiction is a reminder that, just as we never get things exactly right in real life, we also rarely get the story right—hence our cultural repetition compulsion when it comes to a story like "Snow White."

Fairy tales enthrall and entrance in large part because they are constantly taking what seem to be wrong turns. "That's not how I heard it!" or "Why in the world?" are typical reactions. As transparent as some fairy tales may at first seem, they encourage us to think more and think harder as we try to make sense of the world in which the characters move. Asked what stories to read to children, Albert Einstein is said to have responded, "If you want intelligent children, read them fairy tales. If you want more intelligent children, read them more fairy tales."[4] Much as the stories seem to offer closure with "happily ever after," once they come to an end, they call out for a postmortem, an inquiry into who did what and why. Fairy tales move in the optative mode, connecting us with hopes, wishes, and the mode of "if only." For exactly that reason, they are also provocations, leading us to contest, defy, and resist the values they champion. They demand irreverence. And that is part of the reason why we keep listening to their extravagant excesses and trying to make sense of them.

DISNEY'S CHARISMATIC QUEEN

Say Snow White's name, and the first association for many people will be Walt Disney's *Snow White and the Seven Dwarfs,* a US film released in 1937 and inspired by a German fairy tale published by the Brothers Grimm in 1812. Not many Hollywood films have held up so many decades after their premiere, and this animated film created the dominant form of a story that, long before social media, had gone viral on a global scale. Local variants of the story, as it was told all over the world, generally featured a nameless heroine defined solely by her beauty. It was Disney who turned the fairest of them all into Snow White.

Disney's film so dominates the fairy-tale landscape that it is often easy to forget the many versions of it that animated storytelling in times past and still circulate in our own day. Mother-daughter conflicts and the romance of a dashing rescuer know no geographical or chronological boundaries, and the tale—both its deep structure and its standard tropes—flashes out at us in ways both predictable and unexpected as we cross borders and enter new time zones. After all, it gives us what A. S. Byatt has called "the narrative grammar of our minds," a symbolic roadmap for navigating reality, wherever in the world that reality might be.[5]

But has Disney Studios' *Snow White and the Seven Dwarfs,* with its tentacular reach into theme parks, children's toys, dress-up clothes, and beyond, become the only Snow White story, driving out the competition with its cinematic charm and alluring cast? Even back in 1937, when the film was released as the first feature-length animated film, it was accompanied by "one of the biggest merchandising efforts ever for a movie." On the film's fiftieth anniversary, David Smith, chief archivist at Disney Studios, showed off a "tea set, paper dolls, a wind-up Dopey toy, Sleepy holding an egg timer, a board game, a bubble pipe, a sand pail." "Can there ever be too many place mats, crayons, ice shows, commemorative glasses?" a *New York Times* reporter mused. Evidently not, for 1987 marked the beginning of a promotional campaign commemorating the film's rerelease, and it included coloring books, leather-bound collectors' editions of the story, silver candleholders, car sun screens, and so on.[6] And this campaign clearly had the goal of targeting not just little girls but women as well. Suddenly a story from an adult oral storytelling tradition that had moved into the culture of childhood was being repurposed as entertainment for multigenerational audiences. More than that, the story went global, wiping out some of the traces of its many folkloric cousins.

A powerful success story about how a tale once told around the fireside, in workrooms, taverns, and all the many other places where there was *talk,* migrated first into print culture for children and then became a cinematic entertainment "for young and old," Disney's Snow White film is haunted by the specter of its many earlier versions. It is also haunting in its vivid dramatization of an encounter between an innocent child and her cruel stepmother. As in the German source, the sweetly naive heroine contrasts sharply with her dark, devious, yet also beautiful tormentor, a woman bent on destroying her. In fact, the wicked queen's tactics are so excessive that it is almost a wonder that the film was never banned for children, with only a small number of well-publicized moments when glamorous female movie stars declared an unwillingness to let their daughters watch films with Disney princesses. Ironically, their concerns turned on the shallowness of the princess characters and how they send the wrong message to girls about the importance of good hair, skin, wardrobe, and other markers of surface beauty.[7]

Many viewers will assert that the charismatic queen steals the Disney show when she stands before the mirror, addressing it with the words "Magic mirror on the wall" (not "Mirror, mirror, on the wall"), demanding to know who is "the fairest of them all." Unlike the Grimms' tale, which gives us the daughter's story and is marked by Snow White's perspectival dominance, *Snow White and the Seven Dwarfs* is oriented toward the mother's emotional universe.[8] Who can forget the dramatic opening sequence—a stunning meditation on controlled rage—with the queen brooding over the possible diminution of her beauty and summoning her "slave in the magic mirror," demanding to know whether she has any competitors?

"Famed is thy beauty, Majesty," the mirror responds, "but hold, a lovely maid I see. Rags cannot hide her gentle grace. Alas, she is more fair than thee." Alas for the girl, for the now reptilian queen demands to know her name, which she quickly divines from the mirror's description: "Lips red as the rose, hair black as ebony, skin white as snow." (Disney, let it be noted, introduced the connection between the whiteness of snow and skin color by inserting the word "skin" before "white as snow," and the film also changed "red as blood" to "lips red as the rose.") The queen attracts with her resonant voice and repulses with her cold-blooded malice as she utters the name "Snow White" in a way that does not bode well for the "fairest one of all," a girl much diminished by contrast with the regal magnificence of a figure who sits on a peacock throne.

"We just try to make a good picture," Walt Disney once observed in connection with *Snow White and the Seven Dwarfs.* "And then the professors come along and tell us what we do."[9] Disney's emphasis on entertainment—on animation as an art form perfectly calibrated to arouse wonder and deliver enchantment—was exactly what held professors captive, along with the many viewers who flocked to see the film. Having encountered the story of the wicked queen and her beautiful daughter as a child, when the film version of a Snow White play was brought to the Kansas City Convention Hall in 1917, Disney was eager to make a screen version of it, one that would be full of "gags" and "screwiness," with a queen who would be "fat" and "batty" or a "fat, cartoon type."[10] During the planning stages, however, Disney decided that he needed a queen who would be a "high collar—stately beautiful type." At the start, *Snow White* was all "gags, gags, gags," one animator recalled.[11] Before long, the dwarfs, prominent as they remained with their antic behavior, took a back seat to the drama that unfolded between Snow White and the queen. Disney wanted humor, but he also longed to flood the senses of his viewers and to make their pulses race as they watched the screen.

Advertisements for *Snow White and the Seven Dwarfs* may picture the heroine and the prince, but the seven dwarfs and the wicked queen dominate the film both visually and verbally. Snow White and the prince, despite the use of primary colors to represent them, are bleached-out figures, as flat and colorless as their names. The seven dwarfs, by contrast, enliven the film with their capers and song, just as the wicked queen provides surges of emotional energy with her stern beauty and arresting ingenuity. In her underground lair, surrounded by skulls and ravens, she works her magic using dusty tomes and a chemistry set to concoct deadly recipes.

When Walt Disney was asked why he had not stayed closer to the Grimms' script, he responded, "It's just that people now don't want fairy stories the way they were written. They were too rough. In the end, they'll probably remember the story the way we film it anyway."[12] There is indeed much "rough stuff" in earlier versions of the tale, but one could quickly counter that Disney, rather than lightening up the story, not only preserved much of the blood and gore but intensified its dark side, giving the wicked queen more airtime than ever. Note also that Disney did not at all diminish the horrors of the tale's ending. The wicked witch's plunge from a cliff in a thunderstorm is as sudden as the Grimms' tableau of a woman dancing to her death in red-hot iron shoes (a single sentence describes that alarming form of torture), but the ending to the animated film feels more terrifying in its pacing, with dwarfs in hot pursuit and a frenzied scramble up a cliff.

Disney Studios erased the Grimms' prelude, an episode that describes the death of Snow White's biological mother in childbirth. The only maternal figure is the stepmother in her double incarnation as beautiful, vain, and evil queen and as ugly, sinister, and wicked witch. Notes taken at story conferences reveal that the queen was planned as "a mixture of Lady Macbeth and the Big, Bad Wolf," fiercely treacherous and without mercy.[13] Disney himself, who referred to the transformation of the queen into an old hag as a "Jekyll and Hyde thing," seemed unaware that there is no Jekyll component to the figure's personality—only two Hydes.[14] Instead of splitting the mother image into a good mother who dies in childbirth and an evil queen who persecutes her stepchild, Disney gives us a regal figure dressed in majestic purple-and-black robes and seated, tellingly, on that throne with peacock feathers. She is a woman bent on destruction in every way.

The Disney film, like its German source, relentlessly polarizes the notion of the feminine to produce an innocent person accomplished in the art of good housekeeping on the one hand and a murderously jealous and forbiddingly cold woman on the other. We have not so much the Madonna / whore or angel / monster binary as the bifurcation into a range of attributes: young / old, innocent / seductive, naive / calculating, kind / cruel, docile / defiant, sincere / deceitful, hardworking / crafty. Beginning with the Grimms, it is through a combination of labor and good looks that Snow White earns her happily-ever-after. Here is how the Grimms describe the housekeeping contract extended to Snow White by the dwarfs: "If you will keep house for us, cook, make the beds, wash, sew, knit, and keep everything neat and clean, then you can stay with us and we'll give you everything you need."[15] But the dwarfs in the Grimms' tale are hardly in need of a housekeeper, for they appear to be models of tidiness. Everything in their cottage is "indescribably dainty and spotless." The table has a white cloth with tiny plates, cups, knives, forks, and spoons, and the beds are covered with sheets "as white as snow." Compare this description of the dwarfs' cottage with the following one taken from a book based on Disney's Snow White film:

> Skipping across a little bridge to the house, Snow White peeked in through one windowpane. There seemed to be no one at home, but the sink was piled high with cups and saucers and plates, which looked as though they had never been washed. Dirty little shirts and wrinkled little trousers hung over chairs, and everything was blanketed with dust.
>
> "Maybe the children who live here have no mother," said Snow White, "and need someone to take care of them. Let's clean their house and surprise them."
>
> So in she went, followed by her forest friends. Snow White found an old broom in the corner and swept the floor, while the little animals all did their best to help.
>
> Then Snow White washed all the crumpled little clothes, and set a kettle of delicious soup to bubbling on the hearth.[16]

In one post-Disney American variant of the story after another, Snow White makes it her mission to clean up after the dwarfs ("seven little boys") and is represented as serving an apprenticeship in home economics ("Snow White for her part was becoming an excellent housekeeper and cook").[17] The Disney version, made at the height of the Great Depression, has everyone whistling and singing while they work, all the while embracing the work ethic with no grumbling at all. Household drudgery becomes frolicking good fun, less work than play, since it requires no real effort, is carried out with the help of wonderfully nimble, adorable woodland creatures, and achieves dazzling results. And the dwarfs cheerfully extol the joys of spending their days underground in a diamond mine: "To dig dig dig dig dig dig dig is what we really like to do." But their labors are, at the least, productive, yielding sacks of precious stones, while Snow White remains hostage to good housekeeping, locked in an endless cycle of shamelessly flirting with the dwarfs as she picks up after them.

Disney's evil queen plays a commanding role, becoming a source of cinematic fascination that contrasts with a figure so dull that she needs a supporting cast of seven to enliven her scenes. With a chipmunk-like voice in which "the accents of Betty Boop are far too prominent" and with a figure that has been described as a "pasty, sepulchral, sewing-pattern design scissored out of context," the Snow White character lacks the narrative élan so potently present in the representation of the stepmother, whose features are borrowed from Joan Crawford and whose eyebrows resemble the arched back of an angry cat.[18] Ultimately it is the stepmother's disruptive, disturbing, and divisive presence that beguiles us, investing *Snow White and the Seven Dwarfs* with a degree of cinematic allure that has facilitated its widespread circulation and allowed it to take hold in our imaginations. It is she, perhaps more than the eponymous heroine, who has hoodwinked us, turning the story about an innocent persecuted heroine from a communal folk narrative told in many parts of the world into a tale invented by the Hollywood Dream Factory and starring—who else?—herself.

Gender trouble? Incendiary passion? Family violence? No one worried about those things when the film opened in the United States or when it was exported to other countries. Most viewers and critics embraced the film as an artistic triumph for its technical accomplishments and its entertainment value. This was animation as high art and a cinematic experience that would appeal to the entire family.

"SNOW WHITE" AND THE ORIGINS OF FAIRY TALES

Before investigating the domestic disturbances that make "Snow White" so compelling a story for us, it will be useful to consider just how the tale was put together by the Brothers Grimm and made its way from Germany to Burbank, California, in the early part of the twentieth century (and then, in a touch of deep irony, back again, via Disney). As we shall see, the Brothers Grimm, whose "Snow White" inspired Disney, fashioned their tale from many different sources.

When it comes to fairy tales, there are no originals, only endless multiforms, or variations on a theme. Fairy tales stretch back for centuries. Among the earliest is an Egyptian tale about two brothers recorded around 1200 BCE, a Greek "Snow White" that was written down in the early first century CE, and a Roman "Beauty and the Beast" that dates back to the second century CE. We possess nothing more than an infinitesimally small fraction of all the stories once told by kinfolk and kindred spirits as a means of transmitting experience and building communal values. First recorded on stones, parchment, and papyrus, these tales began to flourish in book form after the printing press was invented, with collectors eager to capture indigenous oral storytelling traditions (pure and uncontaminated, as they put it) that were fast fading in an era of rising urbanization and industrialization. Tales that we now know in print versions ("Cinderella," "Jack and the Beanstalk," and "Sleeping Beauty," for example) can be traced back to oral storytelling traditions that demanded melodrama and mystery to help pass time while discharging repetitive household chores. As John Updike told us, these tales were the "television and pornography of an earlier age," as well as the "life-lightening trash of pre-literate peoples."[19] Above all, their narrative energy and verbal sorcery delivered much-needed doses of pleasure to those who told and those who listened in an era when life could be nasty, brutish, and short—but also flat, monotonous, and long.

Fairy tales flash out at us in works by Chaucer, Shakespeare (there are more than echoes of "Snow White" in his play *Cymbeline*), and Boccaccio, but it is only through the efforts of the Venetian Giovanni Francesco Straparola and the Neapolitan Giambattista Basile that we have the first full-blooded fairy-tale collections in the Western world, with Straparola's *Facetious Nights* appearing in the 1550s and Basile's *Pentamerone* in the 1630s. Not much later, Charles Perrault codified stories ranging from "Little Red Riding Hood" to "Sleeping Beauty" and helped to inspire the collecting activities of Jacob and Wilhelm Grimm, two brothers eager to provide a German answer to the Italians and the French. It was the Brothers Grimm who gave us the "Snow White" that has been enshrined as the canonical version of the written story, a tale that has become, for many readers, "the original" from which our modern and postmodern variants derive.

The Grimms' "Snow White" is the story from which writers like Donald Barthelme (*Snow White*), Neil Gaiman ("Snow, Glass, Ice"), Catherynne M. Valente (*Six-Gun Snow White*), and Helen Oyeyemi (*Boy, Snow, Bird*) took their cues, partnering with the German collectors even as they challenged the early version of the tale. Filmmakers, by contrast, have drawn inspiration from the Disney film, with its rich archive of cinematic images. Disney himself was never in an adversarial relationship with the German source material, which he knew well and studied as a warm-up exercise for making his film. Hewing closely to the Grimms' story, he compressed at times (the evil queen visits Snow White only once) and expanded at others (the dwarfs each have individual personalities). But had Disney set his sights on something far grander than the three-thousand-word story that the Grimms published in the first volume of the *Children's Stories and Household Tales* of 1812? That story can be quickly summarized:

A queen sits by a window, sewing and also dreaming of a child as white as snow, as red as blood, as black as ebony. The queen dies soon after the birth of the child. The king remarries, and his wife owns a magic mirror that declares Snow White to be more beautiful than she is. The jealous queen orders a huntsman to take Snow White into the woods and kill her, but he takes pity on the girl, sets her free, and returns to the castle with the heart and lungs of a wild boar (which the queen eats for supper). Snow White discovers a cottage in the woods and goes inside. There she finds food, drink, and a bed in which to sleep. At night, the seven dwarfs who live in the cottage return home, find her there, and agree to let her stay if she keeps house for them. Snow White is told that she must not let anyone in the house. The magic mirror reveals to the queen that Snow White is still alive, and she attempts to kill her stepdaughter three times, first by lacing her up so tightly that she cannot breathe, then by untangling her hair with a poisoned comb, and finally by tempting her to take a bite from an apple, one side of which she has poisoned. The dwarfs place the girl on top of a mountain in a glass coffin and mourn her. A prince finds the coffin and pleads with the dwarfs to let him take it with him. When they finally give in, he orders his servants to take the coffin away. The servants stumble over a branch, and Snow White comes back to life when the piece of apple in her throat is dislodged. She marries the prince, and at her wedding the stepmother is forced to dance in red-hot iron shoes until she collapses and dies.

A new medium demanded resourcefulness, and Disney's team of storytellers, animators, and composers reinvented the story to make it more appealing to American audiences, yet without cleaning it up, as some viewers have asserted, or defanging it. There may be upbeat songs about laboring in mines and tidying up at home, along with dwarfs who playfully allegorize character traits, but Disney Studios left the psychological drama intact. It is the unfolding of that conflict, one that was surely taboo at a time when the nuclear family was considered sacrosanct, that made the film a popular and commercial success. This was a story that enacted unimaginable parental cruelty and profound childhood trauma well before the *Journal of the American Medical Association* identified child abuse as a medical concern and turned it into a social problem that could no longer be ignored.[20]

In 1976, the child psychologist Bruno Bettelheim argued in *The Uses of Enchantment* that fairy tales have survived precisely because they provide therapeutic release through the processing of a symbolic story. He urged parents to accept a narrative corpus that took children on bumpy rides, for the ferocity of fairy tales helps children engage and work through feelings of anger, resentment, and envy. Stories like "Hansel and Gretel" or "Snow White," for example, liberate children from feeling guilty about wanting to get rid of their parents by projecting that wish onto parents who scheme to abandon a child. Bettelheim saw everywhere this process of projective inversion, thereby exonerating the cruel and wicked adults in fairy tales of any blame, for they do nothing but enact a child's furtive longings. For him, the stories provide both wish fulfillment of forbidden desires and cathartic release of toxic feelings. Perhaps Snow White is not so innocent after all? A closer look at how the Brothers Grimm engaged with the story can tell us more about the nature of the family drama played out in it as well as about the source material that informed and inspired "Little Snow White," as it appeared in the first volume of their *Children's Stories and Household Tales* (*Kinder- und Hausmärchen*) of 1812.[21]

THE PERSECUTED HEROINE OF THE BROTHERS GRIMM

Jacob and Wilhelm Grimm both held law degrees, but their real passion was in many ways for language, culture, and folklore. Hailing from the

Hessian region of German-speaking lands, the brothers spent much of their adult life together, quietly publishing massive tomes that included multiple volumes of myths, folktales, poems, and legends, along with philological studies. Unlikely political activists, they were banished from the Kingdom of Hanover in 1837 for protesting the king's abrogation of the constitution, and together they returned to their hometown of Kassel before moving on to Berlin, where they were appointed professors and happily settled into a lifelong research partnership marked by unparalleled patience, diligence, and perseverance. They had what the Germans call *Sitzfleisch,* a willingness to toil silently for hours on end in the spacious book-lined study they shared later in life. Theirs was the first comprehensive German dictionary that, despite herculean efforts, did not get past the letter *F.* Jacob was working on the word *Frucht* (fruit), when he passed away in 1863, just a few years after Wilhelm's death in 1859.

Children's Stories and Household Tales, published in two volumes in 1812 and 1815, was launched as a scholarly project. The brothers wanted to preserve a cultural heritage that was fast vanishing, and they alerted friends, family, and colleagues to their plan to collect folktales and fairy tales, hoping for contributions and collaborations. For "Snow White," the Grimms assembled multiple versions of the tale from their own social milieu and then worked their magic on it, making the story direct and intimate, with an internal logic of its own. Taking baggy oral narratives as their point of departure, they smoothed out contradictions, filled in gaps, trimmed unnecessary, seemingly random, details, and cast the whole in what became a highly appealing and readable fairy-tale style. Written in a tempo that is brisk and bracing, their story of Snow White, like so many entries in *Children's Stories and Household Tales,* became canonical, in large part because the Grimms had mastered a fairy-tale style and crafted the genre of a compact print fairy tale that appealed to multigenerational audiences. Their deceptively simple exercises in fairy-tale miniatures captured the essence of a story with a bewitching mix of broad mythical themes and colorful, local details.

"Little Snow White" (the Grimms' title, *Schneewittchen,* adds a diminutive suffix to the girl's name) gives us what is conventionally seen as the foundational, authoritative, and canonical story in cultures beyond the borders of German-speaking lands. In the commentary to that tale, the brothers suggest that they were indeed trying to create a "standard" version. But far from trying to excavate the "true" version of Snow White (the *Urmärchen*), Jacob and Wilhelm Grimm hoped to craft an "authentic" version true to the culture of the time from material given to them by multiple informants. Facing an overload of source material and discovering many competing narratives even in the relatively circumscribed Hessian locale (which happened to have a rich trove of folkloric resources), they decided to write what is, in the final analysis, their own story.

What the Grimms created was a composite narrative, one revised over a period of several decades, with countless fine calibrations designed to make the story, paradoxically, a pure and unadulterated capture of folk traditions but with a child-friendly orientation. Among the most dramatic changes the brothers made, as the tale moved through successive editions, concerned the villain. In the first edition of the collection, the one closest to vernacular sources, it is a biological mother who cannot curb her murderous impulses. To be sure, she wishes for a beautiful child, one as "white as snow, red as blood, and black as the ebony window frame,"[22] but once the girl grows up, the queen is so tormented by envy that she orders a huntsman to kill her and eviscerate her ("Bring me back her lungs and liver."). The entrails are meant to be more than mere evidence: the queen longs to augment her own beauty by ingesting her rival and, in a ghoulish touch, seasons what she believes to be the innards with salt.

The role of Snow White's father underwent a major shift as well. In the first draft of the story, written down in 1808 and sent by Jacob Grimm to Friedrich Carl von Savigny (the distinguished mentor to both brothers in the field of law), the father happens, by mere chance, to enter the

1 Gustaf Tenggren's hunter may conceal his weapon, but his purpose is evident from the pleading Snow White, presented in all her vulnerability. Tenggren (1896–1970) was a Swedish American illustrator who worked as an animator for the Walt Disney Company in the late 1930s, when *Snow White and the Seven Dwarfs* was being made.

2 In a spooky, otherworldly landscape, Snow White rests peacefully, almost floating in Gustaf Tenggren's haunting illustration for the story.

3 The British illustrator Lancelot Speed (1860–1931) was best known for the images he created for Andrew Lang's rainbow series of fairy-tale books. In a break with tradition, Speed chose to illustrate what no others dared to represent in the story of Snow White: the stepmother dancing to her death in red-hot iron shoes and going up in flames.

4 The younger brother of Jacob and Wilhelm Grimm, Emil Ludwig Grimm (1790–1863), illustrated the 1825 compact edition of the *Children's Stories and Household Tales.* In a rugged landscape and under a star-filled sky, Snow White sleeps peacefully, attended by one of the dwarfs, along with an owl, a raven, and a dove.

5 The British illustrator Walter Crane (1845–1915) provided this image for a popular English edition of the Grimms' fairy tales, translated by his sister Lucy Crane. The peddler woman seems harmless enough as she offers the poisoned apple to the unsuspecting Snow White.

6 The Danish illustrator Kay Nielsen (1886–1957) gives us a Snow White image with a distinctly Nordic sensibility. Dressed in shroud-like apparel, Snow White lies in state, surrounded by dwarfs so grief stricken that they cannot bear to gaze on her.

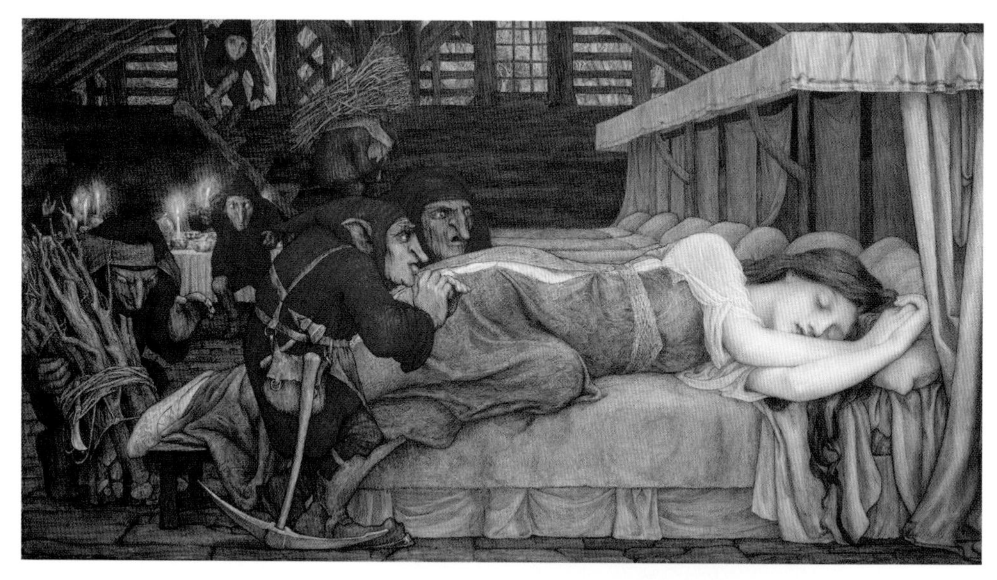

"Looking-glass, looking-glass on the wall,
Who is the fairest of women all?"

(*top*) 7 The industrious dwarfs, setting tables, hauling wood, and tending to the sleeping girl, are both spooky and compassionate in this magnificent work by the British painter John Dickson Batten (1860–1932), who illustrated many volumes of fairy tales.

(*right*) 8 The youthful queen, looking much like a flapper girl (the image is from the 1920s) save for her elaborate costume, finds much to admire in her reflection, as captured by the British illustrator and writer Alice Helena Watson (1896–1984).

(*top*) 9 The Austrian painter Heinrich Lefler (1863–1919) understood the attractions of a highly stylized frame for the scene in which the prince, here a medieval knight, discovers Snow White (anaesthetized and aestheticized) in her coffin in snowy woods.

(*left*) 10 The Austrian painter Hans Makart (1840–1884) became a celebrity in Viennese artistic circles. Known as "the magician of color," he embraced aestheticism and painted in brilliant hues that give us the sculpted beauty of three-dimensional figures. In the far upper right of his painting *Das schlafende Schneewittchen* (*Snow White Asleep*), the dwarfs can be seen, returning home.

"They were very friendly, however, and inquired her name. 'Snowdrop,' answered she."

11 The seven dwarfs, hunched over from their labors and carrying the tools of their trade, display various reactions to the presence of their beautiful intruder. The caption quotes the text of what is translated as "Little Snowdrop" and describes the dwarfs as "very friendly," although Warwick Goble (1862–1943) gives us dwarfs who look both hostile and hospitable.

They laid her in a coffin of glass.

12 In an unusual move, the Austrian-British painter Marianne Stokes (1855–1927) turns the dwarfs into figures cloaked in red, mourning Snow White with woodland creatures and unable to take their eyes off her. Hands clasped as if in prayer, Snow White appears in sharp contrast to her surroundings.

13 The German landscape painter Victor Paul Mohn (1842–1911) represents the home of the seven dwarfs with charm and allure. Startled by the appearance of the girl in white beneath a mature tree lush with growth, the dwarfs come running down an arboreal ladder to greet their nocturnal visitor.

14 The British illustrator Margaret Tarrant (1888–1959) specialized in illustrating books about fairies, but she also created artwork for volumes ranging from Charles Kingsley's *The Water Babies* to Lewis Carroll's *Alice in Wonderland*. There is genius in Tarrant's images for the Snow White stories, with scenes that capture serenity at times, startle viewers at others, as is the case with this image that jolts us into full awareness of the stepmother's hatred of Snow White.

(*top*) 15 In Maxfield Parrish's 1912 painting, *From the Story of Snow White,* a single dwarf stands guard over the heroine, who lies in state under glass on a sculpted platform situated in rocky terrain. Snow White both blends in with the landscape and also stands out from it, a figure frozen in a horizontal pose yet also softened by the folds of fabric beneath her.

(*right*) 16 The Scottish artist Anne Anderson (1874–1952) illustrated several volumes of fairy tales by the Brothers Grimm and Hans Christian Andersen. Her dwarfs seem in desperate need of care and company, with socks and slippers mismatched.

forest in which the seven dwarfs are living. He discovers the coffin, reads the inscription on it, and is "greatly saddened" by the death of his "beloved daughter." But, unlike the prince, he is not content to merely gaze and languish. There are "experienced doctors" in his entourage, and they agree to treat the corpse using unconventional medical practices. "When they took the body, they tied a rope to the four corners of the room, pulled, and Snow White came to life again." Presto, the unique therapy works. Snow White finds a prince and marries him, and the queen perishes after being forced to dance in red-hot iron shoes.[23]

In the notes to "Snow White," the Grimms recorded a second version of the story that gave a more prominent role to the father of the child: A count and countess travel on a sled and see three mounds of snow, whereupon the count wishes for a child as white as snow. The couple then passes three pools filled with blood, and the count wishes for a child with cheeks as red as blood. After seeing three black ravens flying overhead, he wishes for a child with hair as black as ravens. As if on cue, a girl with those exact attributes appears by the side of the road, and the count invites her to ride in the carriage with them. He "likes" the girl, and the countess, "not pleased," drops a glove, tells the girl to retrieve it, and orders the carriage to move on without her. What happens after that? All we know is that the girl discovers a cottage inhabited by dwarfs. We are left in suspense with the phrase "and so on." (Angela Carter's "The Snow Child" is inspired by this version and provides a gothic ending to the story—one with a touch of mischief and a whiff of the macabre, as her fans could easily predict.) What this version of the story provides is concrete motivation for doing harm, since the girl stirs the envy of the countess in understandable ways.[24]

Both Jacob and Wilhelm Grimm displayed uncommon erudition, even for men of learning, in their notes and commentary on the tale. They tip their professorial hats to a story called "Richilde" in *Volksmärchen der Deutschen* (1782), a volume of German fairy tales compiled by their contemporary Johann Karl August Musäus. In that convoluted tale about scheming clerics, imperial physicians, and sleeping potions, a jealous woman named Richilde persecutes her beautiful daughter named Blanca. This is a story with elements drawn from Shakespeare (*Cymbeline*) and from the eighteenth-century German dramatist Gotthold Ephraim Lessing (author of the Enlightenment play *Nathan the Wise*), and it is not without grotesquely comic elements, as when Richilde is forced to dance in red-hot shoes at the wedding feast and complains about burns and blisters.

A more ancient and revered source for the Grimms' "Snow White" came from the Old Norse saga about Harald Fairhair in Snorri Sturluson's *Heimskringla,* a collection of sagas about Norwegian kings. Composed around 1230, the *Heimskringla* (literally "the circle of the world") contains one story remarkably similar to "Snow White." It tells of a young woman named Snæfriðr and how King Harald falls hopelessly in love with her after drinking a cup of mead in her presence. The two have four sons, and the king is so smitten with his wife, even after her death, that he neglects his kingdom: "Afterwards Snæfriðr died, but the color of her skin never faded and she was as rosy as before when she lived. The king always sat over her and thought that she would come to life again, and thus it went on for three winters that he sorrowed over her death and all the people of this land sorrowed over his delusion." A wise counselor suggests giving the dead queen a fresh set of clothes, and at that moment it is revealed that the back of Snæfriðr's body has in fact been decaying. Once the corpse is burned and has turned to ashes, the king comes to his senses and rules his people with strength and intelligence.[25] In the medieval Icelandic manuscript known as *Flateyjarbók,* there is reference to a poem recited by King Harald about the shroud in which Snæfriðr had been draped and how it is a gift from Svási (the dwarf who introduced Harald to his bewitching daughter).

The Nordic tale of Snæfriðr offers a rich feast of interpretive opportunities. For one thing, the story's clear message that there is no resurrection after death runs counter to Christian messages about everlasting life. We are immersed in a pagan cosmology that disavows the possibility of revivification. But the Grimms' interest in the story was piqued by the dead queen's name more than anything else, with Snæfriðr derived from *snæ* (snow) and *fríðr* (beautiful). The optics of the Norse saga seem to coincide with exactly what the Grimms wished their readers to visualize, a beautiful woman, "white as snow." Or do they? The Nordic name Snæfriðr could mean both "beautiful as snow" or "someone who loves snow." As G. Ronald Murphy points out in his study of mythical elements in the Grimms' tales, the name is "best understood as someone who will love the snow and share the snow's loveliness."[26] As for the Grimms' phrase "white as snow," it has a multitude of meanings (like the whiteness ascribed to Snæfriðr) and can imply innocence, purity, blankness, and so on, in short, a host of attributes that have nothing to do with skin color. Our contemporary understanding of Snow White's fair skin may, as it were, color—and reimagine—a story that has little to say about skin pigmentation.

Oral narratives derive their beauty in many ways from layering. Storytellers draw on heterogeneous versions of a story, mixing and mingling, erasing and preserving, destroying and restoring. Each teller adds something new to the accumulated layers to give a story texture and depth. In some ways, the Grimms did exactly what their forebears had done, building and demolishing, all the while leaving traces of the stories antecedent to their new telling of a tale.

RED, WHITE, BLACK

Red, white, black: these have often been seen as the chief elements in the chromatic range of the fairy-tale universe. Jacob Grimm described those hues as "the three colors of poetry."[27] "White as snow, red as blood, and black as ebony." Who can forget the words of the good mother, the one who dies in childbirth, making the way for the wicked queen, in the Grimms' "Snow White"? In the colors she invokes, we are treated to an instant drama of the senses, seeing the hues described by some philosophers as primal: with fire red, air and water white (despite their transparency), and earth black. These are the same color-coded elements alchemists counted on as they puzzled over how to transmute base matter into precious silver and gold, an operation that can be seen as foundational for fairy-tale magic as well, with its enshrining of gold and silver, all that sparkles and shines, with happily-ever-after endings that mark the end of conflict and struggles that are often color-coded in red, white, and black.

Color becomes a powerful shorthand in fairy tales, used to construct an entire visual field without resorting to much description, thin or thick. If we take a quick look in the Russian woods, we discover that the folkloric heroine Vasilisa the Fair encounters three riders there: a white one who represents Day, a second one as red as the Sun, and a third as black as Night. What does she bring back to her stepmother and stepsisters but light, in the form of a tricolored skull-lantern filled with burning coals. In the Grimms' "The Singing, Soaring Lark," a dove flies ahead of the heroine, letting a drop of red blood and a white feather fall at every step taken. An Italian tale has a hero who sees some black jackdaws in the air, cuts his finger over a lump of ricotta cheese, and sets out to find a woman who is like ricotta stained with blood.

Yet for all that, fairy tales also contain all the hues of the rainbow, and we need look no farther than "Fairer-Than-a-Fairy," included in *The Yellow Fairy Book,* one installment in a celebrated series promoted as *Andrew Lang's Fairy Book of Many Colors* or simply as the *Rainbow Fairy Books.* The dozen volumes in that series, published in London over a period of over twenty years, from 1889 to 1910, shift the fairy-tale palette, turning it from an unforgiving red, white, and black to a more child-friendly and variegated palette of pastels. "Fairer-Than-a-Fairy" introduces us to a prince who becomes known, after the curse on him has been lifted, as King Rainbow. Trapped in a fountain, he is released, thanks to the labors of a princess captivated by his polychromatic manifestation. The princess passes by the fountain one day, noticing that "the sun's rays fell on the water in such a manner as to produce a brilliant rainbow. She stood still to admire it, when, to her great surprise, she heard a voice addressing her, which seemed to come from the center of its rays. The voice was that of a young man, and its sweetness of tone and the agreeable things it uttered, led one to infer that its owner must be equally charming; but this had to be a mere matter of fancy, for no one was visible."[28] Color, voices, and scents mingle in the tale's bravura scene of redemption, when Prince Rainbow, a male Sleeping Beauty, is awakened by his beloved.

Why the riot of color? And is this story symptomatic of a shift, not only in the fairy-tale palette but also in a move from the raw emotional power of folktales to the "sweet," "agreeable," and "charming" sentiments in confections oriented toward an audience of children? Suddenly we discover exactly how pastels came to dominate the costumes of Disney princesses yet also have more than an inkling of how Disney did not single-handedly invent a new kind of fairy tale, one that remained universally accessible but also deeply invested in providing child-friendly entertainments.

Walter Benjamin, the prominent German philosopher, cultural critic, and essayist, was a collector of children's books who also wrote about children's literature. He tells us that color is "the instrument of fantasy, the land of dreams for a child lost in games, and not the rigid canon built by artists." Benjamin provided a compelling inventory of objects and activities that stimulate the imagination of the child: "soap bubbles, tea parties, the color-filled evanescence of the magic lantern, drawing with crayons, imaginary friends." What fascinated Benjamin about color in particular is not that it comes from a mere object but that it has an almost otherworldly quality, with a unique "splendor and brilliance."[29] Artifacts derive their luminosity from an unearthly source, mere light rays with no material substance to them at all.

Benjamin's observations help us understand exactly why the fairy-tale palette was transformed into something it had never been. In the universe of adult storytelling, black-and-white chiaroscuro effects trump all else, often with just a splash of red. Fairy tales from times past shied away from blended colors, from airy pastels and subtly nuanced shades, preferring instead saturated colors and even no color at all to the rainbow hues that were once compelling exceptions to the rules of fairy-tale worlds, then de rigueur, almost obligatory.

Thanks to the writings of the Swiss folklorist Max Lüthi, we know that fairy tales are sparing in all things, giving us abstraction in place of richly elaborated concrete details, with minimal descriptive flourishes and only the most basic hues, each charged with an excess of symbolic significance.[30] Red, white, and black can be seen as metaphors for diurnal cycles (dawn, daylight, nighttime) or cosmic forces (a red sun, a white moon, and black darkness). Or they can be connected, as noted earlier, with alchemical rites, in which transfiguration from the base metal of lead into gold moves through purification processes linked to red and white. What remains fascinating is how red, white, and black can be inflected in so many different ways, producing upheavals in meaning and changing dramatically depending on our social and cultural consciousness.

Color in and of itself, then, is no more than an abstraction without meaning, yet we insist on investing it with significance, often endowing it with more than arbitrary values and making claims for certain universal associations. Red is the color of sin, passion, and desire, with white as a symbol of innocence and purity and black as a sign of darkness, doom, and death. There is something sinister, ominous, and threatening about both red and black, with an excess of meaning packed into shades that saturate sight. White, by contrast, can become eerie in its evocation of absence, barrenness, and lack, even if it is also often seen as a marker of saintly innocence.

As the Italian architect Manlio Brusatin tells us, color is a "most serious deception, an adventure in dust and the habitual pain of living."[31] It is all the more curious, then, that we so insistently invest color with stable cultural meaning, turning red into a sign of passion, black into death, and white into innocence, as if those connotations were part of the essence of each shade. Are they? The "color of the world" changes "day by day," as young student revolutionaries sing at the Café Musain, one of the settings in the musical version of *Les Miserables.* There, the forward-looking rebel Enjolras reminds the lovesick Marius that red is "the blood of angry men," not the "color of desire"; and black is "the dark of ages past," not "the color of despair."[32] In other words, we keep inventing meanings for red, white, and black, all the while ignoring the fact that there really can be no consensus on *what* they mean.

The limited chromatic range of the fairy tale does not in any way set limits to our imaginations. To the contrary, minimalism makes surfaces count all the more, and each hue is rarely fixed and stable, challenging us to make sense of a style that veers in the direction of the abstract and stimulates our imaginations. Whiteness, as Herman Melville once told us, when invoked as a "wide landscape of snows" can evoke a "dumb blankness, full of meaning."[33] His paradoxical formulation captures exactly how fairy tales arouse our curiosity as we navigate their worlds. A phrase like "white as snow" or "red as blood" does not fix meaning at all; to the contrary, it can flip a switch in our sensory apparatus as it pushes us to explore the trio of white / snow, red / blood, black / ebony and all the rich reservoirs of meaning contained in those sets of associations.

What becomes clear in reviewing the Grimms' source material, as well as variants from cultures the world over, is how the "white as snow, red as blood, and black as ebony" mantra is a local detail rather than a part of the story's deep structure. The foregrounding of white, red, and black became an important feature of the Grimms' imaginative re-creation of what they considered a folktale with deep *Germanic* roots (is it any coincidence that the German flag was red, white, and black until the end of the empire in 1918?), and the trope came to dominate the story in odd ways, even overshadowing where the real action is: beauty so breathtaking that it arouses maternal jealousy. Yet the name "Snow White" has stuck, and the attributes of the German heroine have come to stand as shorthand for all fairy-tale innocents relentlessly persecuted by their monstrous mothers or stepmothers. More important, once the story migrated into a culture with a history of slavery and of discrimination based on skin color, it was not long before Snow White's name became freighted with new meanings.

BOB CLAMPETT'S *COAL BLACK AND DE SEBBEN DWARFS*

Both the Grimms and Disney catered to general audiences, hoping to capture multigenerational readers and viewers with their melodramatic fairy tale and their animated film. Jacob and Wilhelm Grimm, scholars accustomed to sales in the double digits, were pleasantly surprised by the revenues produced by *Children's Stories and Household Tales.* They were often beset by financial struggles, and the modest royalties actually made a difference for them. The Grimms' commercial success inspired copycats, and the brothers were deeply annoyed that others (one opportunistic collector, in particular, who shared their surname) were trying to capitalize on their accomplishment by producing rival anthologies. It is not surprising, then, that the colossal commercial success of *Snow White and the Seven Dwarfs* also gave rise to competition, with new spins on the Snow White story springing up in a range of media, each seeking to establish a niche by taking advantage of product differentiation and courting specific audiences. There are Snow White musicals, such as *Snow White and the Three Stooges,* produced by Walter Lang in 1961. There are X-rated productions ranging from *Snow White and the*

Seven Perverts, directed in 1973 by Marcus Parker Rhodes, to *Stories Our Nannies Don't Tell,* directed in 1979 by Oswaldo de Oliveira. There are animated sequels such as *Happily N'Ever After* (2007) and its second installment, which gave us another bite of the apple two years later. And there are fairy-tale productions for children, such as the *Faerie Tale Theatre Snow White and the Seven Dwarfs* or the Muppet Babies' Snow White play, or the parody of the story in the Rocky and Bullwinkle cartoon series. And the Walt Disney Company exploits its own success on a regular basis, with productions such as Rupert Sanders's *Snow White and the Huntsman* (2012) and the ABC series *Once upon a Time.* That series featured a fairy-tale paracosm or secondary world populated by many characters but with Snow White and her daughter playing the female leads. In sum, the story will not sit still, constantly roaming into new media and morphing into new versions of itself.

What becomes evident in considering how the Grimm tale and the Disney film are recycled is how sharp the divide is between critical adaptations of the story and nostalgic re-creations. There are versions that aim to shock and startle, and then there are rescriptings designed to do exactly what the Russian film director Sergei Eisenstein found so revolting about Disney films: they soothe, entertain, and distract, lulling us into a passive state. It is, of course, not surprising that stories, novels, films, poems, and musicals deviating from traditional cultural scripts will prove the most revelatory and culturally symptomatic, yet it is still something of a challenge to work out exactly what they disclose. Do they lead us to reassess their source material and to rethink the terms of a familiar tale? Do they speak to us in startlingly new ways—edgy and offensive at times—pushing us to think harder about the cultural stakes in the story?

All of these possibilities are manifestly present in one of the earliest responses to Disney's Snow White film. In 1943, Warner Brothers released a short cartoon, one that has been disavowed and repudiated today, though in its own day it created nothing more than a small ripple of protest. Bob Clampett's *Coal Black and de Sebben Dwarfs* (the original title was *So White and de Sebben Dwarfs*) disrupts and subverts Disney's film in a way that shocks viewers, for the film traffics in and perpetuates racist stereotypes of African Americans. There are many ways to adapt, and the most radical rescriptings of a story give us something that, for better or for worse, dramatically changes its terms. There may be a different point of view (the stepmother becomes the victim of her "innocent" daughter), an upending of our expectations (the handsome prince turns out to be a green monster), or a reversal of key attributes (Snow White becomes Coal Black, or rather "So White"—as the filmmakers first called her—with black skin and black hair).

Clampett's film defamiliarizes Disney in ways that make it impossible to see the 1937 film as culturally innocent. Among many other things, it calls attention to the formulaic, seemingly fixed color-coding of the story. It is here that we would do well to reemphasize that Disney added "skin" to the "white as snow" attribute, ensuring that the innocent heroine would be enshrined as a young white girl and that the color of her skin would be a prominent feature of her beauty. "She seems made of some rare phosphorous alloy," one critic notes. "She is so much whiter than anything around her."[34] And the deeper irony of Disney highlighting, in the 1930s, whiteness by fetishizing a fair-skinned heroine from a Nordic pantheon should not be lost on us. By changing Snow White to Coal Black, Clampett's film, almost like the negative of a photograph, reveals just how profoundly our understanding of that figure is shaped by the girl's name and the attributes ascribed to her. Suddenly it dawns on us that it is no coincidence that the Disney film found favor with political leaders of the Third Reich. For them, as we shall see, the movie was appealing not just on aesthetic grounds but also for ideological reasons, for here was an innocent, white-skinned heroine preyed on by the forces of darkness and evil.

The name Coal Black is charged with intense meaning, and another look at the cultural meaning of blackness goes far toward unpacking the complexities of a cartoon parody so deeply offensive that Warner Brothers tried hard to bury it. We can begin with Greco-Roman associations of black with death and the underworld as well as of Christian hermeneutic traditions that affiliated blackness with sin and with the devil. That legacy is still with us today. "From the simplistic, but readily accepted idea that black is the sign of death and therefore of sin, it was easy to go on to the more dangerous idea that the man whose color was black was a menace, a temptation, a creature of the Devil," David Goldenberg writes in a now classic essay on racism, color symbolism, and color prejudice.[35]

The Grimms themselves, given the intellectual surround and spiritual circumstances in which they grew up, were hardly immune to these cultural associations. In their commentary to "The White Bride and the Black Bride"—a tale in their collection that polarizes chromatic oppositions in particularly stark terms—they refer to the "simple opposition of blackness and whiteness for ugliness and beauty, sin and purity," as well as for the contrast between night and day.[36] Moral and aesthetic categories are collapsed and chromatically coded, with the result that Snow White's name immediately broadcasts innocence and beauty, notwithstanding the fact that she is not fair-haired but rather has hair black as ebony wood. Combining "snow" with "white" produces an excess of meaning that serves as a buffer for the girl's black hair. Red, white, and black are not only the colors of poetry, as it turns out. They also operate as powerful signals for constructing meaning in a fairy-tale universe that aligns whiteness with beauty, innocence, and light and blackness with what is ugly, sinful, and dark.

Instead of opening by pointing to the cultural authority of a written source (as is the case in *Snow White and the Seven Dwarfs,* with pages turning as a voice-over reads the story), Clampett's cartoon situates "Mammy" before a roaring fire, responding to a child's request for a story. Mammy's tale no longer turns on beauty, mirrors, and generational conflicts but on social corruption, politics, and patriotism.

With off-color gags, ribald language, and riotous sexuality on display in a series of oppressively claustrophobic frames, the film is meant less for the young than for war-weary adults craving distraction in anarchic humor. It unsettles and disturbs, and it does so in ways that dare to question the story as it has been handed down to us. At the same time, it reveals that a war fought against Nazi aspirations for a master race triggered a host of anxieties in the United States about skin color and racial superiority. Wartime cartoons, as the film historian Norman Klein puts it, had "more black caricature even than cartoons from the thirties, ripe as they were." And fighting German racism somehow immunized against awareness of homegrown racism: "Lazy 'negroes' and cute piccaninnies mixed in with the patriotic barrage against buck-teethed Japs and bulldog-necked Nazis."[37]

The film, with its profoundly unnerving caricatures of African Americans, has nonetheless found its champions in film scholars and historians of animation. Clampett's autobiographical reminiscences attempt to historicize the project even if they do not try to justify the film's representational practices and use of stereotypes:

> In 1942, during the height of anti-Japanese sentiment during World War II, I was approached in Hollywood by the cast of an all-black musical off-Broadway production called *Jump For Joy*. . . . They asked me why there weren't any Warner's cartoons with black characters and I didn't have any good answer for that question. So we sat down together and came up with a parody of Disney's "Snow White" and "Coal Black" was the result. They did all the voices for that cartoon. . . . There was nothing racist or disrespectful toward blacks intended in that film at all, nor in *Tin Pan Alley Cats* which is just a parody of jazz piano great Fats Waller. . . . Everybody, including blacks had a good time when these cartoons first came out. All the controversy about these

two cartoons has developed in later years merely because of changing attitudes toward black civil rights that have happened since then.[38]

This burst of energy in the "Snow White" landscape left hardly a trace, for the banning of *Coal Black and de Sebben Dwarfs* (it was withdrawn from circulation) proved effective in making the cartoon virtually disappear. What Clampett saw as an employment opportunity and as a benign "good time" was in fact a manifestation of racial anxieties in the United States stirred by a range of changes in the national landscape as well as by events on an international scale. It would take several decades before serious and thoughtful efforts would be made to interrogate and complicate the color-coding in canonical versions of "Snow White."

SNOW WHITE AND THE CULTURE OF DISTRACTION: DISNEY ENVY IN RUSSIA AND GERMANY

Walt Disney may have had ambitious expectations when it came to *Snow White and the Seven Dwarfs,* but he had no premonition whatsoever that poets, philosophers, and even politicians would brood over the film's artistic qualities. The renowned Russian filmmaker Sergei Eisenstein, who improbably actually knew Walt Disney ("we met like old acquaintances"), was one of the first to develop what could best be summarized as a love / hate relationship with Disney and his animated films. On the one hand, Eisenstein saw in the films "a joyful and beautiful art that sparkles with a refinement of form and dazzling purity."[39] But the filmmaker was also quick to perceive a dark side to Disney's cult of beautiful forms, for much as the cinematic artworks produced in Hollywood seemed remote from politics, their very commitment to pure entertainment and their promotion of a culture of distraction raised a red flag and made them deeply suspect in ideological terms.

While watching Disney's *Snow White and the Seven Dwarfs,* Eisenstein had a flashback to three childhood memories, each marking a brief reprieve from a momentous crisis. What he remembered was the "drop of comfort" and "instant of relief" offered by Disney. The American filmmaker, he declared, bestows on viewers, "through the magic of his works," a strong dose of "obliviousness, an instant of complete and total release from everything connected with the suffering caused by the social conditions of the social order of the largest capitalist government." Suddenly the impish charms of Mickey Mouse and the compelling drama of *Snow White and the Seven Dwarfs* collapse, and we learn from the Russian filmmaker the degree to which Disney has created pure entertainment in its most sinister form, a "drop of comfort" in the "hell of social burdens, injustices, and torments, in which the circle of his American viewers is forever trapped."[40] Art has become a narcotic, an opiate for the masses as powerful as what Marx saw in religion. In the end, Eisenstein cast his lot with the revolutionary vector of communism rather than what he condemned as the narcotizing pleasures of capitalism, despite, or rather perhaps because of, the seductions of Mickey Mouse and Snow White.

Eisenstein was undoubtedly onto something big. It was precisely the power of Disney films to entertain, distract, comfort, and soothe that made them so popular in Germany during the Nazi era. And the apparent lack of political or social baggage meant that these movies could travel with ease, crossing borders without incident from one country to the next. But Mickey Mouse and the *Führer*? Joseph Goebbels as a fan of Disney films? As unlikely as it seems, both the chancellor and the propaganda minister of the Third Reich deeply admired the cinematic imagination of Walt Disney. On February 5, 1938, Hitler asked his adjutant to secure a copy of *Snow White and the Seven Dwarfs* for a private screening in Obersalzberg (it would later be publicly screened in Berlin and other German cities), and it is said that he valued the film almost as much as did Goebbels, who declared it to be a "magnificent artistic achievement."[41] The propaganda minister had made no secret of his infatuation with *Snow White and the Seven Dwarfs:* the film was "a fairy tale for grown-ups, thought out into the last detail and made with a great love of humanity and nature. An artistic delight!"[42] It is hard to imagine that ideals about Aryan purity did not play into both Hitler's and Goebbels's appreciation of a film with an innocent white-skinned heroine as the "fairest of them all." Ironically, Disney's "skin white as snow," more than the Grimms' "white as snow," was an ideological bonus for Nazi leaders, who also applauded the revival of folktales from agrarian "Volk" cultures.

It took Theodor Adorno and Max Horkheimer to recognize just how tightly controlled and agenda driven Disney's "magnificent artistic achievements" really were. They believed that the films made by the Hollywood studio were as much about social engineering as what the Walt Disney Company now calls Imagineering. For the two German sociologists from the Frankfurt School, mass culture exists only to distract, soothe, and appease, offering "the freedom to choose what is always the same." In *Dialectic of Enlightenment* (1944), Adorno and Horkheimer made a compelling, if reductive, case for the US film industry operating in much the same way as the entertainment arm of fascist regimes in Europe, with monopoly capitalism creating passive viewers who mindlessly consume cultural products created by hegemonic institutions. Offering the illusion of freedom and escape, mass culture, in a series of cleverly calibrated calculations, reinforces its own power by accommodating within it resistance to its own system: "The escape from everyday drudgery which the whole culture industry promises may be compared to the daughter's abduction in the cartoon: the father is holding the ladder in the dark. The paradise offered by the culture industry is the same old drudgery. Both escape and elopement are pre-designed to lead back to the starting point.

Pleasure promotes the resignation which it ought to help to forget."[43] Pleasure, in other words, has its perils, for it has designs on viewers, doubling back and perpetuating acceptance of the status quo even as it purports to offer an escape hatch from it.

The demonization of Disney as a tranquilizing agent feels in many ways exaggerated and ignores how the film also wakes us up, startling viewers with its special effects and jolts of melodramatic family conflicts. It gets us talking (patently so in a culture attuned to race and gender politics), and it is also a pioneering work in the field of animation, one that kept alive, at a global level, the tale of a beautiful girl and her stepmother. As noted, the story offers a meditation on competition in general, on the way the new supplants the old and the way the next "version" is always more beautiful and attractive than the one before it, displacing and destroying its precursors. In a sense, the Grimms' "Snow White" triumphed for over a century as our master narrative about mother-daughter rivalry, while Disney's *Snow White and the Seven Dwarfs* later became culturally dominant, a kind of global metanarrative that aimed to liquidate the competition and monetize the folktale for all it was worth.

Despite the cultural dominance of Disney, the story of a beautiful girl and her vain, jealous mother continues to surface in a seemingly endless parade of variants, in some ways as a form of resistance to a mass-culture phenomenon that insists on telling the same old story in the same old way. Each new version engages in what fairy-tale DNA does so well, endlessly replicating itself and producing new stories that compel us to think through the psychological stakes in them. The tales in this volume may not dismantle or topple the authority of the Disney version, but they will reveal just how many different narrative possibilities are embedded in the fairy-tale structure we have called "Snow White." Our Snow White, in all her local singularity, deserves to be thought of in the context of an international repertoire, with her many folkloric cousins brought back to life and reanimated.

"SNOW WHITE" VERSUS "THE BEAUTIFUL GIRL"

Why have so many beautiful girls been edged out of the folkloric repertoire? A look at some of the tools used by scholars helps us understand exactly why. Folklorists have long relied on the *Types of International Folktales* to guide them in their research. That three-volume compendium catalogues, summarizes, and assigns tale type numbers to a vast corpus of lore. The classification system was first invented and published by the Finnish folklorist Antti Aarne in 1910 (as *The Types of the Folktale*), then revised by the American folklorist Stith Thompson in 1928 and again in 1961, and finally reworked by the German folklorist Hans-Jörg Uther in 2004. In it you can find 2,499 tale types in all (why exactly 2,499 is a legitimate question), among them ATU 545 ("The Cat as Helper"), ATU 400 ("The Man on a Quest for His Lost Wife"), ATU 505 ("The Grateful Dead"), and ATU 709 ("Snow White").

A survey of global variants of ATU 709 reveals just how misleading it is to adopt the title "Snow White" to designate stories about mother-daughter rivalry, especially since so many versions of the tale are told in climates without snow and with natives whose skin is rarely white. A more capacious designation might be "The Fairest of Them All" or "The Most Beautiful of Them All." "Sleeping Beauty" (ATU 410) is, of course, taken, and Beauty as a character is also unavailable; but "The Beautiful Girl," as the story is sometimes known in African cultures, would be a far more appropriate designation. In this book, I use "The Beautiful Girl" to designate stories that belong to the tale type known to folklorists as ATU 709, though occasionally I use "Snow White" as shorthand for Anglo-American and European versions.

Just what are the standard plot features of what the tale type index refers to as "Snow White" stories, and who are the principal actors and agents in the tale's cast of characters? When the Snow White name is absent, what does it take for us to have that moment when it dawns on us that we are immersed in a mother-daughter psychodrama with a familiar feel to it? Here are the main features as summarized in *The Types of International Folktales:*

> Snow White has a skin white as snow and lips red as blood. . . . A magic mirror tells her stepmother that Snow White is more beautiful than she. . . . The jealous stepmother orders a hunter to kill Snow White, . . . but he substitutes an animal's heart and saves her.
>
> Snow White goes to a house of dwarfs (robbers) . . . who adopt Snow White as their sister. . . . The stepmother now attempts to kill her by means of a poisoned lace, . . . a poisoned comb, . . . and a poisoned apple. . . . The dwarfs succeed in reviving the maiden from the first two poisonings but fail with the third. They lay her in a glass coffin. . . .
>
> A prince resuscitates her and marries her. . . . The stepmother is made to dance herself to death in red hot shoes.[44]

Note that Snow White's attributes have been reduced to fair skin and lips as red as blood and that black hair is no longer a part of her set features. What is problematic here is that a volume with "international" in the title seems to ignore the fact that most "Snow White" figures do not have fair skin, never mind that the Grimms' heroine is just "white as snow"—presumably fair-skinned but not with "skin white as snow." Someone should have detected disturbances in the airwaves once tales from Chile, Morocco, South Africa, and Turkey were added to the folkloric inventory of "Snow White" tale types, though the oversight was no doubt caused by the desire to retrofit the revised version of the tale type index to the original descriptors in Antti Aarne's *Types of the Folktale* rather than to construct an entirely new catalogue.

The motif that evokes the colors of the heroine's blood and skin appears frequently but no more frequently than stories in which the redness of blood is contrasted to the whiteness of milk or some other substance. In one African tale, a woman accidentally pricks her finger while sewing and wishes for a child as beautiful as the red drops of blood. She gives birth to a child and bathes it only in milk. In a Xhosa story, the heroine is restored to life when magic milk is poured over her. Marble, milk, and cheese serve as symbols of whiteness in Italian stories, and one Neapolitan hero finds, on his travels, a raven lying in a pool of blood on a marble stone: "Seeing the bright red blood upon the white, white marble, he heaved a deep sigh and exclaimed, 'Oh Heavens! Why can't I find a wife as white and red as this stone, and with hair and eyebrows as black as the feathers of this raven.'"[45]

Here, in abbreviated form, is the pattern that captures the main features of "The Beautiful Girl," a story well known to African cultures, one that resonates also with the biblical tale of Joseph and his brothers:

> A very beautiful girl arouses jealousy among her friends because she is acclaimed as the most beautiful of all.
>
> Her jealous companions separate her from her family and friends and lure her into a deserted area.
>
> The companions abandon the girl. They persuade her to climb down into a well and promise to help her get back up with a ladder. But they run away, taking the ladder with them.
>
> The girl is found when she sings for help. She is taken home and restored to health, while her treacherous companions are punished.

Flashes of the European "Snow White" can be found in many regions of Africa, and vice versa. In Namibia, there is a Snow White figure described as the daughter of "Frau Koningin [*sic*]" (the queen), and both are also identified as being "German." In African versions, the villain is a blood relative—a mother or sisters. In some of those, the mother has a magic mirror, but in most, it is the sun or the moon that utters the harsh words decreeing the superlative beauty of the daughter (many of the print versions from African cultures were collected by nineteenth- and twentieth-century missionaries and anthropologists from regions that did not have mirrors). It quickly becomes evident that there are many African versions of both "Snow White" and "The Beautiful Girl," with some bearing a resemblance to European tales (particularly in regions colonized by European powers) and some hewing more closely to the plot moves of local tales of magic. At the core of both stories is a beauty contest, and that contest motivates what follows: desperate attempts to snuff out the life of a younger, innocent rival.

The dramatis personae of ATU 709—mother, daughter, a crew of social outcasts or outlaws, and the rescuer—may do things differently from one version to the next, but they are always trapped in the same tightly choreographed drama of sexual rivalry, ostensibly fatal attack, and return to life. To be sure, each telling of the tale vibrates with cultural energy from its own time and place and includes local color and indigenous details, but the presence of a girl, a female persecutor, and a male rescuer, plus the sequence of moves outlined earlier, leads us instinctively to sense that we are in the presence of a "Snow White" / "Beautiful Girl" story.

The reassuring predictability when it comes to the narrative structure and cast of characters in the Snow White tale is paired with tremendous variation in the tropes that make each version of the tale more attractive and relevant. The details of the story fluctuate greatly, as a quick look at its different cultural manifestations reveals. Disney's princess ingests a poisoned apple, but her European counterparts fall victim to toxic combs, contaminated cakes, and, in one case, a suffocating braid. In versions from African cultures, a nail or some other sharp object is thrust into the girl's head. The weapons used in the murderous assaults range from corsets, rings, belts, wine, and gold coins to bread (tainted), raisins (poisoned), shirts, pins, and hats. The companions who offer shelter are sometimes dwarfs and thieves, but they may also be bears or monkeys, giants or ghouls, brothers or knights. Disney's queen, who demands Snow White's heart from the huntsman ordered to take the girl into the woods, actually seems restrained by comparison with the Grimms' evil queen, who instructs the huntsman to return with the girl's lungs and liver. In Spain, the queen is even more bloodthirsty, asking for a bottle of blood she plans to drink, with the girl's toe used as a cork. In Italy, the cruel queen instructs the huntsman to return with the girl's intestines and her blood-soaked shirt. Disney's film has memorialized the coffin made of glass; but in other versions of the story, it is made of gold, silver, or lead, or it is jewel encrusted. While often displayed on a mountaintop, it can also be set adrift on a river, placed under a tree, hung from the rafters, or locked in a room gleaming with candlelight. In the welter of possibilities, folk raconteurs could pick and choose or invent new features designed to shock, startle, or enchant. The poetics of improvisation keep the story fresh, relevant, and full of surprises.

THE MIRROR AND THE COFFIN

Let us linger for a moment longer in the folklorists' universe, looking now not at the figures swept up in the action of fairy-tale worlds but at the tropes and memes that have enabled the story to endure. "I've seen that before," we say, when we trip across a trope, halted in our tracks for a moment to stop and think. Tropes rattle us, leading us, as their derivation from the Greek term for "twist" suggests, to sit up, take notice, and connect with other stories we know. There are narrative tropes ("woman in peril" or "high school student stalked and killed"), but there are also the tropes that folklorists refer to as motifs, instantly recognizable story elements that connect to other tales and produce a pleasing resonance, for example, "haunted castle," "impossible tasks," or "hedge of thorns." These tropes not only arrest our attention but also draw us into a force field that demands intellectual engagement by challenging us to make connections, draw contrasts, and consider how the trope is deployed. Packed with symbolic meaning, fairy-tale tropes invite us to construct our own miniature inquiries into, say, the broader significance of missing shoes or the meaning of invisibility cloaks at different times and in other places.

In a fairy tale that turns on beauty and death, the queen's mirror and Snow White's coffin—as they appear in Anglo-American and European tales from the past few centuries—resonate with cultural meaning. Is it any wonder that one critic proposes calling ATU 709 "Cracking the Magic Mirror"?[46] The queen's divinatory mirror is unforgettable, yet it is also not indispensable, although in many ways it has become central to modern and postmodern retellings. The window through which Snow White's biological mother looks at the beginning of the story as she sits, sews, and dreams of a child "white as snow" introduces the theme of reflective, transparent surfaces, in this case an enclosure that suggests confinement and interiority. The mother remains secluded in a domestic space, but it is an indoor space that does not foreclose the possibility of imagining what is outside and using elements of it in artful ways while performing handicraft work. The looking glass, by contrast, can be seen as a trope for vanity, pride, and narcissism, and it doubles as a symbol of self-division, a sign of lost innocence and the triumph of duplicity, deception, and double-dealing. Helen Oyeyemi foregrounded the "tyranny of the mirror" in her reworking of "Snow White" motifs, showing how it could launch the process of reflection and introspection in its most extreme, unforgiving form.[47]

For the wicked queen, the mirror is also the voice of judgment, authority in its most compelling form. It may be the voice of patriarchal authority, as the feminist critics Sandra Gilbert and Susan Gubar told us, but it also represents a form of self-assessment and judgment.[48] Fiona French turns it into public opinion in her sassy picture book *Snow White in New York* (1990), which cleverly features a newspaper called the *New York Mirror*. Adèle Geras's 1993 Young Adult novel, *Pictures of the Night,* gives us the judgmental voice in the form of a hairdresser who sizes up his clients as he looks at them in the mirror and who fires the jealousy of heroine Bella's stepmother. And Emma Donoghue's "The Tale of the Apple," from her 1997 collection of short stories, *Kissing the Witch,* brilliantly turns the eyes of stepmother and daughter into self-cancelling mirrors "set opposite each other, making a corridor of reflections, infinitely hollow."[49]

The mirror reflects back to the queen an image of beauty, integrity, and autonomy, but it is also a reminder of temporality—the image that looks back at us from a mirror is subject to change: ephemeral and marked by mortality. Beauty may appear to mask death, but its image (both in the mirror and on the face of Snow White in her coffin) has a sinister side, reminding us that everything is subject to decay and must die.[50]

"Snow White" takes up questions of beauty, aging, and mortality, but it also offers a counternarrative that takes us into the territory of death and resurrection; and it is here that the glass coffin figures powerfully. The seven-year-old girl has presumably grown into a young woman before she is poisoned, and when she dies, the dwarfs cannot bear to bury her. They place the body into a transparent coffin designed to ensure that she can be seen "from all sides," and they write her name with gold lettering on one side. "She does not decay," the Grimms wrote, and Snow White, who only looks as if she is dead, is still "white as snow, red as blood," with hair "black as ebony wood." Turning a corpse into a work of art, complete with frame and name, the dwarfs construct a complex icon, one that, in an act of brilliant calculation, links beauty and immortality with maximum collision force. On the one hand, we have the mirror as a palpably direct reminder of beauty and aging; on the other hand, there is the coffin as a memento of beauty and also a container that signifies death even as Snow White is protected from its biological ravages.

Transparent glass and reflective glass: these two surfaces were not available to storytellers in earlier eras. When we consult the folkloric record, we discover versions of the story in which the mother or stepmother consults the sun or the moon to determine who ranks higher when it comes to beauty. These heavenly bodies draw the story into the orbit of the natural world, reminding us that circadian rhythms and seasonal change served as the motors of fairy-tale plots in an earlier age. As sources of illumination, the sun and the moon signal wisdom in ways that link them with patriarchal authority yet without introducing the narcissistic edge added by the presence of a mirror. Representing, reflecting, and also revealing, the mirror is a latter-day bonus that sets up modernist interventions in a tale that originated in premodern rural storytelling cultures.

Borrowing from the tropes of the sacred, "The Beautiful Girl" belongs to a mythical universe that takes on questions fundamental to the human condition and to the natural world around us and is also relevant to the poetics of storytelling. Everything is subject to change, but there is such a thing as resurrection and renewal, it tells us. The tale becomes not only a story about mother-daughter conflict but also a myth about seasonal change. Beyond that, it is also a never-ending story, vital, self-reflexive, and relevant precisely because, as noted, it is always evolving and ready to be reanimated in a more "beautiful" version by the next generation. The tale repeats itself in an endless hall of mirrors, but with new inflection points in its history, as each dominant version is displaced by the next while moving from one time and place to another. Suddenly we witness a decoupling between the tale's manifest content about mothers and daughters on the one hand and on the other the act of narration itself, which is foregrounded as a self-consuming but also self-renewing process. Even the Disney version, the Snow White story in its most enduring and widely dispersed form, is destined to fade and die, for it too is gradually being unseated and displaced by other films that share features of the parent narrative, including *Snow White and the Huntsman* (2012) and the planned live-action version of *Snow White and the Seven Dwarfs.*

BEAUTY, AGING, AND DEATH

Mirrors and coffins have become master-tropes in the "Snow White" plot, and they remind us of the simple deceptions of fairy tales as well as their deceptive simplicity. Take a mirror, and you have suddenly found not only a way to capture vanity, beauty, and fear of aging but also a reflective surface that invites contemplation and thought. Put a beautiful woman on display in a glass coffin, and you have raised the specter of death as well as the hope of forever preserving the beauty of the ones we love. Fairy tales capture dread and desire without explicitly naming what lies beneath them. In our minds, those terrors and wishes may be submerged—repressed and suppressed—but fairy tales bring them right to the surface, making them vivid and palpably real.

When Snow White reaches age seven in the Grimms' story, she displaces the queen as "the fairest of them all," signaling that her mother's beauty is destined to fade and die, that nothing is permanent. And with the loss of beauty comes, especially for women living in an earlier era, the erosion of any power at all.[51] The stepmother in "Snow White," as Garrison Keillor once wrote in "My Stepmother, Myself," is a "victim of the male attitude that prizes youth over maturity when it comes to women." Mocking feminist critiques of the story, he added that the daughter in this case escapes the age trap by knowingly taking a bite of the apple: "The fact is that I *knew* that the apple was poisoned. For me, it was the only way out."[52] It's better to die than to become less attractive to men.

The centrality of the loss-of-beauty trope becomes evident in Disney's compression of the aging process into a brief sequence showing the queen drinking a magic potion, a potent cocktail that is just the opposite of the elixir of youth. Suddenly her hair turns white, her fingers grow talons, her hands become gnarled with age ("Look, my hands!"), her words turn into a throaty cackle ("My voice!"), and finally she emerges from under her dark cloak as a hunchbacked crone. That brilliant allegory of aging, bewitching in its artistic virtuosity, reminds us that just as much is slipped into fairy tales for grown-ups as for the young, even more in many cases.

Fear of aging and anxieties about mortality—these were also the concerns of the poet Anne Sexton when she rewrote the Grimms' fairy tales, turning them with unnerving intensity into poems for adults. Sexton may well have had Disney's hag in mind when, in *Transformations* (the 1972 volume of poems that rewrites the Brothers Grimm in verse only to upend their tales), she writes about an aging queen in the Snow White story ("brown spots on her hand / and four whiskers over her lips") and how she is pitted against a thirteen-year-old "lovely virgin." "Beauty is a simple passion," Sexton declares, "but, oh my friends, in the end / you will dance the fire dance in iron shoes." The scene that stages the queen's death juxtaposes a mobile queen, dancing to death with "her tongue flicking in and out / like a gas jet," with a frozen Snow White, "rolling her china-blue doll eyes open and shut / and sometimes referring to her mirror / as women do."[53] Sexton's inert Snow White will one day gaze into the mirror and become like her mother, galvanized into action and turned into an agent of persecution once she sees that her daughter's beauty exceeds her own.

Snow White's story is, then, about more than mother-daughter rivalry and romantic rescue. It feeds on anxieties about aging and generational succession, showing how time wears beauty away. And it also cues up fears about our own mortality. Snow White may be brought back from the dead—she may be rescued, but we know that her beauty too is subject to aging and that her flesh is mortal. The happy ending may be a salve, but it is also a reminder that our efforts to defy death through the cultural work of creating "everlasting" beauty, "immortal" works of art, and labors of "undying" love are all in vain. And yet, at the same time, like every great myth, the story of Snow White is forever undermining its own terms and confronting us with a paradox. By offering the promise of resurrection and displaying it in the most vivid possible terms, it tells us that in this case some things really are stronger than death.

DARK MAGIC, TRANSFORMATION, AND THE MYTHICAL IMAGINATION

"The Beautiful Girl," in all its rich cultural variation, gives us two things that the best fairy tales unfailingly deliver: magic and transformation. Recall how Jack plants beans, and he returns from the beanstalk not just with wealth (the goose that lays golden eggs) but also with song (the magic harp that plays by itself). A fairy godmother gives Cinderella beautiful clothes and an enchanted coach, and, presto, she moves from rags to riches. Beauty weeps tears of compassion, and Beast turns from a figure of grotesque monstrosity into a handsome prince. Snow White takes a bite from a poisoned apple, falls into a coma, and is revived by a kiss—or, in some instances, by the jolt she feels when the prince's servants drop her coffin, dislodging the apple in her throat. Along with magic and its high coefficient of weirdness come the many odd coincidences, strange accidents, and inspired mischief that belong as much to the logic of fairy-tale worlds as courage, wits, and defiance do.

In the Grimms' "Snow White," magic is concentrated in the figure of the stepmother, who not only possesses an oracular mirror but also has a kind of "witchcraft" that enables her to fashion a poisoned comb and apple to peddle to Snow White. In the Disney version of the story, everything is cinematically enlarged in colossal ways so that the wicked queen does not simply "stain" her face and dress up as a peddler woman. Instead, after the mirror reports that the huntsman has substituted a pig's heart for Snow White's, she descends into her underground lair, a place infested with rats and crows, where she consults the musty tomes in her library for a "formula" that will transform her "beauty" into "ugliness." Taking some "mummy dust" to make her old, the "black of night" to darken her clothes, an "old hag's cackle" to age her voice, a "scream of fright" to whiten her hair, "a blast of wind" to fan her hate, and, finally, a thunderbolt "to mix it well," she works a "magic spell" and drinks the potion that turns her from beautiful queen into ugly hag. In a final hate-filled flourish, she manufactures the poisoned apple that is capable of producing a "sleeping death," a sleep that will, ironically, make her rival even more beautiful than she was while alive.

Since ancient times, when the Iranian term *maguš* was taken as a loan word by the Greeks, magic has carried a negative valence, associated with a threatening foreign power. The Greek *mágos,* for example, was regarded as a swindler and his practices considered fraudulent. Those who practiced magic were seen as marked by alterity—treacherous, subversive, and producing harmful effects. The Grimms' wicked queen is a master of witchcraft, and Disney's animated counterpart is adept at all kinds of arts, ranging from the concocting of brews to the casting of spells. The voice in the magic mirror may be practiced in divination, but the queen draws on the power of words (those volumes in her underground library), the potency of the elements (her chemistry set is the envy of viewers), and the strength of natural forces (the wind and thunderbolts) to work her dark magic. If Snow White makes a natural transition from victimized child to triumphantly happy adult, her rise is shadowed by the sinister art of her mother, an adept relying on magic and other heretical practices to eliminate her rival. Paradoxically, the happily-ever-after of this fairy tale requires some kind of dark, transformative magic, foregrounding sinister scheming for the maternal blessing sought by many fairy-tale heroines.

Still, as we have seen, there is a second story here about magic and transformation—a meditation on death and resurrection that opens up the possibility that bodies do not decay and that you can return from the dead. With that, as we have seen, we are in the realm of the mythical. "Through the forest of fairy tale, the vibrancy of myth passes like a shudder of wind," Italo Calvino once observed, and he no doubt had something like "Snow White" in mind, a story that takes up death and resurrection in terms that are less Christian and sacred than pagan and profane.[54]

It does not require a great leap of imagination to connect Snow White stories with that one "marvelously constant story" that the American mythographer Joseph Campbell identified in *The Hero with a Thousand Faces.*[55] The hero's journey, according to Campbell, traces a trajectory from the womb to the (symbolic) tomb, followed by resurrection in one form or another. Campbell describes the pattern more compactly as Departure, Initiation, Return, and he sees in that move an upward spiral that tracks the hero (his heroes are all emphatically male) "on a perilous journey into the darkness" and draws him into a labyrinth from which he emerges as a charismatic leader.[56] No such glory awaits Snow White, but the stations of her suffering are in fact not so radically different from the nodal points of the hero's journey and suggest that beauty can work a magic of its own. And as the many illustrations showing Snow White in her coffin reveal, there is a distinct Adoration of the Magi feel to scenes with the mourning dwarfs, just as there is also a hint of Christ's entombment and resurrection.

It is easy enough to put the story of Snow White in dialogue with other myths—Demeter and Persephone, to cite just one example—with its daughter abducted and taken into the underworld, only to return, seasonally, in a move that signals resurrection and renewal. What is important in these narratives—all bits and pieces of what anthropologists tell us is a larger myth about life and death as much as about beauty—is how they draw from the same storytelling arsenal to take on the great existential mysteries as they try to create counternarratives to the reality that all living beings must die.

The stepmother's dark magic taps into children's fears about all-powerful mothers as well as into adult anxieties about human mortality. The fairy-tale plot takes us into the arena of domestic disturbances, staging a conflict between a cruel parent adept in the dark arts and an innocent, trembling child, with the two enacting a worst-case family scenario. On another level—and here we are reminded that all fairy tales have mythical features—the story uses magic to unfold an encounter with death, more than a mere brush with death but less than a permanent descent into darkness.

Myth, for all its associations with the invented, fabricated, and made up, has a strange way of reaching into the real. Jean Cocteau surely understood the healing power of fairy tales better than almost anyone when he directed the film *La Belle et la Bête* (1946) in postwar France. "I've always preferred mythology to history," he wrote. "History is truth that becomes an illusion. Mythology is an illusion that becomes reality."[57] Just how have stories and films about beautiful girls touched readers and viewers? What kind of cultural work do they do, and how do we harness their energy in ways that can be therapeutic rather than toxic?

OUR COLLECTIVE FICTIONS

In *Sapiens: A Brief History of Humankind,* Yuval Noah Harari describes a "Cognitive Revolution" that enabled *Homo sapiens* to reach the top of the food chain. What Harari sees as pivotal is not so much the invention of language as a tool for transmitting knowledge as the capacity of language to create fiction—stories about things that have no grounding in reality. These collective fictions take the form of myth, legend, and religion, and they enable humans to cooperate in large groups. But those stories are also nothing but invented constructs, Harari insists: "There are no gods in the universe, no nations, no money, no human rights, no laws, and no justice outside the common imagination of human beings."[58] We take that on faith, and we have survived precisely because we create collective fictions and improbably turn ourselves into true believers.

Harari does not pay much attention to the collective fictions we know to be lies and to which we bring skepticism from the start. The "big old lies" (to use Zora Neale Hurston's phrase) we tell each other are patently counterfactual and false, and they take the form of the symbolic stories we use, not so much to build the foundations of the legal, political, and commercial world of *Homo sapiens* as to make sense of the world and to develop an understanding of who we are and why we do the things we do.[59] When we tell fairy tales, myths, or legends and create literary fictions, we are supremely aware that the stories are not true. Yet we keep telling them, not because they give us historical facts but because they traffic in higher, spiritual truths to help us understand what could be, should be, and might be.

Taken literally, these kinds of narratives can turn toxic. But understood as symbolic stories, they engage our imaginations and oblige us to start thinking about perils and possibilities. As Marina Warner tells us, fairy tales are "above all acts of imagination, conveyed in a symbolic Esperanto," with "building blocks" that include "certain kinds of characters (stepmothers and princesses, elves and giants) and certain recurrent motifs (keys, apples, mirrors, rings, and toads)."[60] Unlike foundational myths and charter narratives that can lead to the creation of belief systems, fairy tales welcome incredulity and invite skepticism, challenging us to think hard about the terms of a story and reimagine it in our own minds as we listen to one version of it. They generate talk, gossip, chatter, and conversation—all those lines of communication that turned *Homo sapiens* into a master of collective bartering, bickering, bargaining, and, most important, brainstorming.

And yet not all would agree that every collective, communal story is worth preserving and bringing back to life in new shapes and forms. Ellen Datlow and Terri Windling, two experts on fairy tales, describe "Snow White" as "the most disturbing" in the fairy-tale canon. The story, they argue, "remains chilling in its evocation of a mother's hatred toward her child and an aging beauty's obsession with a younger rival in a world where beauty is the basis of power."[61] As we have seen, there is much in versions of the story to give offense, but that may be exactly why we should not let the story of the beautiful girl go and instead struggle with all the things in that story that we rebel against, simply because they take us out of our comfort zone.

We have more to gain than to lose when we confront and contest a story like "Snow White." To take one spectacular example, the weighty effects of reading fairy tales and embracing them, rather than challenging them, can be found in the life of Alan Turing, the father of theoretical computer science. When Turing went to see Disney's *Snow White and the Seven Dwarfs,* a year after its Hollywood debut, he fell under the spell of the scene in which the wicked queen labors in her underground hideout, preparing the poisonous brew that will put her stepdaughter in a coma.

According to his running partner Allan Garner, Turing would go over the scene in detail, describing the apple as red on one side, green on the other (the wicked queen actually starts with a green apple, which is turned red). He would ritually chant the couplet, "Dip the apple in the brew / Let the Sleeping Death seep through." On June 8, 1954, Turing's landlady discovered his inert body. At his bedside: half an apple; and in the kitchen: a jam jar with a cyanide solution.[62] In some ways, this is the true Turing enigma, a posthumous challenge from the man who established the foundation for artificial intelligence to those who defend the uses of enchantment. Turing's reading reminds us of just how important it is to break the magic spell of a tale rather than to embrace its seductive appeal, even if his obsession with the Disney film had no real-life consequences and was nothing more than a way of giving expression to deep-rooted anxieties. The stories are there to quicken our imaginations, to envision alternatives to their plots, and to be inventive and adventurous as we make the stories our own.

Does "Snow White," we might ask, nourish the very anxieties it aims to soothe? Is there a way that the story might amplify the high stakes in the drama of mother-daughter rivalry? If Turing gives us a reason to worry about fairy tales and their possibly toxic properties, we have even more reason to fear the power of fantasy when we watch Erin Lee Carr's

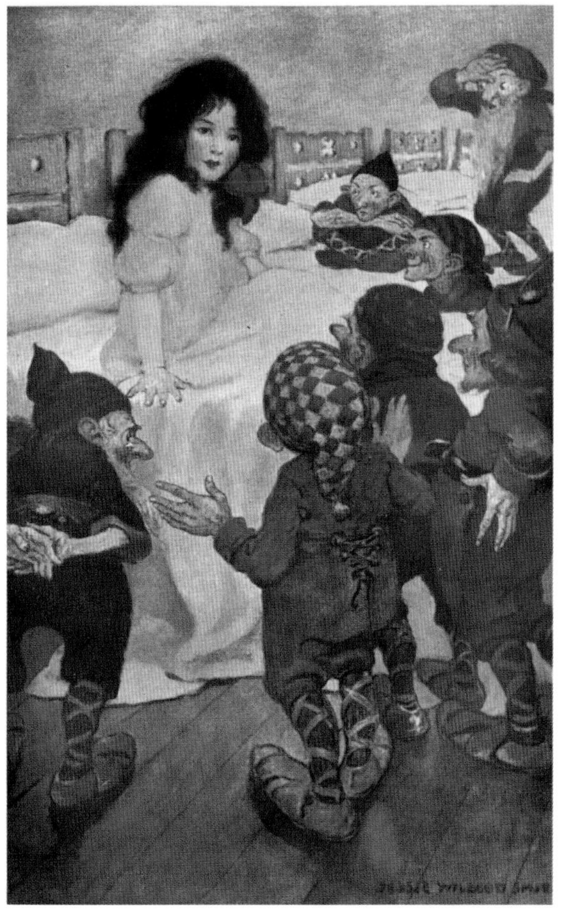

(*top*) 17 The German illustrator Lothar Meggendorffer (1847–1925) created a dozen images for the Grimms' "Snow White," and, in this first one, the blond-haired, biological mother has just pricked her finger while sewing, with a single drop of red blood contrasting with the white of her handiwork. Like Walter Crane, who produced fairy-tale "toy books" for the British public, Meggendorffer used vibrant colors and brought the outdoors indoors with plants and animals, along with fabrics and furnishings with floral designs.

(*left*) 18 Jessie Willcox Smith (1863–1935), best known for her family scenes, especially of mothers and their children, gives us a Snow White considerably younger than the one appearing in most illustrations for the story. All eyes are fixed on the rosy-cheeked girl, who fits the Grimms' description of her perfectly.

19 Theodor Hosemann (1807–1875), a German painter, illustrator, and caricaturist, reveals the full terror felt by a traumatized Snow White, as she pleads for her life before a huntsman poised to stab her.

20 The German illustrator Franz Jüttner (1865–1926) created a series of eight colorful images for the Grimms' "Little Snow White." Off the hunter goes on the far right (between two trees), while Snow White, in luminous white, makes her way through a gloomy forest with predators lurking all around and birds, bugs, and squirrels as part of the sylvan fauna.

21 The sharp edges of the wicked queen's magnificent costume and regal bearing form a strong contrast with Snow White's soft features. Here the queen holds the potion that will be used to let the "sleeping death" seep through the apple she plans to offer Snow White.

22 In the 2012 film *Snow White and the Huntsman,* Kristen Stewart plays a Snow White true to the Grimms' chromatic register. Queen Ravenna, played by Charlize Theron, entices Snow White into taking a bite of the poisoned apple at her side in the film still.

23 A young, blond Snow White frolics with doll-like dwarfs in a rustic idyll, tightly choreographed and contained within the picture frame. The German illustrator Hermann Vogel (1854–1921) strengthened Snow White's connection with nature with the beauty of the flora and fauna surrounding the girl.

24 The Scottish artist Katharine Cameron (1874–1965) added a touch of chinoiserie to *Snowdrop,* her portrait of the wicked queen interrogating her magic mirror. The investment in image and surfaces becomes evident not only in the reflection but also in the vase and artwork on the wall.

25 “The Dwarfs, when they came in the evening, found Snowdrop lying on the ground.” Frantically attentive to the comatose young woman, the captivating dwarfs take her pulse, bring water, and try to make her more comfortable. Dressed entirely in white, Snowdrop, as she is called, contrasts sharply with the dwarfs, all wearing eccentrically stylish bandanas, checked and striped in this classic Arthur Rackham (1867–1939) illustration for the Grimms’ story.

(*top*) 26 A pampered queen admires herself in a mirror while courtiers tend to her every whim in an exoticized illustration created by Jennie Harbour (1893–1959) for a volume of fairy tales.

(*left*) 27 The American illustrator Dorothy Dulin gives us a dramatic rendering of the mirror scene, with a queen enthralled by appearances.

(top) 28 A raven, owl, and dove keep watch over Snow White, along with one of the dwarfs and forest creatures. The luminous moon and coffin lit up by it hold forth the promise that the girl will be restored to life in Thekla Brauer's (1871–1960) illustration for the Grimms' tale.

(right) 29 Charles B. Falls (1874–1960) provided many somber illustrations for an American fairy-tale play inspired by the Grimms' "Little Snow White." The harsh moonlit landscape is dominated by a stepmother up to no good.

documentary film *Mommy Dead and Dearest* (2017). Carr includes a remarkable sequence that begins with a girl named Gypsy Rose Blanchard, victim of Munchausen syndrome by proxy (her mother's need to turn a healthy child into a dangerously ill patient), sitting in Cinderella's castle at Disney World, eating "some real mashed potatoes," as she calls the food on her plate. As we discover, this is a girl who never learned how to distinguish fantasy from reality. "Life is not a fairy tale," she later reflects while awaiting trial for plotting with her boyfriend to kill her mother. "I learned that the hard way," she admits after she has been charged with second-degree murder.

What fairy tale did Gypsy Rose use to make sense of her life? "I liked the Disney film *Tangled,*" she says, looking directly into the camera. "It's about Rapunzel. She's a princess in this kingdom, and she's kidnapped by Mother Gothel from her real family. And Mother Gothel keeps her in this tower for all of her life and tells her 'Don't leave this tower,' so that is all she knows. . . . At the end Mother Gothel dies. She got thrown out a window because Rapunzel tried to stand up for herself and leave her tower." In many ways, *Tangled* is just another version of *Snow White and the Seven Dwarfs,* with the tower as a kind of coffin imprisoning and limiting a young woman in ways that make her dead to the world.

Gypsy Rose never had a chance to learn to distinguish fantasy from reality, and in an odd way, like Turing, she identified and wanted to reenact rather than talk back to the fairy tale. The desperate need to follow scripts that are pure fantasy turned her life into what one court officer describes in the film as a "fairy-tale nightmare," a worst-case scenario that replicated the colossal excesses of fairy tales and never enabled her to experience the redemptive therapeutic value of stories understood as story. Never told in a safe space that creates the opportunity to use the symbolic to navigate the real, the stories modeled behavior that, in her case, turned horrifyingly real.

Fairy tales can, to be sure, feed pathologies and turn toxic, particularly when they become weary retreads of the tried and true and do nothing more than retell the same old story. Our ancestors used these narratives to keep themselves woke as well as awake—to shock, startle, and generate talk rather than to invite identification and imitation in solitary pursuits. Fairy-tale plots can move us to engage with and work through the many conflicts and taboos they so unceremoniously invoke. The question for us today is, How do we recruit stories about beautiful girls so that they function as cure rather than curse?

HOW "SNOW WHITE" CONNECTS US TO THE DARK SIDE OF THE MOTHER-DAUGHTER BOND

Fairy-tale drama turns on moments of existential crisis. Beauty is sacrificed by her father to appease a beast; a child loses her mother just moments after being born; a predatory witch invites children in for a meal; and a girl is evicted from the tower where she has spent her childhood. Few existential crises can match the one in which a girl becomes the victim of maternal malice, and nowhere is that malice more vividly on display, as we have seen, than in the story we call "Snow White." Two rivals—one evil, cunning, and determined; the other sweet, innocent, and naive—are locked in mortal combat, with one destined to die while the other will survive and thrive. Staged as a beauty contest, the story, as we have seen, actually gives us much more than that, drawing us, with lightning speed, into matters ranging from generational conflict and narcissistic pathologies to seasonal change and the promise of rejuvenation. It is a tale that takes up the unspeakable—the possibility that maternal love may not be rock solid—and it gives us an opportunity to talk about things that are ordinarily not the subject of polite conversation.

"Whatever else is unsure in this stinking dunghill of a world a mother's love is not," James Joyce famously wrote in *A Portrait of the Artist as a Young Man* (1916).[63] Our stories about beautiful girls and their jealous mothers give the lie to that dead certainty about maternal love, which has almost universally been seen as robust, enduring, and always available, even as fatherhood has long been associated with the moment of begetting rather than the protracted process of nurturing and raising. Motherhood has implied not just the biological capacity to give birth but also the social activity of empathetic parenting.

It took courage for the poet Adrienne Rich to describe, in 1970s America, the "exquisite suffering" of being a mother. "It is the suffering of ambivalence: the murderous alternation between bitter resentment and raw-edged nerves, and blissful gratification and tenderness." Sometimes a mother will see herself as a "monster of selfishness and intolerance," barely able to manage her "held-in rage." Caught up in "waves of love and hate, jealousy even of the child's childhood, hope and fear for its maturity," she is the quintessence of ambivalence.[64] Rich is uncompromising in her effort to chart the full emotional spectrum of maternal dedication to child rearing.

"I have *never* heard a mother say she does not love her daughter," Nancy Friday tells us in *My Mother / My Self*, her best-selling study of the conflicted feelings in mother-daughter relationships. And she quickly adds, "I have heard daughters say they do not love their mothers."[65] Clearly there is some kind of taboo at work, and the excesses of maternal cruelty and craft with regard to daughters in fairy tales are rich with implication and raise a red flag that requires attention. Why are there so many cold and calculating (step)mothers in tales that were once part of an adult storytelling culture? And do they somehow provide an outlet for talking about things otherwise considered unmentionable?

Perhaps it is precisely because maternal anger and antagonism toward a child is so off limits as an affect and as a topic of conversation that we have so many stories dramatizing those feelings. Mothers may feel "love and resentment, affection and anger," but they cannot afford to "*know* it," Nancy Friday tells us.[66] In some ways, stories can express the feelings we suppress in real life and then discharge culturally unacceptable toxic feelings through imaginative work. The less we are able to talk about hostile feelings toward a child, the stronger the impulse to release those emotions. And what better way to release them is there than to make up a story so outrageous that it *cannot possibly* be true?

The father of psychoanalysis understood exactly how the symbolic functions as a cover for forbidden fantasies and thoughts rooted in real life. Sigmund Freud described, in an essay on writers and their day-dreams, how most people would not consider divulging the content of idle dreams, for they are usually tainted with too much guilt and shame about the feelings at their core. But poets, he tells us, use artistic flourishes and disguises to mask the kinds of anxieties that find expression in dreams, and then they work their magic to present them in an appealing format. They enable us "to enjoy our own day-dreams without self-reproach or shame."[67] And the genre best suited for restoring the pleasure principle in the face of guilt and self-censure is—what else but the fairy tale?

Fairy tales are known for the economy of means with which they operate. Even as stories about maternal cruelty may provide expressive outlets for women, these same tales help children give free rein to their hostile feelings to mothers. We have seen how powerfully the taboo against revealing maternal rage toward a child operates, and there is an equally powerful taboo against exposing the myth about the purity of a young child's love for mother. The Swiss psychotherapist Alice Miller has noted that "there is one taboo that has withstood all the recent efforts at demystification: the idealization of mother love."[68] By splitting the mother into a good (often dead) mother and an evil stepmother, mother-in-law, or witch, fairy tales enable children to preserve positive feelings about their own parent even as they indulge in all manner of morbid fantasies about the "bad" mother. As Bruno Bettelheim put it in his landmark study of fairy tales, *The Uses of Enchantment*, "such a splitting up of one person into two to keep the good image uncontaminated occurs to many children as a solution to a relationship too difficult to manage or comprehend." And, with this strategy, "all contradictions are suddenly solved."[69] That conclusion may feel somewhat facile, but it reminds us that emotional ambivalence has always been the stuff of fairy tales.

A story like "Snow White" succeeds in giving voice to all the feelings of resentment harbored by a mother whose physical capacities and mental reserves are stretched by care for a child. The genius of the story is that it enables the child as well to preserve the positive image of a protective, nurturing mother, all the while projecting onto an evil double or impostor all the hostile feelings harbored toward a real-life mother who engages at times in withholding love or denying pleasure. The story can become a productive contact zone for all kinds of pairings ranging from mother and child to therapist and patient, with the potential for deep insight even as the tale enacts the dark side of the mother-daughter relationship.

But what about the child left alone with stories like "Snow White"? In 1997, Michael Cohn made a film adaptation of "Snow White" to which he gave the subtitle *Tale of Terror,* with a descriptor that captures exactly what a child might experience when exposed to this story. Left alone in the woods with a huntsman who, in many illustrations, is poised with dagger in hand, Snow White, through the protective power of her beauty, manages to escape. In Disney's *Snow White and the Seven Dwarfs,* she flees the huntsman and enters a haunted forest in which logs turn into crocodiles and tree branches snatch at her clothes. In the 1937 film, we see her full frontal, open-mouthed, wide-eyed, arms akimbo, scrambling in terror across perilous terrain.

Today we have turned many of these innocent, persecuted heroines into warrior princesses who wield weapons and use their wits to outsmart opponents. But there may also be value in displaying frailty, weakness, and terror—the entire range of a child's sense of vulnerability and helplessness—and showing how, despite all those feelings, it is possible to navigate your way to safety. Snow White's defenselessness enables adults to go back and feel just what it was once like to imagine yourself without resources, even as it lets children experience, in a safe place, the rush of emotions attached to feelings of abandonment, peril, and lack of adult protection. Perhaps this is one explanation for the uses of enchantment in therapeutic sessions—as a means of remembering not just the kinds of trauma suffered in childhood but also the feelings associated with those remembered moments.

Let us forget what the priests of high culture chanted in times past. Today, we are discovering that we can change the narrative about narratives. Instead of placing stories in the service of constructing imagined communities with shared allegiances to a nation state (as the Brothers Grimm did, along with the many collectors who followed in their footsteps), we can begin to identify links in the chain of what the folklorist William Wells Newell described as the "golden net-work" linking worlds radically different in terms of their political order, legal practices, and economic arrangements.[70] Stories that we once imagined to be a constructed collective "theirs" or "ours" turn out to be yours as much as mine, and these fictions are used around the world, not just to entertain and distract but also to engage our imaginations, define our aspirations, and forge our identities. In endless forms most beautiful and wonderful, the same stories keep coming back (always in new ways) to reveal that we live not only by collective fictions in the world of politics, finance, and law—all those institutions that make the human world—but also by all those big old lies that make the world human. These stories are about families, but they also tell us about family in the larger sense, reminding us that we are all next of kin and that we share far more than we ever imagined. As we have seen, "beautiful girls" in fairy tales from around the world are forever reminding us that our collective fears and desires are heterogeneous and complex but also at their core related and relatable in powerful ways.[71]

FOR THE READER

The tales in this volume will take readers on a high-spirited ride, often far away from the here and now into storytelling cultures from long ago and far away. What kinds of tales did our ancestors tell about mothers and daughters and the generational conflicts that arose between them? How were those tales inflected in times past, and are those new twists revelatory in some way?

Each story in this volume has its own gravitational pull and can be painlessly detached from its neighbors in this anthology. But fairy tales about beautiful girls can also be read consecutively, if not necessarily in the chronological order of publication set forth in the table of contents. Readers may want to travel to India one evening, to Italy on another, and they may be inclined to make a stop in Portugal the next night. For those interested in exploring additional versions of the tale, everything from "The Story of Chione" in Ovid's *Metamorphoses* and the tale of Snæfriðr in Snorri Sturluson's Nordic epic to contemporary picture books, novels, and films about Snow White and other beautiful girls, the Bibliography offers many opportunities for deeper exploration.

The stories presented here were collected under a variety of social and cultural circumstances, in some cases by native collectors to consolidate national identity, but in other cases by non-native anthropologists and colonial administrators invested in understanding the minds of the colonized. The stories they published, as Sadhana Naithani reminds us, were "temporally and spiritually disconnected from the narrators" and repurposed as entertainment for those with no understanding of social context. Still, what they recorded lets us see, if only through a glass darkly, something of the connectivity between worlds set apart in geographical and cultural terms.[72]

NOTES TO THE INTRODUCTION

1 "Fairness" can, of course, be read as a sign of Snow White's instinct for justice, and that attribute points to the possibility that beauty and justice, as Elaine Scarry has pointed out, are more closely akin that we realize. "In periods when a human community is too young to have yet had time to create justice, as well as in periods when justice has been taken away, beautiful things . . . hold steadily visible the manifest good of equality and balance." Scarry, *On Beauty and Being Just* (Princeton, NJ: Princeton University Press, 2001), 97.

2 J. R. R. Tolkien, "On Fairy-Stories," in *The Tolkien Reader* (New York: Ballantine, 1966), 26–27.

3 Sandra M. Gilbert and Susan Gubar, *The Madwoman in the Attic: The Woman Writer and the Nineteenth-Century Literary Imagination* (New Haven, CT: Yale University Press, 1979), 36.

4 Wikiquote, "Albert Einstein," accessed October 31, 2019, https://en.wikiquote.org/wiki/Albert_Einstein#Disputed.

5 A. S. Byatt, "Happily Ever After," *The Guardian,* January 3, 2004, https://www.theguardian.com/books/2004/jan/03/sciencefictionfantasyandhorror.fiction.

6 Aljean Harmetz, "A Promotional Blitz for Snow White," *New York Times,* April 29, 1987, https://www.nytimes.com/1987/04/29/movies/a-promotional-blitz-for-snow-white.html.

7 Helen Holmes, "Keira Knightley and Kristen Bell Are Not Down with Disney Princesses," *Observer,* October 18, 2018, https://observer.com/2018/10/no-disney-princesses-keira-knightley-and-kristen-bell/.

8 Shuli Barzilai, "Reading 'Snow White': The Mother's Story," *Signs* 15 (1990): 523.

9 "Mouse & Man," *Time,* December 27, 1937, 21.

10 Neil Gabler, *Walt Disney: The Triumph of the American Imagination* (New York: Vintage Books, 2007), 216.

11 Ibid., 221.

12 Maria Tatar, "Introduction: Snow White," in *Classic Fairy Tales,* ed. Maria Tatar, 2nd ed. (New York: Norton, 2017), 84.

13 Richard Holliss and Brian Sibley, *Walt Disney's "Snow White and the Seven Dwarfs" and the Making of the Classic Film* (New York: Simon and Schuster, 1987), 14.

14 Ibid.

15 All quotations are taken from Jacob Grimm and Wilhelm Grimm, *The Annotated Brothers Grimm: The Bicentennial Edition,* ed. Maria Tatar (New York: Norton, 2012), 246–61.

16 *55 Favorite Stories Adapted from Disney Films* (n.p.: Western, 1960).

17 The phrase about the dwarfs is from *Snow White,* illus. Rex Irvine and Judie Clarke (n.p.: Superscope, 1973). The description of Snow White comes from *Storytime Treasury* (New York: McCall, 1969).

18 "The accents of Betty Boop" quoted in Holliss and Sibley, *Disney,* 65; "pasty, sepulchral" quoted in "The Snow White Fiasco," *Current History,* June 1938, 46.

19 John Updike, "Fiabe Italiane," in *Hugging the Shore: Essays and Criticism* (New York: Knopf, 1983), 662.

20 C. Henry Kempe, Frederic N. Silverman, Brandt F. Steel, et al., "The Battered Child Syndrome," *JAMA* 181 (1962): 17–24.

21 Jacob Grimm and Wilhelm Grimm, "Sneewittchen (Schneeweißchen)," in *Kinder- und Haus-Märchen, gesammelt durch die Brüder Grimm* (Berlin: Realschulbuch-handlung, 1812), 238–50.

22 For Jacob Grimm, red, white, and black appear frequently in folktales because "in them and in their intermixing the human body appears: the white in skin, nerves, tendons, and bones; the red in blood; the black in hair and in the vision of the eyes; and all three colors express themselves in particular in the chyle and in the red and black blood." Ann Schmiesing, "Blackness in the Grimms' Fairy Tales," *Marvels & Tales* 30 (2016): 219.

23 Heinz Rölleke, *Die älteste Märchensammlung der Brüder Grimm: Synopse der handschriftlichen Urfassung von 1810 und der Erstdrucke von 1812* (Cologny-Genève: Fondation Martin Bodmer, 1975), 381–83.

24 Jacob and Wilhelm Grimm, *Kinder- und Hausmärchen,* vol. 3, ed. Heinz Rölleke (Stuttgart: Reclam, 1984), 99–102. Angela Carter's tale appears in *The Bloody Chamber and Other Stories* (New York: Penguin, 1990), 91–92.

25 Snorri Sturluson, *Heimskringla: History of the Kings of Norway,* trans. Lee M. Hollander (1964; repr., Austin: University of Texas Press for the American-Scandinavian Foundation, 2005), 80–81.

26 G. Ronald Murphy, *The Owl, the Raven, and the Dove: The Religious Meaning of the Grimms' Magic Fairy Tales* (Oxford: Oxford University Press, 2000), 161.

27 Red, white, and black as the three colors of poetry ("die drei Farben der Poesie") are discussed by Jacob Grimm, "Die Bedeutung der Blumen und Blätter," in *Altdeutsche Wälder,* vol. 1 (Kassel: Thurneissen, 1913), 1–30.

28 Andrew Lang, *The Yellow Fairy Book* (London: Longmans, Green, 1894), 127.

29 Walter Benjamin, "A Glimpse into the World of Children's Books," in *Selected Writings,* vol. 1, ed. Marcus Bullock and Michael W. Jennings (Cambridge, MA: Harvard University Press, 1996), 443.

30 Max Lüthi, *The European Folktale: Form and Nature* (Bloomington: Indiana University Press, 1986).

31 Manlio Brusatin, *History of* Colors (Boulder, CO: Shambhala, 1991), 7. The tellers of tales seem almost instinctively to recognize the strong correlation between color, even in a reduced palette, and imagination. And in addition, what we discover in the stories written down is an understanding of color as an abstraction but always also with a mysterious specificity. Writing about colors, as Victoria Finlay tells us, is something of a challenge, because "they don't really exist." When we see red, she tells us, we are actually seeing "that portion of the electromagnetic spectrum with a wavelength of about 0.0007 millimeters, in a situation where the other wavelengths are absent." Victoria Finlay, *Color: A Natural History of the Palette* (New York: Random House, 2002), 4. Red: we need light to see that color, and when we see blood, roses, or apples, we perceive their color from the light rays that remain unabsorbed by those objects, bouncing off them. Without light, there is black. The sum of all the colors in light is white. The popular scientific explanation for understanding these hues speaks volumes already in symbolic terms, and the fairy-tale world knows exactly how to exploit them.

32 "The Complete Libretto," *Les Misérables* website, accessed March 21, 2018, http://www.angelfire.com/ms/shows/LesMizScript.html.

33 Herman Melville, *Moby-Dick* (New York: Norton, 2017), 163.

34 Norman M. Klein, *Seven Minutes: The Life and Death of the American Animated Cartoon* (London: Verso, 1993), 142.

35 David Goldenberg, "Racism, Color Symbolism, and Color Prejudice," in *The Origins of Racism in the West,* ed. Miriam Eliav-Feldon, Benjamin Isaac, and Joseph Ziegler (Cambridge: Cambridge University Press, 2009), 104.

36 Grimm and Grimm, *Kinder- und Hausmärchen* (ed. Rölleke), 230.

37 Klein, *Seven Minutes,* 188.

38 Wikipedia, "Censored Eleven," accessed March 16, 2019, https://en.wikipedia.org/wiki/Censored_Eleven.

39 Sergei Eisenstein, *On Disney,* trans. Alan Upchurch (London: Seagull, 2017), 4, 20.

40 Ibid., 15, 16.

41 J. P. Storm and M. Dreßler, *Im Reiche der Micky Maus: Walt Disney in Deutschland, 1933–1945* (Berlin: Henschel, 1991), 80.

42 Ibid.

43 Max Horkheimer and Theodor W. Adorno, *Dialectic of Enlightenment* (New York: Continuum, 1994), 143.

44 Hans-Jörg Uther, *The Types of International Folktales,* vol. 1 (Helsinki: Suomalainen Tiedeakatemia, Academia Scientiarium Fennica, 2004), 383–84. The ellipses used here replace only motif numbers.

45 Giambattista Basile, *The Pentamerone; or, The Story of Stories,* trans. John Edward Taylor (London: David Bogue, 1850), 308.

46 Jack Zipes, *The Enchanted Screen: The Unknown History of Fairy-Tale Films* (New York: Routledge, 2011), 115.

47 Helen Oyeyemi, *Boy, Snow, Bird* (New York: Riverhead, 2014).

48 "His [the King's], surely, is the voice of the looking glass, the patriarchal voice of judgment that rules the Queen's—and every woman's—self-evaluation." Gilbert and Gubar, *Madwoman in the Attic*, 38. See also Laurence Anholt, *Snow White and the Seven Aliens*, illus. Arthur Robins (New York: Orchard Books, 2002).

49 Fiona French, *Snow White in New York* (Oxford: Oxford University Press, 1986); Adèle Geras, *Pictures of the Night* (London: Red Fox, 2002); Emma Donoghue, "The Tale of the Apple," in *Kissing the Witch* (New York: HarperTeen, 1999), 48.

50 Elisabeth Bronfen, *Over Her Dead Body: Death, Femininity, and the Aesthetic* (New York: Routledge, 1992), 104–5.

51 As Roger Sale puts it, "For an older woman to fight against these facts and values made her frightening, and no fairy tale can imagine defeating such a woman without also destroying her." Sale, *Fairy Tales and After: From Snow White to E. B. White* (Cambridge, MA: Harvard University Press, 1978), 43.

52 Garrison Keillor, "My Stepmother, Myself," *The Atlantic*, March 1982.

53 Anne Sexton, *Transformations* (Boston: Houghton Mifflin 1971), 3–9.

54 Italo Calvino, *The Uses of Literature* (New York: Harcourt Brace, 1986), 18.

55 Joseph Campbell, *The Hero with a Thousand Faces*, 3rd ed. (Novato, CA: New World Library, 2008), 1.

56 Ibid., 84.

57 Quoted in Richard Paul Janaro and Thelma C. Altschuler, *The Art of Being Human: The Humanities as a Technique for Living* (New York: HarperCollins, 1993), 328.

58 Yuval Noah Harari, *Sapiens: A Brief History of Humankind* (New York: Harper Perennial, 2015), 28.

59 The phrase "big old lies" is attributed to B. Moseley, one of the men who told the tales recorded by Zora Neale Hurston in *Mules and Men* (New York: HarperCollins, 2008).

60 Marina Warner, *Once upon a Time: A Short History of Fairy Tale* (Oxford: Oxford University Press, 2016), xix.

61 Ellen Datlow and Terri Windling, *Snow White. Blood Red* (New York: William Morrow, 1993), 105.

62 Andrew Hodges, *Alan Turing: The Enigma* (London: Burnett Books, 1983), xxv–xxvi, 615–16.

63 James Joyce, *A Portrait of the Artist as a Young Man* (New York: B. W. Huebsch, 1922), 285.

64 Adrienne Rich, *Of Woman Born: Motherhood as Experience and Institution* (New York: Norton, 1986), 21–22.

65 Nancy Friday, *My Mother / My Self: The Daughter's Search for Identity* (New York: Delta, 1977), 10.

66 Ibid., 16.

67 Sigmund Freud, "Creative Writers and Day-Dreaming," in *The Freud Reader*, ed. Peter Gay (New York: Norton, 1989), 443.

68 Alice Miller, *The Drama of the Gifted Child* (New York: Basic Books, 1981), 4.

69 Bruno Bettelheim, *The Uses of Enchantment* (New York: Vintage Books, 1976), 67. The psychoanalyst Melanie Klein writes about how infants feel a sense of having harmed "the breast" that nourishes them and transform that guilt into "persecutory anxiety"—the object that "arouses guilt" is turned into a persecutor or "the retaliating, devouring, and poisonous breast." Klein, *Envy and Gratitude and Other Works, 1946–1963* (New York: Free Press, 1975), 231.

70 William Wells Newell, *Games and Songs of American Children* (New York: Harper & Brothers, 1884), 225.

71 Studying the wonder lore of the world today means accepting what Donald Haase has called the challenge of understanding "fairy-tale production and reception precisely as acts of translation, transformation, and transcultural communication" and realizing that "nineteenth-century romantic models of national, cultural, and ethnic purity" will no longer dominate (30). Haase, "Decolonizing Fairy-Tale Studies," *Marvels & Tales* 24, no. 1 (2010): 17–38. Once upon a time, it seemed logical to frame cultural spaces in national terms (our academic disciplines have long been organized that way and are only gradually giving way to new interdisciplinary formations), but in an era of global awareness that self-consciously acknowledges hybridity, multivocality, transmediation, and hypertextuality, fairy-tale production and analysis remind us that the cultural work performed by these "simple stories" has always been marked by heterogeneity and sophistication at the deepest levels. On this point, see especially Cristina Bacchilega, *Fairy Tales Transformed? Twenty-First Century Adaptations and the Politics of Wonder* (Detroit: Wayne State University Press, 2013); and Lee Haring, "Techniques of Creolization," *Journal of American Folklore* 116 (2003): 19–35.

72 Sadhana Naithani, *The Story-Time of the British Empire: Colonial and Postcolonial Folkloristics* (Jackson, MS: University Press of Mississippi, 2010), 128.

LITTLE SNOW WHITE

The Grimms' "Little Snow White" appeared in its canonical form in the final edition of their *Children's Stories and Household Tales,* published in 1857. It was cast in a literary style that reflected the brothers' investment in writing down the story in its most "poetic" form. The earlier manuscript version of "Snow White" (the second story printed below) represented an effort to set down a "first draft," a tale that combined features from the many Snow White stories available to the Grimms. That version has a rough-hewn quality to it, a patchwork in some instances, with a queen who hails from England. An alternative beginning to that tale follows the two stories below. The value of white, red, and black as the colors of poetry and as fairy-tale colors becomes evident in the mantra-like repetition of Snow White's attributes, a coding that is not a vital element in other German folk narratives about beautiful girls who arouse the envy of their mothers.

ONCE UPON A TIME in the middle of winter, when snowflakes were falling down from the sky like feathers, a queen was sitting by a window with a black ebony frame. She was sewing, and while she was looking out at the snow, she pricked her finger with her needle. Three drops of blood fell down onto the snow. The red looked so beautiful against the white snow that she thought to herself, "If only I had a child as white as snow, as red as blood, and as black as the wood on this window frame." Not much later she gave birth to a little girl, who was white as snow, red as blood, and black as ebony, and she was called Snow White. The queen died soon after the child was born.

A year later the king married another woman. She was a beautiful lady but proud and arrogant. She could not bear being second to anyone when it came to beauty. She owned a magic mirror, and when she stood before it and looked at herself, she would repeat the words,

"Mirror, mirror, on the wall,
Who's the fairest of them all?"

The mirror would reply,

"Oh, my queen, you are the fairest of them all."

Then she felt satisfied, for she knew that the mirror always spoke the truth.

In the meantime, Snow White was growing up and becoming more and more beautiful with each passing day. By the time she was seven years old, she was as beautiful as the bright day and more beautiful than the queen herself. One day the queen asked the mirror,

"Mirror, mirror, on the wall,
Who's the fairest of them all?"

The mirror replied,

"My queen, you are the fairest one here,
But Snow White is a thousand times fairer!"

When the queen heard those words, she began to tremble, and she turned green with envy. From that moment on, she hated Snow White, and whenever she set eyes on her, her heart became cold as a stone. Envy and pride grew like weeds in her heart. Day and night, she never had a moment's peace. One day she summoned a huntsman and said, "Take the girl out into the forest. I never want to set eyes on her again. Kill her and bring me her lungs and liver as proof of your deed." The huntsman obeyed and took the girl out into the woods, but just as he was pulling out his hunting knife and about to plunge it into her innocent heart, she began weeping and pleaded with him, "Alas, dear huntsman, spare my life. I promise to run into the woods and never return."

Snow White was so beautiful that the huntsman took pity on her and said, "Just get out of here and run away, you poor child."

"Wild animals will devour you before long," he thought to himself. He felt as if a great weight had been lifted from his shoulders, for at least now he would not have to kill her. Just then a young boar ran past him, and the huntsman stabbed it to death. He took out its lungs and liver and brought them to the queen as proof that he had murdered the girl. The cook was told to boil them in brine, and the wicked woman dined on them, thinking that she had eaten Snow White's lungs and liver.

The poor child was left all alone in the vast forest. She was so frightened that she could only stare in silence at all the leaves on the trees and had no idea what to do next. She started running and sped over sharp stones and raced through bushes with thorns in them. Wild beasts darted near her at times, but they did her no harm. She ran as far as her legs could carry her. When night fell, she saw a little cottage and went inside to rest. Everything in the house was tiny and indescribably dainty and spotless. There was a little table, with seven little plates on a white cloth. Each little plate had a little spoon, seven little knives and forks, and seven little cups. Against the wall were seven little beds in a row, each made up with sheets white as snow. Snow White was so hungry and thirsty that she ate a few vegetables and some bread from each little plate and took a sip of wine from each little cup. She didn't want to take everything away from one place. Later, she was so tired that she tried out the beds, but they did not seem to be the right size. The first was too long, the second too short. But the seventh one was just right, and she stayed in it. Then she said her prayers and fell fast asleep.

Once it was completely dark outside, the owners of the cottage returned. They were seven dwarfs who spent their days in the mountains, mining ore and digging for minerals. They lit their seven little lanterns, and when the cottage brightened up, they saw that someone had been there, for some things were not the way they had left them.

The first one asked, "Who's been sitting on my little chair?"
The second asked, "Who's been eating from my little plate?"
The third asked, "Who took a bite out of my little loaf of bread?"
The fourth asked, "Who's been eating from my little plate of vegetables?"
The fifth asked, "Who's been using my little fork?"
The sixth asked, "Who's been cutting with my little knife?"
The seventh asked, "Who's been drinking from my little cup?"

The first one turned around and noticed that the sheets on his bed were wrinkled, and he said, "Who climbed into my little bed?"

The others came running and shouted, "Someone's been sleeping in my bed too."

When the seventh dwarf looked in his little bed, he saw Snow White lying there, fast asleep. He called to the others, who came running and who were so astonished that they raised their seven little lanterns to let the light shine on Snow White.

"My goodness, oh my goodness!" they exclaimed. "What a beautiful child!"

The dwarfs were so delighted to see her that they decided not to wake her up, and they let her continue sleeping in her little bed. The seventh dwarf slept for an hour with each of his companions until the night was over.

In the morning, Snow White woke up. When she saw the dwarfs, she was frightened, but they were friendly and asked, "What's your name?"

"My name is Snow White," she said.

"How did you find our house?" asked the dwarfs.

Then she told them how her stepmother had tried to kill her and how the huntsman had spared her life. She had run all day long until she found their cottage.

The dwarfs told her, "If you will keep house for us, cook, make the beds, wash, sew, knit, and keep everything neat and tidy, then you can stay with us, and we'll give you everything you need."

"That's perfect," Snow White replied, and she stayed with them.

She kept house for the dwarfs. In the morning, they went up to the mountains to search for minerals and gold. In the evening, they returned, and dinner had to be waiting for them. Since the girl was by herself during the day, the good dwarfs gave her a stern warning: "Beware of your stepmother. She'll know soon enough that you're here. Don't let anyone in the house."

After the queen had finished eating what she thought were Snow White's lungs and liver, she was sure that she was once again the fairest of all in the land. She went to the mirror and said,

"Mirror, mirror, on the wall,
Who's the fairest of them all?"

The mirror replied,

"Here you're the fairest, dear queen,
But little Snow White, who plans to stay
With the seven dwarfs far, far away,
Is now the fairest ever seen."

When the queen heard those words, she was horrified, for she knew that the mirror could not lie. She realized now that the huntsman had deceived her and that Snow White must still be alive. She thought long and hard about how she could kill Snow White. Unless she herself was the fairest in the land, she would never be able to feel anything but envy in her heart. Finally, she came up with a plan. Once she stained her face and dressed up as an old peddler woman, she was completely unrecognizable. She traveled beyond the seven hills to the seven dwarfs in her disguise. Then she knocked on the door and called out, "Pretty wares for a good price."

Snow White peeked out the window and said, "Good day, old woman, what are you selling?"

"Nice things, pretty things," she replied. "Staylaces in all kinds of colors," and she took out a silk lace woven in many colors.

"I can let this good woman in," Snow White thought to herself, and she unbolted the door and bought the pretty lace.

"Oh, my child, what a sight you are! Come, let me lace you up properly."

Snow White wasn't the least bit apprehensive. She stood in front of the old woman and let her put on the new lace. The old woman laced her up so quickly and so tightly that Snow White's breath was cut off, and she fell down as if dead.

"So much for being the fairest of them all!" the old woman shouted and rushed away.

Not much later, in the evening, the seven dwarfs came back home. When they saw their beloved Snow White lying on the ground, they were horrified. She wasn't moving at all, and they were sure she was dead. They lifted her up, and when they saw that she had been laced too tightly, they cut the staylace in two. Snow White began to breathe, and gradually she came back to life. When the dwarfs heard what had happened, they said, "The old peddler woman was none other than the wicked queen. Beware, and don't let anyone in unless we're at home."

When the wicked woman returned home, she went to the mirror and asked,

"Mirror, mirror, on the wall,
Who's the fairest of them all?"

The mirror replied as usual,

"Here you're the fairest, dear queen,
But little Snow White, who plans to stay
With the seven dwarfs far, far away,
Is now the fairest ever seen."

The blood froze in her veins when she heard those words. She was horrified, for she knew that Snow White was still alive. "But this time," she said, "I will dream up something that will destroy you."

Using all the witchcraft in her power, she fashioned a poisoned comb. Then she changed her clothes and disguised herself as a different old woman. Once again she traveled beyond the seven hills to the seven dwarfs, knocked on the door, and called out, "Pretty wares at a good price."

Snow White peeked out the window and said, "Go away. I can't let anyone in."

"But how about just taking a look?" said the old woman, and she took out the poisoned comb and held it high up in the air. The child liked it so much that she was completely fooled and opened the door. When the two had agreed on a price, the old woman said, "Now I'll give your hair a good combing."

Poor Snow White suspected nothing and let the woman go ahead, but no sooner had the comb touched her hair than the poison took effect, and the girl collapsed and fell to the ground.

"There, my beauty!" said the wicked woman. "Now you're finished," and she hurried away.

Fortunately, it was almost evening, and the seven dwarfs were on their way home. When they saw Snow White lying on the ground as though dead, they suspected the stepmother right away. They examined Snow White and found the poisoned comb. As soon as they pulled it out, Snow White came back to life and told them what had happened. Again they warned her to be on guard and not to open the door to anyone.

At home, the queen stood before the mirror and said,

"Mirror, mirror, on the wall,
Who's the fairest of them all?"

The mirror answered as before,

"Here you're the fairest, dear queen,
But little Snow White, who plans to stay
With the seven dwarfs far, far away,
Is now the fairest ever seen."

When the queen heard the words spoken by the mirror, she began trembling with rage. "Snow White must die!" she cried out. "Even if it costs me my life."

She went off into a remote chamber, hidden away where no one ever set foot, and there she made an apple full of poison. On the outside it looked beautiful—white with red cheeks—so that once you set eyes on it, you longed to eat it. But anyone who took the tiniest bite would die. When the apple was finished, she stained her face, dressed up as a peasant woman, and traveled beyond the seven hills to the seven dwarfs. She knocked at their door, and Snow White put her head out the window to say, "I can't let anyone in. The seven dwarfs won't allow it."

"That's all right," replied the peasant woman. "I'll get rid of my apples one way or another. Here, let me give you one."

"No," said Snow White, "I'm not supposed to take anything from anyone."

"Are you afraid that it's poisoned?" asked the old woman. "Here, I'll cut the apple in two. You eat the red half; I'll eat the white."

The apple had been made so artfully that only the red half was poisoned. Snow White felt a craving for the beautiful apple, and when she saw the peasant woman eating it, she could no longer stop herself. Putting her hand out the window, she took the poisoned half. But as soon as she took a bite, she fell down on the ground dead. The queen stared at her with savage eyes and burst out laughing, "White as snow, red as blood, black as ebony! This time the dwarfs won't be able to bring you back to life!"

At home, she asked the mirror,

"Mirror, mirror, on the wall,
Who's the fairest of them all?"

And finally it replied,

"Oh, queen, you are the fairest in the land."

Her envious heart was finally at peace, as much as an envious heart can be.

When the little dwarfs returned home in the evening, they found Snow White lying on the ground. Not a breath of air came from her lips. She was dead. They lifted her up and looked around for something that might be poisonous. They unlaced her, combed her hair, and washed her with water and wine, but it did no good. The dear child was dead, and nothing could bring her back. They placed her on a bier, and all seven of them sat down by it and mourned her. They wept for three days. They were about to bury her, but she still looked just like a living person with beautiful red cheeks.

"How can we possibly lower her into the dark ground?" they asked. They had a transparent glass coffin made so that you could see Snow White from all sides. They put her in it, wrote her name in golden letters, and added that she was the daughter of a king. They brought the coffin up to the top of a mountain, and one of them was always there to keep vigil. Animals also came to mourn Snow White, first an owl, then a raven, and finally a dove.

Snow White lay in the coffin for a long, long time. But she did not decay and looked as if she were sleeping, for she was still white as snow, red as blood, and with hair as black as ebony.

One day the son of a king was traveling through the woods and arrived at the dwarfs' cottage. He wanted to spend the night there. On top of the mountain, he saw the coffin with beautiful Snow White lying in it, and he read what had been written in golden letters. Then he said to the dwarfs, "Let me have the coffin. I will give you whatever you want for it."

The dwarfs answered, "We wouldn't give it to you for all the gold in the world."

Then he said, "Make me a gift of it, for I can't live without seeing Snow White. I will honor and cherish her as if she were my beloved."

The good dwarfs took pity on him when they heard these words, and they gave him the coffin. The prince ordered his servants to hoist the coffin up on their shoulders and take it back home. It happened that they stumbled over a shrub, and the jolt freed the poisonous piece of apple lodged in Snow White's throat. She returned to life. "Good heavens, where am I?" she cried out.

The prince was overjoyed and said, "You are with me," and he described what had happened and said, "I love you more than anything else on Earth. Come with me to my father's castle. You shall be my bride." Snow White had tender feelings for him, and she agreed to go with him. A marriage was soon celebrated with great splendor.

Snow White's wicked stepmother was also invited to the wedding feast. She put on beautiful clothes, stood before the mirror, and said,

"Mirror, mirror on the wall:
Who's the fairest of them all?"

The mirror replied,

"My queen, you may be the fairest here,
But the young queen is a thousand times fairer."

The wicked woman let loose a curse, and she was so upset that she had no idea what to do. At first she didn't want to go to the wedding feast. But she never had a moment's peace after that and had to go and see the young queen. When she entered the castle, Snow White recognized her right away. The queen was terrified and just stood there, unable to budge an inch. Iron slippers had already been heated up over a fire of coals. They were brought in with tongs and set right in front of her. She had to put on the red-hot iron shoes and dance in them until she dropped to the ground dead.

LITTLE SNOW WHITE, OR, THE UNLUCKY GIRL

One winter day, snow was coming down from the heavens. A queen was sitting at a window with a frame made of ebony, and she was sewing. She had been dreaming about a child, and while she was imagining it, she pricked her finger with a needle. Three (a few) drops of blood fell on the snow. She made a wish and said, "Oh, if I only had a child as white as the snow here, with cheeks red as this blood and with eyes as black as this window frame."

Before long she gave birth to a wondrously beautiful little girl, as white as snow, as red as blood, as black as the wood on the frame. The queen was the most beautiful woman in the kingdom, but Snow White was hundreds of thousands times more beautiful. The queen turned to her mirror and asked,

"Mirror, mirror on the wall,
Who is the loveliest in all of England?"

The mirror answered, "You, oh queen, are the most beautiful, but Snow White is hundreds of thousands of times more beautiful."

The queen could no longer stand to see Snow White, who had now become the most beautiful in the kingdom.

One day the king had to march off to war. The queen harnessed up a carriage and ordered the coachman to drive deep into the dark woods.

She took little Snow White along with her. There were many beautiful red roses in those woods. After making a stop in the woods, she said to the girl, "Oh, Snow White, climb out of the carriage and pick one of those beautiful roses for me." The moment Snow White obeyed her order and left the carriage, the carriage took off at high speed, for that is what the queen had ordered. She was hoping that wild animals would make a meal of the girl.

Snow White was all alone in the forest and began to weep. She started walking and kept walking and was growing very tired when she saw a little house before her. Seven dwarfs were living in the house, but they were working in the mines and not at home just then. Snow White walked into the house and saw a table, and on the table were seven plates and next to them seven spoons, seven forks, seven knives, and seven glasses. There were also seven little beds in the room. Snow White ate some of the vegetables and bread from each plate, and she took a small sip from each glass. She was tired and wanted to go to sleep. She tried each bed and found them all uncomfortable except for the last one, where she lay down to sleep.

When the seven dwarfs returned home from their workday, each one asked,

"Who ate from my plate?"
"Who took some of my bread?"
"Who used my fork?"
"Who cut things up with my knife?"
"Who drank from my glass?"

And then the first dwarf asked,

"Who tried out my bed?"

And the second said that someone had tried his bed out too. And the third one and the fourth said the same thing, and so on until they all realized that Snow White was lying in the seventh bed. They found her so enchanting that they took pity on her and let her continue sleeping, and the seventh dwarf ended up sharing a bed with the sixth.

When Snow White woke up the next morning, the dwarfs asked her how she had found her way there. She explained everything to them and told them how her mother, the queen, had taken her into the woods and left her there, all alone. The dwarfs felt sorry for her and invited her to stay with them. She could cook their meals while they were at the mines, but she would have to watch out for the queen and not let anyone in the house.

When the queen learned that Snow White was living with the seven dwarfs and that she had not perished in the forest, she dressed up as a peddler woman, found the house, and asked to be let in to show her wares. Snow White did not recognize her and spoke to her from the window, telling her that she was not allowed to let anyone in. The peddler woman said, "But look, dear child, I have such beautiful laces with me, and I'll give them to you for a good price!"

Snow White thought to herself, "I really need some new stays, and it won't hurt to let the woman in. I will strike a good bargain with her," and she opened the door and bought some laces. After selling the laces, the peddler woman said, "My but your laces are poorly tied! That's not right. I'll lace you up nice and tightly." The old woman, who was really the queen, took the laces and pulled them so tight that Snow White fell down as if dead, and then she left.

The dwarfs returned home and saw Snow White lying on the ground. They quickly figured out who had been there and unlaced her, and she came back to life. The dwarfs warned her to be more careful.

When the queen learned that her daughter was still alive, she was beside herself with rage and disguised herself again. She went back to the house in the woods and tried to sell Snow White a stunning little comb.

Snow White was quite taken with the comb, and so the queen got the better of her again and walked right into the house through the door and began combing Snow White's beautiful hair. She stuck the comb in her head so hard that she fell down dead.

When the seven dwarfs reached home, they saw that the gate was open, and there was Snow White, lying on the ground. They knew right away who was responsible for this calamity. They pulled the comb out of her hair as fast as possible, and Snow White returned to life. The dwarfs told her that the next time she fell for one of these tricks, they would not be able to help her.

The queen was furious when she learned that Snow White was still alive, and she dressed up a third time as the peasant woman and took an apple with her. One side of it, the red half, was poisoned. Snow White did not let the woman in. But the woman handed the apple to Snow White through the window, and then she positioned herself in a way that you could not see who she was. Snow White took a bite of the beautiful apple, from the part that was red, and she fell down on the floor, dead. When the seven dwarfs returned home, there was nothing they could do. They were miserable and felt great sorrow. They placed Snow White in a glass casket, and she stayed exactly as she was. They inscribed her name and her ancestry on the casket and kept watch carefully day and night.

At last the king, Snow White's father, returned home, and on the way he passed through the woods in which the seven dwarfs were living. When he saw the casket and the words engraved on it, he went into deep mourning over his daughter. His entourage included some expert doctors, and they asked the dwarfs to give them the body in the casket. Then they tied ropes to the four corners of a room, pulled, and Snow White came back to life. They all returned home. Snow White was married to a handsome prince. At the wedding, a pair of slippers was heated up over a fire. The queen had to put them on, and she danced in them until she fell down dead.

In another version, the dwarfs hammer thirty-two times with their little magical hammers, and that is how they succeed in waking up Snow White.

A DIFFERENT BEGINNING

Once there lived a count and a countess. They drove in a carriage past three mountains of white snow. The count said, "I wish I had a little girl as white as this snow." They traveled a little farther and passed by three pools filled with red blood. The count made another wish: "If only I had a little girl with cheeks as red as this blood!" Not much later three ravens black as coal flew overhead, and the count wished for a little girl again, one with hair as black as the ravens. Finally, they met a girl, as white as snow, as red as blood, and as black as the ravens, and she was named Snow White. The count invited her to take a seat in the coach, but the countess did not care for her. She could not stop herself and dropped a glove and asked Snow White to pick it up. When she climbed out, the carriage took off at a high speed.

THE YOUNG SLAVE

Giambattista Basile (1575–1632) wrote fifty tales that were published shortly after his death as *The Tale of Tales* and became a literary landmark as one of the first collections of print fairy tales in Europe. Despite a subtitle that suggested the stories were for children (*Entertainment for Little Ones*), *The Pentamerone,* as it was also known, gives us fairy tales tailored for a sophisticated audience, with adult themes that turn on infidelity, marital intrigue, and family conflict. Writing in a Neapolitan dialect, Basile used ornate language, subtle wordplay, and literary conceits to craft lively narratives that were bawdy, vulgar, and full of rough truths. "The Young Slave" gives us an unusual twist on the Snow White story, with a heroine persecuted by her uncle's wife rather than by a stepmother or mother-in law. What is especially striking about Basile's tale is the transformation of private confession into public revelation. When Lisa confides in her doll, she simultaneously as good as broadcasts the story of her persecutor's misdeeds. She repeats the story of her sufferings in public, at a banquet. Many versions of "Bluebeard," a story about a serial murderer with a secret chamber that houses the corpses of his previous wives, similarly end by self-reflexively alluding to the power of telling your story as a way to remove yourself from the narrative and live to tell it.

THE YOUNG SLAVE

There once lived a Baron of Selvascura who had an unmarried sister. This girl used to go and play in a garden with other girls her age. One day they found a beautiful rose in full bloom, and they decided to give a prize to the girl who could jump over it without touching a single leaf. The girls were all able to leapfrog over it. But each one ended up brushing against it, and not one of them could clear it perfectly. When it was the turn of Lilla, the Baron's sister, she backed up a little, took a running start, and jumped over the bush without touching the rose. Still, one petal fell to the ground, but she picked it up and swallowed it so quickly that no one noticed. And she won the wager.

Three days went by, and suddenly Lilla realized that she must be with child. She was just dying of humiliation, for she knew that she had not done anything sneaky, nor had she taken part in any kind of shameful behavior. How was it possible that her belly was swelling up? She made her way to the house of some fairies who had once befriended her, and when she told them her story, they told her not to worry, for it was all just the fault of the leaf she had swallowed.

When Lilla heard this, she took precautions to conceal her condition as much as possible, and when her time came, she went into seclusion and gave birth to a lovely little girl whom she named Lisa. She sent the girl to the fairies, and each one put a different charm on her. The last one slipped and twisted her foot so badly in her haste to see the child that the sharp pain unleashed a curse by mistake. That meant that when the girl turned seven, her mother, while combing out her hair, would forget to remove the comb, and it would remain stuck there and lead to her death.

At the end of seven years everything happened as foretold. The despairing mother, in mourning, placed the girl's body in seven caskets of crystal, one within the other, and moved her to a distant room in the palace, keeping the key in her pocket. Grief drained her of life, and when she felt the end was near, she summoned her brother and told him, "My brother, I can feel Death's hook dragging me away bit by bit. I am leaving all my earthly possessions to you, and you can do with them what you like. All I ask is that you give your word never to open the door to the far room in this house and that you keep the key in this writing desk." The brother, who loved his sister with all his heart, gave his word, and at the same moment she said, "Adieu, for the beans are ripe."

A few years later, this lord, who had in the meantime taken a wife, was invited to a hunting party. He left the care of the house in his wife's hands, and he pleaded with her not to open the room, the key to which he kept in the writing desk. However, as soon as his back was turned, she began to feel suspicious, and driven by jealousy and consumed by curiosity, which is woman's first attribute, she took the key and unlocked the door. There she saw the young girl, clearly visible through the crystal caskets, and she opened them one by one and found Lisa, who seemed to be sleeping. She had grown like any other woman, and the caskets had lengthened with her, keeping pace as she grew.

As soon as the wife set eyes on this beautiful creature, the jealous woman at once thought, "By my life, this is a fine thing! Keys at my waist, yet nature makes horns! No wonder he never let anyone open the door and see the Mohammed that he was worshiping inside the caskets!" Saying this, she seized the girl by the hair and dragged her out. As she did so, the comb fell to the ground, and the sleeping Lisa awoke, calling out, "Mother, mother, help me!"

"I'll give you mother—and father too!" cried the Baroness, who was as bitter as a slave, as angry as a bitch with a litter of pups, and as venomous as a snake. She straightaway cut off the girl's hair and thrashed her with the tresses, dressed her in rags, and every day landed blows on her head and put bruises on her face, blackening her eyes and making her mouth look as if she had eaten raw pigeons.

When the Baroness's husband returned from the hunting party and saw this girl being treated so badly, he asked who she was. His wife replied that she was a slave sent by her aunt, only fit for the rope's end, and that one had to be forever beating her.

Now it happened one day, when the Baron had occasion to go to a fair, that he asked everyone in the house, including the cats, what they would like him to buy for them, and when they had all chosen, one one thing and one another, he turned at last to the slave. But his wife flew into a rage and acted in a way unbecoming to a Christian, saying, "That's right, put this slave in the same class as the rest of us. Let everyone be brought down to the same level, and we can all piss in the same chamber pot. Don't pay any attention to that ugly animal, and just let her go to hell." But the Baron, who was kind and courteous, insisted that the slave girl should also have something. And she told him, "I want nothing but a doll, a knife, and a pumice stone; and if you forget them, may you never be able to cross the first river that you come to on your journey!"

The Baron brought back all the things requested save for what his niece had wanted. He reached a river that carried stones and trees down from the mountains to its shores to lay foundations of fears and raise walls of wonder—and he found it impossible to cross. Then he remembered the spell put on him by the slave and turned back and bought the three articles in question. When he arrived home, he gave everyone what they had asked for.

When Lisa had what she wanted, she went into the kitchen and, after setting the doll before her, began to weep and wail and recount the story of her troubles to that bundle of cloth just as if it were a real person. When it did not reply, she took the knife, sharpened it on the pumice stone, and said, "Mind, if you don't answer me, I am going to plunge this knife in my chest, and that will put an end to our game!" And the doll, swelling up like a reed when you blow into it, answered at last, "All right, I heard you! I'm not deaf!"

This music had already gone on for a few days when the Baron, who had a little room on the other side of the kitchen, chanced to hear the song and, putting his eye to the keyhole, saw Lisa telling the doll all about her mother's leap over the rose bush, how she had swallowed a petal, her own birth, the spell, the curse of the last fairy, the comb left in her hair, her death, how she had been shut in the seven caskets and placed in that distant room, her mother's death, the key entrusted to the brother, his departure for the hunt, the jealousy of his wife, how she opened the room against her husband's commands, how she cut off her hair and treated her like a slave, and the many, many torments to which she had been subjected. And all the while she was weeping and telling the doll, "Answer me, or I will kill myself with this knife." And sharpening it on the pumice stone, she would have stabbed herself had the Baron not kicked down the door and snatched the knife from her hands.

The Baron made her tell the story again in all its details, and then he embraced her as his niece and removed her from the house, putting her in the care of one of his relatives so that she could recover from the distress inflicted on her by that heart of a Medea who had made sure she would become half of what she could be.

In just a matter of a few months, Lisa had become as beautiful as a goddess. The Baron brought her back home and told everyone that she was his niece. He ordered a great banquet, and after the tables had been cleared, he asked Lisa to tell the story of the suffering she had endured and of his wife's cruelty—a tale that made all the guests weep. And after that, he drove his wife away, banishing her to the home of some relatives. He found for his niece a handsome husband of her own choosing, one whom her heart desired. Thus Lisa could truly say,

Heaven rains favors down on us when we least expect it.

THE DEATH OF THE SEVEN DWARFS

The historian and folklorist Ernst Ludwig Rochholz (1809–1892) collected over five hundred legends and tales from the Swiss canton of Aargau in an effort to preserve a robust tradition that he appreciated as more than mere curiosities and amusing household stories. He was drawn to folklore out of a nostalgic desire to feel more "at home" in Switzerland by uncovering similarities between his native land (Germany) and the region in which he lived for over twenty years. His Snow White story is a shocker, a tale that clearly belongs to adult storytelling traditions and that captures exactly how sex and violence are at the core of stories told to pass time on long evenings devoted to household chores and agricultural labors.

In one of the deep valleys between Brugg and Waldshut near the dark forests, seven dwarfs were living together in a small hut. Late one evening a pretty, young peasant girl appeared at the door asking for shelter. She was hungry and had lost her way in the woods. The dwarfs had only seven beds, and they fell to arguing with each other, since each one wanted to give up his bed for the girl. Finally the oldest in the group gave his bed up. Just as they were all about to go to sleep, an old peasant woman started knocking at the door and wanted to be let inside. The girl climbed out of bed when she heard the knocking, and she told the woman that there were only seven beds and not enough room for another person.

The woman flew into a rage and accused the girl of being a slut and of sleeping with all seven of the men. Threatening to make a quick end to such a scandalous business, she stormed off. That very night she returned with two men whom she had found down by the banks of the Rhine. They broke into the house and killed the seven dwarfs. They buried the bodies outdoors in the garden and burned the house down. No one has any idea what happened to the girl.

MAROULA AND THE MOTHER OF EROS

Maroula's trials are more severe than those of most innocent persecuted heroines, and her story, here from a version published in 1877, bears traces of Apuleius's "Cupid and Psyche" as well as the Grimms' story "The Girl without Hands" and the version of "Sleeping Beauty" written down by Charles Perrault. The guardian angel in the form of a monk who protects her is most likely a Christian overlay to a pagan story about sexual jealousy and its evils. Maroula's silence about her mother-in-law's cruelty and the failure to assert her own innocence contrast sharply with the scenes of storytelling at the end of the tale, each of which suggests that confession, reporting, and narrating can lead to healing and restore justice. The golden apple evokes the Judgment of Paris, with three goddesses vying for that prize, which is inscribed with the words "To the Fairest."

ONCE THERE WAS a princess, and she was by far the most beautiful of all the women in the world. When the mother of Eros was told of her beauty, she decided to kill her, for she could not bear the idea of anyone more beautiful than she was. She disguised herself as an old woman and traveled to the princess's castle with an enchanted golden apple that she planned to offer for sale. The princess was an orphan, but she had many brothers. They were all very protective and locked her in the palace whenever they left so that no one would be able to do her any harm. And so the doors were locked when the old woman arrived and showed her the golden apple. The princess wanted to buy the apple, and Eros's mother told her to toss a rope out the window. She would then wind it around the apple, and the princess could pull it up through the window. And that's what happened. All it took was one bite of the apple, and the girl fell down on the floor unconscious. That's how the brothers found poor Maroula—that was the girl's name—when they returned home. They saw the apple and realized that it might have harmed their sister if it was poisoned. They took the piece of apple she had bitten off out of her mouth, and suddenly she was alive again.

The mother of Eros wanted to know for certain that the beautiful princess had died after tasting the apple. And so she held a mirror up to the sun and said,

"O sun that shines so brightly,
Let your eyes flash lightly,
And see the most beautiful woman of all."

"You are very beautiful," the sun replied, "but Maroula does not have her equal on Earth." When the mother of Eros discovered that Maroula was still alive, she was more enraged than ever and went back to the castle, this time with an enchanted ring. The princess bought the ring from her, but as soon as she put it on her finger, she fell to the ground, lifeless. When the brothers returned home this time, they did not notice that the ring on their sister's finger was enchanted. Once they gave up the hope of restoring Maroula to life, they put her in a large golden casket and placed it in a meadow near the castle.

One day a prince went out hunting, and a little bird drew his attention to the casket by flying through the sky around him and then landing on it. The prince ordered his servants to pick up the casket and carry it to his castle. Then he opened it up and gazed on the beautiful maiden lying in it. Just by chance he removed the enchanted ring from her finger, and instantly she came back to life.

The prince married the maiden, and after the two had been living together for some time, the young woman became pregnant and gave birth to twins. The prince's mother was incensed that her son had stopped paying attention to her because he was so devoted to his wife. She was determined to ruin the life of her daughter-in-law. One evening she slipped into her chambers, found the two children and chopped off their heads, then threw the knife she had used to commit the murders on Maroula's bed to throw suspicion for the terrible deed on her. The next morning the prince discovered what had happened, and since his mother blamed Maroula for the deed, he was convinced that she had committed the murders. He issued a command to have his wife's hands cut off, to sew them up in a sack with the bodies of the children, and to hang the sack around Maroula's neck. And so it happened that Maroula was banished from the country.

Maroula walked on and on, and on the way she met a monk to whom she told her entire story. The monk took the heads of the children and fastened them back on their bodies, and suddenly the children returned to life. He also joined Maroula's hands back to her arms. He tapped the ground with his staff, and a castle appeared out of nowhere. He said to Maroula, "Stay here with your children and live in happiness. I am your guardian angel, and I'll come back to see how you are faring." At that he disappeared, and Maroula did not even have time to bid him farewell.

Maroula lived in the castle with her children. One day the husband who had driven her from their home was on an expedition with some friends and passed by the castle. He caught sight of his wife but did not recognize her. But she recognized him, and following the advice of the monk who was her guardian angel and who had mysteriously appeared just then, she invited him to come in with his entourage. While the prince was climbing the stairs with his friends, Maroula instructed her children to grab hold of two balls and throw them, while chanting, "We hope you are well, Father, but we are longing for our grandmother to burst into pieces, because she was moved by Eros's mother to tell you to punish our mother by cutting off her hands, even though it was she who murdered us." When the prince heard those words, he turned to his friends and said, "I want you to know that this is my wife and these are my children." And then he told them everything that had happened. Maroula then told her husband about what had happened afterward, how the monk had healed her and her children and had told her that Eros's mother had caused all her troubles because she was jealous of her beauty. The prince returned to his castle with his wife and children and kept them hidden. A few days later he invited his friends to a banquet, revealed everything to them, and invited them to determine the punishment his mother deserved. They reached a decision to put her in a barrel of tar and set fire to it on the sea. And that is exactly what happened. The young couple lived happily from then on, for Eros's mother found enough satisfaction in all the suffering she had inflicted on Maroula and left her alone from then on.

THE ENCHANTED STOCKINGS

Collected by the renowned French folklorist Paul Sébillot, this story, published in 1880, was told by a fifty-eight-year-old cooper named Pierre Derou de Collinée. The touching contrasts between murderous hostility and warm hospitality, both triggered by beauty, fuel the story's narrative power, which gives us everything from hunger pangs and aerial suspension to costume changes and startling reanimation, reminding us that even the simplest of tales can sound full dramatic chords.

Once upon a time there lived a queen who had a grown daughter, almost old enough to be married. The queen was renowned for her beauty, and she was still so graceful and pretty that she was often taken for the elder sister rather than the mother of the princess.

One day, when the queen and her daughter were standing on the balcony of the palace, some soldiers walked by and said, "The queen is very beautiful, but her daughter is even more beautiful."

When the queen heard those words, she grew jealous of her daughter, whom she could no longer bear to have near her, and she made up her mind to get rid of her. She ordered two of her servants to take the girl into the forest and kill her. The poor princess followed them into the woods, without even an inkling of their intentions. When they reached the middle of the forest, the two servants looked at her and were so taken by her beauty and innocence that they did not have the heart to carry out the queen's orders. They said to each other, "It would be a sin to kill a princess who is so pretty and who has never spoken a harsh word to a soul. We will leave her here in the woods, where she will lose her way, for we are very far from the castle. No one will ever know what became of her."

They completed their task and disappeared. The princess called after them and tried in vain to find her way back. For four days she wandered around in the forest, unable to find anything to eat or drink, trembling at the slightest noise and fearful that at any moment wild beasts would devour her. Then suddenly a beautiful castle appeared in a clearing, and she entered it, hoping to beg for a crust of bread.

Three brothers lived in that castle. Every day two of them went off to hunt, while the third stayed at home to attend to the household. It was around noon when the princess reached the castle. The brother guarding the house had just gone down into the cellar to find some wine for dinner. He had removed a roast chicken from the spit, and it was on the table, where the princess caught sight of it. She had not eaten for four days, and when she saw the chicken and took in its smell, she grabbed it, planning to take just a leg or a wing. But she heard a noise and fled, taking the chicken with her and hiding in the stable where the dogs were kept.

The two brothers returned from the hunt with hearty appetites and found nothing but an empty platter on the table. They asked the brother who had stayed home, "Why didn't you prepare anything for dinner?"

"I did," he replied. "I roasted a whole chicken, took it from the spit, and put it on the table. Then I went down to the cellar to fetch some wine. Who in the world could have taken it?"

"The dogs must have swiped it," one of the brothers said.

They whistled, and the dogs came running, but one of them was missing. They walked over to the stable to make sure he was not ailing or had not run away, and they discovered a young girl there, feeding the bones of the chicken to the dog.

When the girl saw them, she cried out, "Oh, my dear sirs! You are probably ready to kill me for stealing from you, but I have had nothing to eat for four days."

"No, no," they replied. "We have no intention of harming you. The only thing we want is to make sure that you are safe and have a home."

They took her over to the castle, and the girl charmed all three brothers with her beauty and her endearing manner. A few days later they said, "We can't all three marry this beautiful girl, and if one of us were to marry her, the others might grow jealous. If she stays here as our sister, we can keep the peace in our home. She can look after the household while we go out to hunt."

The princess happily agreed to this arrangement, and she did her best to manage the household for the three brothers.

One day, when she was by herself in the castle, an old woman came begging for alms and recognized the girl as the queen's daughter. The old woman, who had imagined the girl to be dead, hurried back to the palace and told the queen that her daughter must be alive, for she had seen her with her own two eyes.

The queen was shocked by the news and said to the poor woman, "Take these stockings to the princess, but don't tell her they are from me. If you manage to persuade her to put them on, your future will be secure."

The beggar woman returned to the castle. When the princess was alone, the old woman made her way to her chamber and presented the girl with the stockings. The girl suspected that they were a gift from her mother, who was up to no good. Still, she put them on. As soon as she pulled up the second stocking, her eyes closed, and she fell into a deep trance, unable to move. The old woman took her leave as quickly as possible.

The three brothers returned home and began to worry when their adopted sister seemed to have disappeared. They went up to her room and found her stretched out on a chair, looking as if she were dead. They suspected that the old woman had cast a spell on her, and they ran after her; but they were unable to catch up with her. When they returned to the castle, they were distraught, for they loved the girl with all their heart.

"What shall we do with our sister?" asked the eldest.

"Let's put her in a casket with a glass lid, and that way we will be able to keep her with us. Even in death, she is beautiful."

They placed her gently in a glass-covered casket, and they went to see her often. But she never stirred.

Now it came to pass that the three young men were sent into battle. Before setting off, they took the casket from the castle and hoisted it up into the branches of one of the trees in the forest.

Before long a hunter, who was roaming through the forest in search of game, saw a flicker of light in the branches of a tree. The next day he noticed a shining object up in the same place, and he made up his mind that if he saw that light a third time, he would climb up the tree and get to the bottom of things.

The next day he climbed up the tree and discovered the casket and saw through the glass lid the most beautiful woman you could imagine, but motionless and with her eyes closed, as if she were dead.

He managed to bring the casket down to the ground and carried it back home, where he lived with his three sisters. The girls were enraptured by the beauty of the sleeping princess, and the youngest of the three, who was playful and loved to giggle, said, "Yes, she is pretty, but she would be even prettier if she put on my fine stockings and one of my dresses."

"What are you thinking?" her sisters said. "How did you come up with that? Just leave her alone."

The youngest sister was given permission to keep the glass casket in her chamber. One day, when her sisters were away, she opened it up, slipped one of her dresses on the girl, and took off the girl's stockings so that she could put on the finer ones she owned.

As soon as she pulled off the second stocking, the princess opened her eyes, sat up, and cried out, "Oh!" just like a person who has been woken up. The young girl raced down the stairs on all fours, as frightened as if she had seen a ghost.

"Don't be afraid!" the princess shouted. "Come back here. I am as alive as you are, but I have been asleep for a long, long time."

When the sisters realized that the beautiful young girl had come back to life, they were overjoyed, and their brother was even happier. He fell in love with the princess and asked her to marry him, and she consented, for he was a handsome young fellow.

PRINCESS AUBERGINE

Collected in the region that lies today in the border areas between Afghanistan and Pakistan, this story was told by an "old woman," and not by the "little children" credited for the tales in the anthology's title, *Wide-Awake Stories: A Collection of Stories Told by Little Children, between Sunset and Sunrise* (1884). The editors were keen to emphasize authenticity and to differentiate what they collected from literary fare. Their stories, they claimed, were "procured at first-hand from the lips of purely village children, who have never been inside a school" (viii). One of the editors, Flora Annie Steel, lived for twenty-two years in India with her husband, who was in the Indian Civil Service. She published many collections of folktales, British and Indian, and the anthology from which this tale is taken was reprinted in 1917, with a radically different title, as *Tales of the Punjab: Told by the People.*

This story bears a resemblance to "Sodewa Bai," an Indian Cinderella tale collected by Mary Frere in *Old Deccan Days; or, Hindoo Fairy Legends,* published in 1868 (Philadelphia: J. B. Lippincott). The prince who finds Sodewa Bai's "tiny slipper" marries his beloved but also has a "first Ranee," who despises the new wife and engineers her downfall by removing the necklace she is wearing. But the young woman, who appears to be dead, does not "decay," nor does the "color of her face change." She looks "as fair and lovely as on the night on which she died," and in that story, restoration of stolen property brings the princess back to life. The "nine-lakh necklace" in the story below contains the term for a unit in the Indian numbering system equal to one hundred thousand.

Once upon a time there lived a poor Brahman and his wife, so poor that often they did not know where to turn for a meal and were reduced to wild herbs and roots for their dinner. One day, while the Brahman was gathering herbs in the wilderness, he came upon an aubergine, or eggplant. Thinking it might prove useful in some way, he dug it up, took it home, and planted it by his cottage door. Every day he watered and tended it so that it grew wonderfully and at last bore one fruit as large as a pear, purple and white and glossy. It was such a handsome fruit that the good couple thought it a pity to pick it, and they let it hang on the plant day after day, until one fine morning when there was absolutely nothing to eat in the house.

The Brahman said to his wife, "We must eat the egg-fruit. Go cut it down and prepare it for dinner." The Brahman's wife took a knife and cut the beautiful purple and white fruit off the plant. Suddenly she thought she heard a low moan. And when she sat down and began to peel the egg-fruit, she could hear a tiny voice saying quite distinctly, "Watch out!—oh, please watch out! Peel more gently, or the knife will cut into me!"

The good woman was terribly perplexed, but she went on peeling the fruit as gently as she could, wondering all the while what had bewitched it, until she had cut all the way through the rind, when—what do you think happened?—why, out stepped the most beautiful little girl imaginable, dressed in purple and white satin! The poor Brahman and his wife were astonished but also delighted, for they had no children of their own and looked on the tiny girl as a godsend.

They made up their minds to adopt the girl and took great care with her, petting and spoiling her and always calling her Princess Aubergine. If she was not really a princess, the couple thought, she was still dainty and delicate enough to be a king's daughter.

Not far from the Brahman's hut lived a king with a beautiful wife and seven stalwart young sons. One day a slave girl from the palace, happening to pass by the Brahman's cottage, went in to ask for a light, and there she saw the beautiful Aubergine. She went straight home to the palace and told her mistress how a princess was living nearby in a hovel, and she was so lovely and charming that, were the king to set eyes on her just once, he would immediately forget not only his wife but every other woman in the world.

The queen had a very jealous disposition and could not bear the idea of anyone being more beautiful than she was, so she cast about in her mind how she could destroy the lovely Aubergine. If she could only lure the girl into the palace, she could easily do the rest, for she was a sorceress and adept in all sorts of magic. So she sent a message to Princess Aubergine to say that the fame of her great beauty had reached the palace and that the queen would like to see with her own eyes if the report was true.

Lovely Aubergine was proud of her beauty and fell into the trap. She went to the palace, and the queen, pretending to be wonderstruck, said, "You were born to live in castles! From now on you must never leave me. You will be my sister." This flattered Princess Aubergine's vanity, and she remained in the palace and exchanged veils with the queen and drank milk out of the same cup with her, as is the custom when two people say they will be sisters.

But the queen, from the very first moment she set eyes on Princess Aubergine, had seen that she was not a human being but a fairy, and she knew she must be very careful how she set about using her magic. She placed powerful spells on her while she slept and chanted,

"Beautiful Aubergine! Tell me true—
In what thing does your life lie?"

And the princess answered, "In the life of your eldest son. Kill him, and I will also die."

The very next morning the wicked queen went to where her eldest son was sleeping and killed him with her bare hands. Then she sent the slave girl to the princess's apartments, hoping to hear she too was dead, but the girl returned saying that the princess was alive and well. The queen wept tears of rage, for she knew her spells had not been strong enough, and she had killed her son for nothing. Nevertheless, the next night she laid even more powerful spells on Princess Aubergine, saying,

"Princess Aubergine! Tell me true—
In what thing does your life lie?"

And the sleeping princess replied, "In the life of your second son. Kill him, and I too will die."

The wicked queen killed her second son with her bare hands, but when she sent the slave girl to see whether Aubergine was dead as well, the girl returned again saying the princess was alive and well. Then the sorceress queen cried with rage and spite, for she had killed her second son for no reason. Still, she refused to abandon her wicked project, and the next night she put even more powerful spells on the sleeping princess, asking her,

"Princess Aubergine! Tell me true—
In what thing does your life lie?"

And the princess replied, "In the life of your third son. Kill him, and 1 will also die!"

The very same thing happened. Though the young prince was killed by his wicked mother, Aubergine remained alive and well. And so it went on day after day, until all seven young princes were slain. The cruel mother wept tears of rage and spite at having killed her seven sons for no reason.

The sorceress queen summoned up all her art and cast such powerful spells on Princess Aubergine that she could no longer resist them and was obliged to speak the truth. When the wicked queen asked,

"Princess Aubergine! Tell me true—
In what thing does your life lie?"

the poor princess was obliged to answer, "In a river far away there lives a red and green fish. Inside the fish there is a bumblebee, inside the bee a tiny box, and inside the box is the wonderful nine-lakh necklace. If you put it on, I shall die."

The queen was finally satisfied, and she set about finding the red and green fish. When her husband, the king, came to see her, she began sobbing so hard that he asked her what was the matter. She told him that she had set her heart on procuring the wonderful nine-lakh necklace.

"But where is it to be found?" asked the king. And the queen replied with the words of Princess Aubergine: "In a river far away there lives a red and green fish. Inside the fish there is a bumblebee, inside the bee a tiny box, and in the box is the nine-lakh necklace."

Now the king was a very kind man, and he had long been in mourning for the loss of his seven young sons, who, the queen said, had died suddenly of an infectious disease. Seeing his wife so distressed and being anxious to comfort her, he gave orders that every fisherman in his kingdom was to fish all day long until the red and green fish was found. And so all the fishermen set to work, and before long the queen's desire was fulfilled—the red and green fish was caught. When the wicked sorceress opened it, there was the bumblebee, and inside the bee was the box, and inside the box was the wonderful nine-lakh necklace, which the queen put on at once.

No sooner had the queen's magic forced Princess Aubergine to reveal the secret of her life than she knew she must die. She returned sadly to the hut of her foster parents and, telling them of her approaching death, begged them not to burn or bury her body.

"Here is what I want you to do," she said. "Dress me in my finest clothes, lay me on my bed, scatter flowers over me, and carry me to the farthest reaches of the wilderness. There you must place the bed on the ground and build a high mud wall around it so that no one will be able to see over it." The poor foster parents, weeping bitterly, promised to do as she wished. When the princess died (which happened at the very moment the wicked queen put on the nine-lakh necklace), they dressed her in her finest clothes, scattered flowers over the bed, and carried her out to the farthest reaches of the wilderness.

Now when the queen sent the slave girl to the Brahman's hut to inquire if Princess Aubergine was really dead, the girl returned saying, "She is dead but neither burnt nor buried. She is lying out in the wilderness to the north, covered with flowers, and she looks as beautiful as the moon!"

The queen was not satisfied with this reply, but since there was nothing more she could do, she had to be content. The king was still mourning his seven young sons, and in an effort to forget his grief, he went out hunting every day. The queen, who feared that he might find the dead Princess Aubergine while hunting, made him promise never to travel north, for she said, "Some evil will surely befall you if you do."

But one day, having hunted to the east and the south and the west without finding game, he forgot his promise and set off to hunt in the north. During his wanderings he lost his way and came upon a high enclosure with no door. Curious about what was inside, he climbed over the wall. He could scarcely believe his eyes when he saw a lovely princess lying on a bed strewn with flowers, looking as if she had just fallen asleep. He could not believe she was dead, and kneeling down beside her, he spent the entire day praying and begging her to open her eyes. At nightfall he returned to the palace, but with the dawn he took his bow and, dismissing all his attendants on the pretext of wanting to hunt alone, flew to his beautiful princess. So he passed day after day, kneeling distractedly beside the lovely Aubergine, beseeching her to rise, but she never stirred.

A year passed, and one day he found the most beautiful little boy imaginable lying beside the princess. He was greatly astonished; but taking the child in his arms, he cared tenderly for it all day long, and at night he placed it next to its dead mother. After some time the child learned to talk, and when the king asked if his mother had always been dead, he replied, "No! At night she is alive and cares for me as you do during the day."

Hearing this, the king asked the boy the cause of his mother's death, and the next day the boy replied, "My mother says it is the fault of the nine-lakh necklace your queen wears. At night, when the queen takes it off, my mother comes back to life, but every morning, when the queen puts it back on, my mother dies." The king was puzzled, for he could not imagine what his queen could have to do with the mysterious princess, so he told the boy to ask his mother who his father was. The next morning the boy replied, "Mother asked me to tell you that I am your son, sent to console you for the loss of the seven fair sons your wicked queen murdered out of jealousy of my mother, the lovely Princess Aubergine."

The king grew enraged at the thought of his dead sons and told the boy to ask his mother how the wicked queen should be punished and by what means the necklace could be recovered.

The next morning the boy said, "Mother says I am the only person who can recover the necklace, so tonight, when you return to the palace, you should take me with you." The king carried the boy back to the palace and told all his ministers and courtiers that the child was his heir. Hearing this, the sorceress queen, thinking of her own dead sons, became mad with jealousy and was determined to poison the boy. To this end she prepared some tempting sweetmeats and, caressing the child, gave him a handful, bidding him eat them. But the child refused, saying he would not do so until she gave him the glittering necklace she wore round her neck so that he could play with it.

Dead set on poisoning the boy and seeing no other way of inducing him to eat the sweetmeats, the sorceress queen slipped off the nine-lakh necklace and gave it to the child. No sooner had he touched it than he ran off so fast that none of the servants or guards could stop him. He did not catch his breath until he reached the place where the beautiful Princess Aubergine lay dead. He threw the necklace over her head, and she rose up lovelier than ever. Then the king came and asked her to return to the palace as his bride, but she replied, "I cannot be your wife until that wicked sorceress is dead, for she would murder me and my son just as she murdered your seven young sons. If you dig a deep ditch at the threshold of the palace, fill it with scorpions and snakes, throw the wicked queen into it, and bury her alive, I will walk over her grave, and then I can be your wife."

The king ordered a deep ditch to be dug and had it filled with scorpions and snakes. Then he went to the sorceress queen and asked her to come see something very wonderful. She refused, suspecting a trick. The guards seized her, bound her, flung her into the ditch among the scorpions and snakes, and buried her alive. As for Princess Aubergine, she and her son walked over the grave and lived happily in the palace ever after.

SNOW-WHITE-FIRE-RED

The predictable drama of stories about beautiful girls is overturned by this Italian tale that sets up distinct expectations through the name of its protagonist. Kisses turn toxic, not as the kiss of death but as a means of producing amnesia, a loss of memory that has distinctly death-like overtones. Quirky in its originality, the tale was written down by a college professor at Cornell, who, in the introduction to his *Italian Popular Tales* (1885), declared that he wanted to preserve tales "exactly as they were taken down from the mouths of the people." Breaking free from canonical versions of stories about beautiful girls, "Snow-White-Fire-Red" has the kind of playful irreverence found in tales close to oral traditions, even as it still fetishizes feminine beauty.

SNOW-WHITE-FIRE-RED

Once there lived a king and a queen who had no heir. They were determined to have one, and they swore that if they had a son, or even a daughter, they would keep two fountains flowing for seven years: one running wine, the other oil. After they made that vow, the queen gave birth to a handsome boy.

As soon as the child was born, the two fountains were set up, and everyone gathered there to collect wine and oil. After seven years both fountains began to run dry. An ogress, wishing to collect the last few drops still in the fountain, went there with a sponge and a pitcher. She sopped up the last drops with her sponge and then squeezed them into her pitcher. After she had done all that work to fill up the pitcher, the young son of the king, who was playing ball nearby, tossed a ball her way and broke the pitcher. When the old woman realized what had happened, she said, "Listen to me! I can't do much to you because you are the king's son, but I can put a curse on you. May you never marry until you find Snow-white-fire-red!"

The wise child took a piece of paper and wrote down the words of the old woman, put the paper in a drawer, and said not a word about what had happened. When he was eighteen, the king and the queen wanted to make plans for his marriage. Suddenly he remembered the old woman's curse, took out the slip of paper, and said, "Oh, if I do not find Snow-white-fire-red, I will not be able to marry!" When the time was right, he took leave of his father and mother and set out on a journey on his own. Months passed without his encountering a soul. One evening, just when it was turning dark, a large house appeared before him in the middle of a clearing.

The next morning, at sunrise, an ogress appeared before the house. She was massive and stout, and she cried out, "Snow-white-fire-red, lower your braids and let me climb up them!" When the prince heard these words, he took heart and said, "Here she is at last!" Snow-white-fire-red lowered her braids, which seemed never to end, and the ogress used them to climb up to the window. The next day the ogress climbed back down, and when the prince saw her leaving, he jumped down from the tree where he had hidden and cried out, "Snow-white-fire-red, lower your braids and let me climb up them!" The girl lowered her braids, for she thought it was her mother who was calling her (she called the ogress "Mother"). The prince climbed up the braids. When he came in through the window, he said, "Oh! My dear little sister, how far I have traveled to find you!" And he told her about the curse uttered by the old woman when he was a boy of seven.

The girl gave him something to drink and then said, "When the ogress returns and finds you here, she will eat you up. Go hide somewhere!" And sure enough, the ogress returned, but by then the prince was in a hiding place.

After the ogress finished her meal, her daughter gave her some wine and, before long, made her drunk. Then she said, "Mother, what do I have to do to get away from here? Not that I want to go, because I really want to stay with you. I'm just curious to know. Tell me!"

"To get away from here, you will have to cast a spell on everything that is in this room to slow me down," the ogress said. "I will call out your name, and instead of you, the chair, the cupboard, the chest of drawers, all those things will answer for you. When you are not to be seen, I will rise up and follow you. You must take the seven balls of yarn I have hidden away. When I come after you and can't find you, I will still be on your trail. When you see me hot in pursuit, toss the first ball down and then the others after it. I will keep overtaking you, but not after you throw down the last ball."

The daughter listened carefully to everything said to her and remembered every word. The next day the ogress left, and Snow-white-fire-red and the prince did what was required for them to leave. They went through the entire house, saying, "Table: you must answer if my mother calls; chairs: answer when my mother calls; chest of drawers: answer when my mother calls."

And so they cast spells on everything in the house. Then the girl and the prince left in such a hurry that they looked as if they were flying away.

When the ogress returned, she cried out, "Snow-white-fire-red, let down your braids so that I can climb up them." The table answered, "Come up, Mother, come up!" The ogress waited a while, and when no one appeared at the window, she called up again, "Snow-white-fire-red, lower your braids so that I can climb up them!" The chair replied, "Come up, Mother, come up!" She waited a while again, but no one appeared at the window. Then she called up again, and the chest of drawers replied, "Come up, Mother, come up!" Meanwhile the lovers were fleeing as fast as possible.

The ogress asked so many times for the braids that finally there were no items left in the house to answer, and she cried out, "Treason! Treason!" Then she found a ladder and climbed up to the window. When she realized that her daughter had left and had taken the balls of yarn, she shouted, "Oh, wretch! I will drink your blood!" Then she sped after the fugitives, following their scent. They saw her from a distance, and when she caught sight of them, she shouted, "Snow-white-fire-red, turn around so that I can see you." (If Snow-white-fire-red had turned around, she would have been cursed.)

When the ogress had nearly overtaken them, Snow-white-fire-red tossed the first ball of yarn, and suddenly there appeared a massive mountain. The ogress was undaunted. She started climbing up the mountain and kept climbing until she almost overtook the two. Then Snow-white-fire-red, seeing her gaining on them, tossed down the second ball, and suddenly a clearing appeared, covered with sharp blades and knives. The ogress, wounded and dripping with blood, continued to chase after the lovers.

When Snow-white-fire-red saw her drawing near again, she tossed down the third ball, and a torrent appeared, forming a river. The ogress jumped into the river and continued her pursuit, even though she was half dead. Then a fourth ball was tossed, and a fountain sprang up, spewing vipers and other terrible things. At last the ogress, so worn out that she was near death, stopped and cursed Snow-white-fire-red, saying, "When the queen kisses her son, the prince will forget all about you!"

And with that the ogress could no longer bear the pain, and she died in great anguish.

The lovers continued on the journey and reached a town near the prince's birthplace. The prince said to Snow-white-fire-red, "Stay here, for you need to have some proper clothing before you meet my father and mother, and I will go get something for you to wear." She agreed and stayed right where she was.

When the queen saw her son, she rushed toward him to embrace and kiss him. "Mother," he said, "I have taken a vow and sworn not to let anyone kiss me." The poor mother was paralyzed with fear. Late that night, while her son was still asleep, the mother, dying to kiss her son, went to his bedroom and kissed him. From that moment on he could remember nothing of Snow-white-fire-red.

Let us leave the prince behind with his mother and return to the poor child left in the streets without any idea of where she was. An old woman saw the girl, who was as beautiful as the sun, and noticed that she was weeping. "What on Earth is the matter, my daughter?"

"I have no idea where I am!"

"My daughter, do not despair. Come with me." And the old woman took the girl to her house. The young girl was skillful with her hands and could work spells on objects. She made things with her hands, and the old woman sold them. That's how they made a living. One day the girl told the old woman that she needed two little pieces of cloth from the palace for something she was making. The old woman went over to the palace and begged the servants to give her two bits of fabric until finally they did. Now the old woman had two doves, a male and a female, and with those two pieces of cloth, Snow-white-fire-red made clothing for the doves and whispered in their ears, "You are the prince, and you are Snow-white-fire-red. The king is sitting down and having a meal. Fly to him and tell him about everything we have endured together."

While the king, queen, prince, and many others were sitting down for a meal, the beautiful doves flew in the window and alighted on the table. "How beautiful you are!" the royal ones exclaimed, and everyone was greatly pleased. Then the dove that represented Snow-white-fire-red began, "Do you remember when you were young how your father vowed, in honor of your birth, to build two fountains, with oil flowing from one and wine from the other?"

The other dove replied, "Yes, I remember."

"Do you remember the old woman whose pitcher filled with oil you broke? Do you remember?"

"Yes, I remember."

"Do you remember the curse she put on you, that you could not marry until you found Snow-white-fire-red?"

"I remember," the other dove replied.

In short, the first dove recalled everything that had happened and finally said, "Do you remember how the ogress was at your heels and how she cursed you, declaring that a kiss from your mother would make you forget Snow-white-fire-red?"

When the dove mentioned the kiss, the prince suddenly remembered everything, and the king and queen were astonished by everything the doves had said.

When the doves finished their conversation, they nodded and flew away. The prince called out, "Hey there! Hey there! Keep track of where those doves are going! Follow them!" The servants followed them and saw the doves settle on the roof of a country house. The prince followed them and rushed in to find Snow-white-fire-red right there before him. As soon as he caught sight of her, he threw his arms around her, exclaiming, "Oh, my dear sister, how you have suffered for me!" Straightaway they dressed Snow-white-fire-red in beautiful clothes and escorted her to the palace. When the queen set eyes on her, she said, "What a beauty!" Everything was quickly settled, and the two were married.

THE MAGIC SLIPPERS

This Portuguese tale, translated into English in 1888, resembles other Romance-language versions of the tale, with hospitable robbers in the place of dwarfs. Set in a mountainous region of Portugal, the tale's symbolic landscape of rolling hills, winding rivers, gloomy forests, and dark passages contrasts with the various interior spaces—inns, havens, dens, and castles—on the heroine's journey from the perils of home to a joyful wedding in a castle. The story is unique in its emphasis on dainty, lovely feet and the use of a slipper to suffocate and produce a catatonic sleep. The detail about the feet and slippers brings the story into the orbit of Cinderella tales. Many variants of stories about beautiful girls pick and choose tropes from a range of stories including "Goldilocks" and "Sleeping Beauty" to produce maximum dramatic effects.

THE MAGIC SLIPPERS

A LONG TIME AGO there lived a very beautiful woman who ran a roadside inn patronized by muleteers and merchants who stopped there with their merchandise. This woman had a daughter who had the great misfortune of being more beautiful than her mother. The mother was so jealous of her daughter that she locked her in a dark room with all the windows shut so that no one would be able to see her. Poor girl, she often wished that she had been born plain so that she could have her freedom and enjoy life like other young people.

When any muleteers stopped at the inn, the first question put to them by the innkeeper was whether they had ever seen a woman more beautiful than she was. Since they generally said no, she was sure that they had not seen her daughter. One day, however, the girl managed to open a window, and one of the muleteers who had stopped at the inn and had been asked the same question as always replied that he had just seen a girl at the window who surpassed her in beauty.

"Ah, I know who that is then," the woman said. "What business does she have looking out the window? She will pay for that." And full of spite and rage, she resolved to do away with her daughter. She ordered two of her men to take the girl to a remote place on a mountain, a few miles away, and to put her to death there.

The men took the girl to the chosen spot. But just as one of them was raising the hatchet to sever her head from her body, the girl sank to her knees, and with tears rolling down her beautiful cheeks, she pleaded with them to spare her life, promising never to return to her mother. They could just pretend they had executed her mother's orders. The men were so moved by her appeal that they raised her up from the ground, and bearing no ill feelings against her, they said, "No, no, we do not have the heart to kill you. But you must leave this part of the country, for if your mother were ever to find you alive, we would be in real trouble with her."

"I thank you for this good deed," the girl replied, "and I hope someday to have the means of rewarding you."

The girl decided to leave the place as quickly as possible. She took a winding path that led down to a stream at the foot of the mountain, and she followed its course until she reached a house situated between two hills. Now that it was dark, she went up to the house, and finding the door open, she entered all the way into the great hall of the place. Seeing no one, she called out, "Can anyone here give a poor girl shelter for the night?" Since her call was unanswered, she walked farther into the house, and wandering from one chamber to the next through dark passages, she found that the place was deserted. There was also no furniture in the house, save for a few broken chairs and a collapsed table. She decided to take up her quarters there until daybreak, and she made herself as comfortable as possible.

The girl was hungry, and she went down to the kitchen and pried into every corner of the pantry with the hope of finding some food. Among some trash and broken crockery, she discovered a brown earthenware pot containing flour and a jar of rancid oil, all of which was like a feast to her. Then she went down to the garden, and after gathering some kindling and lighting a fire, she made herself a hearth cake with the flour and oil. Just as she was putting her meager meal on the kitchen table—in addition to the cake there were a few small radishes she had dug up in the garden and a cupful of water from the well—she heard a noise so frightening that she hid and listened. She soon realized that the noise was being made by a band of robbers returning home to conceal their booty. When they saw that supper was on the table, they cried, "Hallo? Who prepared this meal? If anyone is here, let them show themselves."

The poor girl came out of her hiding place trembling with fear, and she stood before the robbers. But the men, astonished by her beautiful face and charming figure, asked what misfortune had befallen her that she had come to their house all alone. The robbers felt great compassion for her and said, "Don't be afraid and don't be sad. You can stay with us, and we promise to protect you and treat you like a sister."

What could the poor girl do but agree to their proposal? She stayed with the men and made herself useful by preparing their meals and keeping house for them. The robbers become fonder of their newly adopted sister with each passing day. She was so gentle and good that they treated her with respect and tried to let her enjoy every possible comfort they could provide.

I must now tell you that the girl's mother was acquainted with an old woman who often stopped by her inn and whose business it was to run errands and carry messages.

"Tell me," the innkeeper said one day to the old woman. "You have been everywhere and have seen so many different faces. Have you ever seen a woman more beautiful than I am?"

"Well, to tell you the truth, I have seen one face more attractive than yours. Once, in a town at Trás-os-Montes, I saw a girl more charming than any woman I have ever seen in my life. She had a lovely figure and the sweetest and tiniest feet imaginable."

"Indeed," replied the innkeeper. "Then I know who she is. I want you to take a present to her the next time you are near there." She took a small pair of slippers out of a drawer and gave them to the old woman, saying, "Here, take these to her and tell her that her loving mother is sending a gift to her. But you must promise not to leave until you have seen her put the slippers on. Be very exacting on that point and follow my instructions precisely, and I can promise you that I shall pay you handsomely."

The woman did as she was told and went to the house where the girl was living. She said, "My dear child, I am bringing you some slippers sent by your loving mother. She wants you to wear them for her sake."

"I don't need any shoes. My brothers give them to me whenever I need them, and so you can just take them back to my mother."

But the old woman insisted that the girl try them on, and she tormented her for so long that she agreed at last to try them on, just to get rid of the old woman. Hardly had she put one of the shoes on when one eye shut completely. She put on the other shoe, and the other eye closed.

And then she fell down on the floor, dead. The old woman, surprised and frightened by what she saw, ran away and left the house as quickly as she could.

When the robbers returned home and saw their beloved sister lying on the ground dead, they could not imagine what had happened to her. They were in deep mourning and wept as they stood over her corpse.

"It is such a shame for this face and figure to be hidden away underground," they said. "Let's put her in a coffin with a glass lid and put it in the hills where the king's son goes to hunt with his friends. It is fitting that he should have the chance to see such a rare and lovely flower."

The robbers had a beautiful coffin made, and they put the body of their dear sister in it, strewed flowers over her, and then, fastening the glass cover down, they carried her to a remote place in the hills.

Now it so happened that the king's son, while hunting one day with a number of courtiers, passed the very spot where the girl's body had been placed. He and his men saw the coffin and wondered why it had been put in such an unusual location. The prince looked into the coffin and was immediately taken by the beauty of the dead girl's countenance and by the eyelids that were fringed with long, silken lashes. He could not help but admire the pretty hands and feet, along with the silver band entwined in the luxuriant tresses of the hair. His heart skipped a beat as he looked down into her face, and he wondered if it could be possible to summon a fairy who, with her magic wand, would bring back to life the little beauty whom he longed to snatch from death and call his own.

When the prince recovered from his reverie, he decided that he would at least take a keepsake with him. Lifting the cover of the coffin, he pulled one of the pretty little slippers from the girl's feet. But hardly had he done that when one of her eyes opened, and the king's son, seeing this, took off the other slipper. And behold! the other eye opened as well, and the girl came back to life. The prince was overjoyed, and he took her by the hand and helped her climb out of the coffin. She emerged fresher and fairer than ever, if that was even possible.

The prince now sent one of his attendants for a carriage to take the maiden to the palace and to present her to the king. A few weeks later the prince married the girl amid great rejoicing. Among all the court beauties there was not a one who could rival the grace and loveliness of the sweet bride.

The prince took his bride to the inn owned by her mother so that the cruel woman would finally know that she had not succeeded in killing her daughter, a woman who, in her unrivaled beauty, had captivated a prince of royal blood and had married him.

The chronicles from these times relate that the wicked innkeeper, steadfast in her iron resolve, tried again to destroy her daughter, so consumed was she by jealousy and revenge. But now her daughter was so far removed from her clutches and her domain that she could not carry out any more of her cruel intentions. Thus ends this wonderful history of a beauty and her magical slippers.

THE WORLD'S MOST BEAUTIFUL WOMAN

The introduction of exotic elements ranging from allusions to the Garden of Eden to the insertion of a Persian prince suggests a certain worldliness to this Hungarian story published in 1889. If intrigue and maneuvering are more sharply profiled in this tale, it seems in part to be a consequence of a self-conscious literary style that offers some elaboration on motivation and also emphasizes the value of beauty yet also deprecates vanity. The toxic alliance between the two older women in the story is an unusual example of same-sex sibling solidarity even if the alliance is short-lived.

THE WORLD'S MOST BEAUTIFUL WOMAN

In the beautiful land of Asia, where Adam and Eve may have lived, where all animals, including cows, live wild, where the corn grows wild and even bread grows on trees, there lived a pretty girl whose palace was built on a low hill that looked over a pretty valley from which you could see the whole world. In the same country there lived a young king who decided not to marry until he succeeded in finding the prettiest woman in the world.

One day it struck the young king that it would be a good thing to marry. He told his noble friends to travel everywhere in his kingdom until they found the prettiest girl in the land. Then they were to write the king, and he could go have a look at all of them and choose for himself the one he liked best among the beauties.

After a year the king received letters from all seventy-seven of his friends, and all seventy-seven letters arrived from the same town, where, on a low hill above a pretty little valley, there stood a golden palace in which there lived a young lady with a nice old man and a maid. From the four windows of the palace, you could see the whole world.

The young king set out with a retinue of wedding guests to the place where the girl lived. He found all seventy-seven friends there, and they were all lovesick, lying about on the pavement of the palace, on hay that was like fine silk grass. There they lay, every one of them. The moment the young king saw the beautiful girl, he cried out, "The Lord has created you just for me. You are mine and I am yours! And it is my wish to find peace in the same grave with you."

The young lady also fell in love with the handsome king. She was so smitten that she could not utter a word but only put her arm around his waist and took him to her father. Her father wept tears of joy that at last a man had appeared whom his daughter could love. Up until then she had thought every man ugly. The ceremony was very short. As the wife wished, the king came to live in the beautiful spot, for there was no prettier one in the whole world!

Near the palace there was a hut. A witch lived in it, and she knew all the young lady's secrets and helped her with advice whenever she needed it. The witch praised the young lady's beauty to everyone she met, and it was she who had gathered the seventy-seven young noblemen in the palace. On the evening of the wedding she called on "the world's most beautiful lady" and praised the young king's looks and wealth. After a while the witch let out a deep sigh. The pretty young lady asked her what was wrong, for she had praised the king as handsome, rich, and honorable.

"My pretty lady, my beautiful queen, if you two live for some time here, you will no longer be the prettiest woman in the world. You are very pretty now, and your husband is the handsomest of all men. But should a daughter be born, she will be more beautiful than you. She will be more beautiful than the morning star—that is why I'm so sad, my beautiful lady."

"You are quite right, my good woman, I will do whatever you tell me to do to remain the most beautiful woman in the world."

The witch said to the beautiful lady, "I will give you a handful of cotton wool. When your husband is asleep, put this wool on your lips, but be careful not to wet it, because it will have poison on it. When your husband returns home from the dance, he will come to kiss you, and he will die from the poison." The young lady did as the witch told her, and the king was found dead the next morning. The physicians were not able to figure out why he had died.

The bride was left a widow and went back to live with her maid and her father. She took a vow never to marry again, and she kept her word. As it happened, however, by some miracle, after a few months she discovered that she was with child. She hurried over to see the witch and ask her what she should do. The witch gave her a looking glass, along with some advice: "Every morning you must ask the mirror whether there is a more beautiful woman. If it says there is not, there really won't be one for a long time, and you can rest easy.

But if it says that there is one, there will be one, and I will tell you that myself as well."

The beautiful lady snatched the mirror from the witch with great joy, and as soon as she reached her dressing room, she placed it on the window ledge and asked, "Well, my dear little mirror, is there a woman in the world more beautiful than I am?"

The mirror replied, "Not yet, but soon there will be one, and she will be twice as beautiful as you."

The beautiful woman nearly lost her mind and told the witch what the mirror had said. "Don't worry," she replied. "Let her be born, and we shall soon get rid of her."

The beautiful lady was confined, and a pretty little daughter was born. It would have been a sin to look at her with an evil eye. The bad woman did not even look at the pretty little creature but fetched her mirror and asked, "Well, my dear little mirror, is there a creature more beautiful than I am?" and the looking glass replied, "You are very beautiful, but your little daughter is seven times prettier than you." As soon as she left her bed, she sent for the witch to ask for advice. When the witch took the babe in her arms, she declared that she had never seen such a beautiful creature in all her life. While gazing at the beautiful child, she spat into her eyes and covered her face. Then she told the beautiful woman to look at the child again in three hours, when she would find that it had become a monster. The beautiful lady was troubled and asked the witch if she could question the mirror again. "Certainly," the witch replied, "for I know that at this moment you are the most beautiful woman alive." But the mirror replied, "You are beautiful, but your daughter is seven times more beautiful than you." The beautiful woman nearly died of rage, but the witch only smiled, confident of her magic power.

Three hours went by, and the little girl's face was uncovered. The witch fainted away, for the the little girl had become not only seven times but seventy-seven times more beautiful than ever from something that usually disfigured babies. When the witch was revived, she advised the beautiful lady to kill the baby, for the devil himself had no power over it.

The father of the beautiful woman died suddenly, his heart broken by what his daughter had done. The beautiful woman was bereft, and in order to forget her troubles, she spared her daughter until she turned thirteen. The little girl grew more beautiful every day, until one day the woman could no longer bear her daughter's beauty and handed her over to the witch to be killed. The witch was only too glad to carry out the deed and took the girl deep into the woods. She tied the girl's hands together with wisps of straw and placed a wreath of straw on her head and a bundle of straw around her waist. She was going to light them and burn this beautiful child to death. All of a sudden loud shouts were heard in the forest, and twelve robbers came running as swiftly as birds toward the witch and the pretty girl. One of the robbers grabbed the girl, while another knocked the witch on the head and gave her a sound beating. The witch pretended to be dead, and the robbers left the wicked wretch behind, carrying off the pretty girl (who had fainted in her fright) with them.

After some time, the witch got up and rushed over to the castle where the beautiful woman was living and said, "Well, my queen, don't ask your mirror any more questions, because you are now the most beautiful creature in the world. Your beautiful daughter is dead and buried." The lady jumped for joy and kissed the ugly witch.

When the pretty girl recovered, she found herself in a nice little house guarded by twelve men, who whispered among themselves about her unmatched beauty. The sweet young thing looked at the men with their long beards and their gaping eyes. She got up from her soft bed and thanked the good men for having rescued her from the witch and then asked them where she was and what they planned to do with her. If they were going to kill her, she begged them to do it swiftly, since anything would be better than being killed by that horrible witch, who was going to burn her to death. None of the robbers could speak, for their hearts were so softened by her words—words they had never heard from human lips. Her sweet expression would have tamed even a wild bull. At last one of the robbers said, "You lovely creature: you are in the house of twelve robbers, men with good hearts but bad morals. We would never kill you. Stay here and keep house for us, and let us feast our eyes on you! Whatever you want, even if you are seeking a husband, we will bring to you! Be our daughter, and we will be everything to you! your fathers! brothers! guardians! and, if you should need it, your warriors!"

The little girl smiled and was pleased. She found more happiness among the robbers than she had ever felt in her mother's palace. The robbers went back to their plundering with great joy—singing and whistling because they now had the most beautiful queen in the world.

One day the girl's mother was feeling weary and listless, for no one had praised her looks for a long time. She took the mirror and said, "My dear, sweet little mirror, is there a more beautiful creature in all the world than I?"

The little mirror replied, "You are very beautiful, but your daughter is a thousand times better looking."

The woman nearly had a fit, for it had not dawned on her that her hated daughter might still be alive. She ran to the witch's hut to report what the mirror had said. The witch heard her words and at once disguised herself. She reached the fence of the place where the pretty girl was living. In the garden were flowers and rose bushes. Among the flower beds she could see the pretty girl walking around in a dress fit for a queen. The witch's heart nearly broke in two when she saw the young girl, for never, not even in her imagination, had she ever seen anyone so beautiful. She stole into the garden among the flower beds and could see that the young girl's fingers were covered with precious diamond rings. She kissed the girl's hand and begged her to put on a ring more precious than any she had. The girl gave her consent and even thanked the woman for it. When the girl returned to the house, she fell down as if dead. The witch rushed back home and brought the good news to the beautiful queen, who asked the mirror if there was anyone prettier than she, and the mirror replied that there was not.

The woman was delighted and nearly went mad with joy on hearing that she was again the most beautiful creature in existence. She gave the witch a handful of gold.

At noon the robbers returned home from their plundering and were thunderstruck when they saw that the jewel of their household appeared to be dead. After much weeping and wailing they made preparations to lay out their adored queen. They took off her shoes in order to put even more beautiful ones on her feet. They removed the rings from her fingers so that they could clean them. One of the robbers took off the very last one, and the girl suddenly sat up and smiled. She told them that she had slept very well and had had the most beautiful dreams. She also said that if they had not taken off the ring from her little finger, she would never have woken up.

The robbers smashed the murderous ring to pieces with their hatchets and pleaded with their dear queen not to speak to anyone. For several weeks nothing happened to the young lady. But a few weeks later her mother again felt bored and asked her mirror, "Is there anyone on Earth more beautiful than I am?" The mirror replied, "You are very beautiful, but your daughter is one thousand times more beautiful."

The beautiful lady began to tear her hair out and went to see the witch to complain that her daughter was still alive. The witch found the young lady again. She disguised herself as a peddler and began to praise the gold and diamond pins on the young lady's shawl. She begged her to add another pin as a keepsake. The young lady thanked her for it and went indoors to look after the cooking. As soon as she was back in the house, she dropped down dead.

The mother was overjoyed when the witch returned, and once again the mirror declared that the girl was dead. In the meantime the robbers returned home and saw the beautiful corpse stretched out on the ground and began to weep again. Three of the robbers got everything needed for the funeral, and the rest undressed the corpse and washed it. When they were taking the pins off her shawl, they found one that sparkled more brilliantly than the others, and two of the robbers snatched it away, each being anxious to make sure she would be wearing it for her burial. Suddenly the young queen sat up and told them that the old woman had tried to kill her. The robbers buried the pin five fathoms deep in the ground so that no evil spirit could find it. No creatures on Earth are more anxious than women. It is a misfortune when they are pretty and a misfortune when they are not. When they are pretty, they constantly need reassurance; if they are not, they want to be. Once again the evil one tempted the beautiful lady, and she asked whether any living being was prettier than she. The mirror replied that her daughter was prettier.

In a rage the lady called the witch all kinds of bad names and threatened to betray the witch to the world for persuading her to do evil. It was the witch who had convinced her to murder her handsome husband. It was the witch who had given her the mysterious mirror. The old hag did not reply but went off in a confident manner. She turned herself into a pretty girl and went straight to where the young lady was living and told her that the robbers had hired her to guard the house. The innocent girl believed everything the witch said. The witch did up the girl's hair in accordance with the latest fashion, braided it, and fastened it with all kinds of hair pins, one of which was a pin she had brought with her. She hid the pin in the girl's hair so that no one would notice it. Once she had finished, she asked permission to leave for a moment but never returned. The young lady fell down dead again, and once more the robbers began sobbing and wept bitter tears. The men began the painful duty of laying the girl out for burial. They took off all her rings, jewelry, and hairpins. They even smoothed out the folds of her dress, but still they did not manage to bring the young girl back to life.

The mother was really thrilled this time, because whenever she talked to the mirror now, it answered as she wanted. The robbers, however, were weeping and wailing and unable to eat. One of them proposed not burying the girl but staying by her side and praying. Some also believed it would be a pity to bury her. Others thought it would be too heartbreaking to look on her beauty for any length of time. Finally, they ordered a splendid coffin made of gold. They wrapped her in fine, purple linen. Then they caught an elk and placed the coffin on its antlers so that the body would not decompose. The elk carried the precious coffin around and took the greatest care to make sure it would not fall from its antlers.

This elk happened to be grazing in Persia just when the Persian king's son was out hunting all alone. The prince was twenty-three years old. He caught sight of the elk and also the splendid coffin between its antlers, and he took a sack of sugar from his bag and gave it to the elk to eat. Lifting the coffin from the antlers, the Persian king's son opened the gold coffin with trembling hands. He discovered in it a corpse, the likes of which he had never before seen, not even in his dreams.

He began to shake the coffin, hoping to waken the young woman and kiss her. Finally, he got down on bended knee and prayed for her to return to life, but she was still not moving. "I will take her home with me," he said, sobbing. "Although she is a corpse in a coffin and she must have been dead for some time, there is no sign of decay. This girl is prettier in death than all the living girls in Persia." It was late at night when the prince returned home with the golden coffin. He mourned the dead girl for a long time and then went off to supper. The king looked anxiously into his son's eyes but did not dare to ask for the cause of his grief. Every night the prince locked himself in his room and did not go to sleep until he had spent some time mourning, and when he woke up at night, he started weeping again.

The prince had three sisters, and they were very fond of their brother. They watched him every night through a keyhole but could not tell what was happening. But they could hear their brother's sobs and were upset.

The king of a neighboring country declared war against the Persian king. The Persian king, who was advanced in age, asked his son to go in his place to fight the enemy. The good son agreed, but he was tortured by the thought of leaving the beautiful dead girl behind. He knew that he would be able to see his dear one once the war was over, and so he locked himself in his room for two hours, weeping the entire time and kissing his sweetheart. Then he locked the door to his room and put the key in his satchel. The good-hearted princesses were patiently waiting for their brother to leave, and as soon as he was gone, they went to a locksmith to get every key he had. They tried each one out until at last one of the keys fit.

The princesses looked all around in the cupboards, and they even took the bed to pieces. While they were removing the planks from the bed, they suddenly caught sight of the glittering gold coffin, opened it, and found the sleeping angel. All three kissed her, and when they realized that they could not bring her back to life, they began weeping. They rubbed her limbs and held balsam under her nose but without success. Then they removed her rings and jewelry and dressed her up like a pretty doll. The youngest princess brought combs and perfumed oils for the girl's hair. They pulled out her hairpins, parted her golden hair, combed it, and adorned each lock with a hairpin. While they were combing the hair at the nape of her neck, the comb stuck fast, and they realized that a golden hairpin was caught in the hair. The eldest princess removed it carefully, and suddenly the beautiful girl opened her eyes, began to smile, and stepped out of the coffin.

The girls were not at all afraid, and the youngest ran to the king and told him what had happened and how they had discovered the source of their brother's grief. The king wept for joy and went to see the beautiful young woman, declaring, "You shall be my son's wife, the mother of my grandchildren!" And he embraced and kissed her. The king asked how she had made his son's acquaintance and where they had first met. But the pretty princess knew nothing about it and simply told him that she knew she had two enemies who would, sooner or later, kill her. And she also said that she had been living among robbers. The king told her not to be afraid, for neither her mother nor the witch would be able to find her.

The girl sat down to a meal with the king's daughters and asked about the young prince, wondering whether he was handsome or ugly. She said that his looks did not matter. If he was willing to marry her, she would consent. The princesses gave her a portrait of the prince, and the young girl fell so deeply in love with him that she carried the portrait around with her and kissed it from time to time. One morning the news spread that the prince had conquered the enemy and was returning home. The news turned out to be true, and clouds of dust could be seen in the distance as horsemen approached. The princesses asked their pretty new sister to come with them into the room next to her brother's, the place where her coffin had been kept under the bed.

The moment the prince arrived, he jumped off his horse, raced to his room, and opened the lid of the coffin, but all he found was a hairpin. He rushed out of the room like a madman, leaving the door open and demanding to know who had robbed him of his angel. But the angel, over whom he had shed so many tears, stood smiling before him. The young man hugged her tightly and covered her with kisses. He took his betrothed to his father and told him how he had found the pretty corpse resting in the antlers of an elk. The girl also told the story of her life. And the princesses confessed how they had broken into their brother's room and how they restored his sweetheart to life again. The king was overjoyed, and he sent for a priest so that the wedding could be celebrated.

One day the young queen, who was as beautiful as a fairy, informed her husband that she was being persecuted and that while her mother was alive, she could not have any peace. "Don't be afraid," said the prince, "for no human or diabolic power can harm you while you are here."

A year passed, and the queen's mother was still content. Her mirror was covered with dust, and she never for a moment dreamed that her daughter was still alive. But one day she dusted her mirror and asked, "Is there a creature anywhere prettier than I am?" The mirror replied,

"You are very pretty, but your daughter is seventy-seven thousand times more beautiful than you." The beautiful woman fainted, and they had to sprinkle cold water over her for two hours before she came to. Again she went to the witch and begged her to save her from that girl, or else she would have to go and commit suicide. The witch promised she would do everything in her power to get rid of her.

Eight months later the prince had to go back to war, and with a heavy heart he took leave of his wife, who was with child. He promised to return soon. The prince left instructions to send news as soon as the child was born. Not much time had passed after his departure when the queen gave birth to two beautiful boys with golden hair. The princesses swaddled the babies in purple silk and showed them to everyone as miracles of beauty. The king's father sent out a soldier with news to his son about the birth of the boys.

While angels were rejoicing, devils were wracking their brains and making mischief!

The witch put a flask under her apron and got a head start on the soldier. She pitched a small tent by the roadside, using some dirty sheets she had brought with her, and then put the flask in front of her, waiting for passersby. She waited for a long time, but no one appeared. Suddenly clouds began to gather in the sky, and the witch was delighted. A fierce storm set in. The witch saw the soldier running to escape the rain. When he ran past her tent, the wicked old soul shouted to him to come in and sit down in her tent until the rain stopped. The soldier, who was afraid of thunder, accepted her offer and took shelter in the tent. The old woman put some spirits before him, and the soldier drank up. She offered him more, and he drank that too. The witch had put a sleeping potion in the drink, and the soldier soon fell fast asleep and was as still as a fur cloak. The old woman searched his bag for the letter, and imitating the king's handwriting perfectly, she wrote a new letter informing the prince that there was much sorrow at home, for his wife had given birth to two pups. She sealed the letter and woke the soldier up. He raced off and did not stop until he had reached the camp. The prince was upset by his father's letter, but he did not want anyone to harm the creatures born and ordered that they be treated with care. He told the messenger not to stop anywhere and to hurry back with a reply. But the soldier could not forget the good dose of spirits, and so he went into the tent again and had some more. The witch again mixed the spirits with a sleeping potion and searched the bag while the soldier slept. She stole the letter, and imitating the prince's handwriting, wrote back to the king that he should kill his wife and her pups, because a woman who gave birth to pups must be a bad person. The king was surprised by his son's reply but said not a word. At night he summoned the soldier and put his daughter-in-law in a black carriage. The soldier had orders to take the woman and her two children into the middle of the forest and kill them. But when he ordered the mother to get out of the carriage in the woods, he started weeping. Three times the soldier tried to raise his club to kill her, but each time he stopped, overcome by grief. The mother implored him not to kill her and told him she was willing to go away and never be seen again. The old soldier let her go, and she took her two babes and found shelter in a hollow tree. There she stayed, living off roots and fruit.

The soldier returned home and was questioned by the king. The king did not want to disappoint his son, who was to return the next day. The soldier swore that he had killed the prince's wife and the children too and that he had thrown their bodies into the water. The prince arrived home and feared seeing his unfortunate wife with her two pups.

The king had left his son's letter on his desk, and when the prince picked it up and read it, he was enraged. "This looks just like my writing," he said, "but I did not write it. It must be the work of some devil." He then produced his father's letter and handed it to him. The king was horrified at the lies written by some devil in his hand. "No, my dear son," he said, weeping, "I did not write this letter. I wrote that two sons with golden hair had been born to you."

"And I," replied the prince, "said that my wife and her offspring should not be harmed. Where is my wife? Where are my boys?"

"My dear son," said the king, "I thought I was carrying out your orders. I sent them into the woods and had them killed by one of my soldiers. He threw their bodies into the water."

The old soldier happened to be listening through a crack in the door to the conversation of the two. He entered the room without being summoned and said, "I was unable to carry out your orders, my lord and king. I did not have the heart to destroy the most beautiful creature in the world, and I let her go free in the forest. If she and her children have not been devoured by wild beasts, they are still alive."

The prince did not touch his supper and had his horse saddled at once. For three days and three nights he searched the woods with his men. On the fourth night, at midnight, the prince thought he heard a baby crying. He jumped off his horse and found his beautiful wife and children. He took the family home, and there were celebrations throughout the realm.

The prince's wife was still afraid of her mother and the witch and knew they would try to kill her again. The prince issued a warrant for the witch, and the soldier found her and tied her up. She was a fearsome creature, her body covered with frightful boils with an immense horn sprouting from her forehead. The prince's wife recognized the witch and interrogated her. Then the witch revealed that she was in fact her aunt. "When I was just a baby, your grandmother gave orders to drown me. A devil rescued me and educated me. I went along with my sister's madness because I wanted to protect her. But the Lord has preserved you, and your mother did not go mad until I put a pox on her and her face became pitted and scarred. Her mirror made fun of her, and she lost her mind and is now wandering the face of the Earth, with children pelting her with stones. She grieves for you all the time."

The beautiful woman told her husband what she had learned, and the witch was strangled, strung up in a tree, and burned at the stake. Once her soul had left its wicked body, a horse was tied to each of her hands and to her feet, and her body was torn into four pieces, with one quarter of her body sent to each of the points of the compass, as an example to other witches.

The "most beautiful woman in the world" had now become ugly. One day she happened to reach the palace where the princess was living. Her daughter wept to see her and had her kept in a beautiful room, every day showing her, through a glass door, her own beautiful children. The poor lunatic wept and tortured herself until one day she jumped out the window and broke her neck. The prince loved his beautiful wife as a dove does its mate. He obeyed her every wish and protected her from danger.

The two little sons with golden hair became powerful and valiant heroes, and when the king died, his two golden-haired grandchildren carried him to his vault.

The young couple survived so many trials, and they are still alive and well, if they have not yet died.

SILVER-TREE AND GOLD-TREE

The Australian folklorist Joseph Jacobs (1854–1916) collected this tale and published many anthologies of British folklore, among them *English Fairy Tales, Indian Fairy Tales,* and *Celtic Fairy Tales,* from which this tale is taken. He settled in New York in 1900 to become editor of the *Jewish Encyclopedia.* Jacobs was an active member of the Folklore Society in England and was a key figure in preserving British fairy tales. Jacobs was always eager to disavow "foreign" borrowings in the tales he collected. Horrified by the possibility that a tale from the Highlands might normalize bigamy, he was anxious to attribute the story to another culture. "It is unlikely," he wrote in the commentary to "Silver-tree and Gold-tree," "that this tale, with the incident of the dormant heroine should have arisen independently in the Highlands: it is most likely an importation from abroad. Yet in it occurs a most 'primitive' incident, the bigamous household of the hero. . . . It is probable, the story came from abroad, this trait may have come with it, and only implies polygamy in the original home of the tale" (252). Instead of the fairy-tale triad of white, red, black, we have in this case the highly valued metallic gleam of silver and gold.

Once upon a time there was a king who had a wife, whose name was Silver-tree, and a daughter, whose name was Gold-tree. On a certain day of the days, Silver-tree and Gold-tree went to a glen, where there was a well, and in it there was a trout.

Said Silver-tree, "Troutie, bonny little fellow, am not I the most beautiful queen in the world?"

"Oh! indeed you are not."

"Who then?"

"Why, Gold-tree, your daughter."

Silver-tree went home, blind with rage. She lay down on the bed and vowed she would never be well until she could get the heart and the liver of Gold-tree, her daughter, to eat.

At nightfall the king came home, and it was told him that Silver-tree, his wife, was very ill. He went where she was and asked her what was wrong with her.

"Oh! only a thing which you may heal if you like."

"Oh! indeed there is nothing at all which I could do for you that I would not do."

"If I get the heart and the liver of Gold-tree, my daughter, to eat, I shall be well."

Now it happened about this time that the son of a great king had come from abroad to ask Gold-tree for marrying. The king now agreed to this, and they went abroad.

The king then went and sent his lads to the hunting hill for a he-goat, and he gave its heart and its liver to his wife to eat; and she rose well and healthy.

A year after this Silver-tree went to the glen, where there was the well in which there was the trout.

"Troutie, bonny little fellow," said she, "am not I the most beautiful queen in the world?"

"Oh! indeed you are not."

"Who then?"

"Why, Gold-tree, your daughter."

"Oh! well, it is long since she was living. It is a year since I ate her heart and liver."

"Oh! indeed she is not dead. She is married to a great prince abroad."

Silver-tree went home and begged the king to put the longship in order and said, "I am going to see my dear Gold-tree, for it is so long since I saw her." The longship was put in order, and they went away.

It was Silver-tree herself who was at the helm, and she steered the ship so well that they were not long at all before they arrived.

The prince was out hunting on the hills. Gold-tree knew the long-ship of her father coming.

"Oh!" said she to the servants, "my mother is coming, and she will kill me."

"She shall not kill you at all; we will lock you in a room where she cannot get near you."

This is how it was done; and when Silver-tree came ashore, she began to cry out, "Come to meet your own mother, when she comes to see you."

Gold-tree said that she could not, that she was locked in the room, and that she could not get out of it.

"Will you not put out," said Silver-tree, "your little finger through the keyhole, so that your own mother may give a kiss to it?"

She put out her little finger, and Silver-tree went and put a poisoned stab in it; and Gold-tree fell dead.

When the prince came home and found Gold-tree dead, he was in great sorrow, and when he saw how beautiful she was, he did not bury her at all but locked her in a room where nobody would get near her.

In the course of time he married again; the whole house was under the hand of this wife but one room, and he himself always kept the key of that room. On a certain day of the days he forgot to take the key with him, and the second wife got into the room. What did she see there but the most beautiful woman that she ever saw!

The wife began to turn and try to wake the woman, and she noticed the poisoned stab in her finger. She took the stab out, and Gold-tree rose alive, as beautiful as she was ever.

At the fall of night the prince came home from the hunting hill, looking very downcast.

"What gift," said his wife, "would you give me that I could make you laugh?"

"Oh! indeed, nothing could make me laugh, except Gold-tree were to come alive again."

"Well, you'll find her alive down there in the room."

When the prince saw Gold-tree alive, he made great rejoicings, and he began to kiss her and kiss her and kiss her. Said the second wife, "Since she is the first one you had, it is better for you to stick to her, and I will go away."

"Oh! indeed you shall not go away, but I shall have both of you."

At the end of the year, Silver-tree went to the glen, where there was the well, in which there was the trout.

"Troutie, bonny little fellow," said she, "am not I the most beautiful queen in the world?"

"Oh! indeed you are not."

"Who then?"

"Why Gold-tree, your daughter."

"Oh! well, she is not alive. It is a year since I put the poisoned stab into her finger."

"Oh! indeed she is not dead at all, at all."

Silver-tree went home and begged the king to put the longship in order, for that she was going to see her dear Gold-tree, as it was so long since she saw her. The longship was put in order, and they went away. It was Silver-tree herself who was at the helm, and she steered the ship so well that they were not long at all before they arrived.

The prince was out hunting on the hills. Gold-tree knew her father's ship coming.

"Oh!" said she, "my mother is coming, and she will kill me."

"Not at all," said the second wife; "we will go down to meet her."

Silver-tree came ashore. "Come down, Gold-tree, love," said she, "for your own mother has come to you with a precious drink."

"It is a custom in this country," said the second wife, "that the person who offers a drink takes a draught out of it first."

Silver-tree put her mouth to it, and the second wife went and struck it so that some of it went down her throat; and she fell dead. They had only to carry her home a dead corpse and bury her.

The prince and his two wives were long alive after this, pleased and peaceful.

I left them there.

KING PEACOCK

King Peacock has many of the motifs and tropes of "Snow White and the Seven Dwarfs"—a cruel mother, a benevolent servant, and a young woman who falls into a deep sleep from which she is awoken by an adoring person of royal blood. The tale, here from a version published in 1895, shifts into a female version of "Jack and the Beanstalk," in an unusual twist, with an ogress who uses brilliantly beautiful peacock feathers to fan the girl—with the feathers anticipating the name of the rescuer. The seeds given to the girl suggest, as in many variants of "The Beautiful Girl," a connection with the story of Persephone, who is tricked by Hades into returning to the underworld when she eats the pomegranate seeds he gives her.

KING PEACOCK

THERE WAS ONCE a lady who was so pretty—so pretty that she never wanted to marry. She found something to criticize in all the suitors who presented themselves, saying of them, "Oh, you are too ugly," "You are too short," "Your mouth is too large."

One day a man arrived in a golden carriage drawn by eight horses. He asked the lady to marry him, but she refused. He threw a fit and then told her that in a year she would have a daughter who would be much prettier than she was. The lady felt nothing but contempt for him and sent him away.

A year later she gave birth to a pretty little girl. When she saw how pretty the girl was, she locked her up in a room at the far end of the house, with only a nurse to attend to her. The girl became more beautiful with each passing day. The nurse never allowed her to leave her room or even to look out the window.

One day, while the old woman who was her nurse was sweeping the floor, she left the door open, and the young girl saw a large bird.

"Nurse," she said, "what is the name of that beautiful bird?"

The woman replied, "That is a peacock."

"If I ever marry," the girl said, "I want to marry King Peacock."

"May God hear you, my child."

That very day the mother appeared and went into a corner with the nurse. She drew a long knife from under her skirt and said, "I want you to kill my child. She has become prettier than I am."

The nurse began to cry and begged the lady to spare the poor child, but it was no use. That evil heart could not be softened. When night fell, the nurse said to the girl, "My poor child, your mother wants you to die, and I am supposed to kill you."

The girl was so good that she replied, "Well, kill me, nurse, if that's what my mother wants."

But the nurse said, "No, I don't have the heart to do any such thing. Here, take these three seeds and jump down into the well as if you were going to drown yourself. But before jumping in the well, swallow one of these seeds, and nothing will be able to harm you."

The girl thanked the nurse and walked down to the well to throw herself into it. But before touching the water she took one of the seeds and put it in her mouth. The seed fell into the water, and all at once the well became dry. The young lady was very sad to see that there was no water left in the well. She climbed out and walked into the woods, where she found a small house. She knocked at the door, and an old woman appeared. When the old woman saw the pretty young girl, she said, "Oh! my child, why have you come here? Don't you know that my husband is an ogre? He will eat you up!"

The girl replied, "That's what I'm hoping for. My mother wants me to die."

The woman replied, "If that is the case, come in. But what a pity."

The girl sat down in a corner and began crying while she was waiting for the ogre. All at once they heard loud footsteps, and as soon as he opened the door, the ogre said, "Wife, I smell fresh meat in here." And he ran toward the girl. She looked at him with her big eyes, and he stopped himself, saying to his wife, "How can I possibly have a pretty girl like that for supper? She is so beautiful that all I want to do is look at her."

The girl said she was tired, and so the ogre took her to a beautiful room and ordered his wife to fan her with peacock feathers while she was sleeping.

The girl thought to herself, "It would be better for me to die now, since the ogre might change his mind by tomorrow and decide to have me for dinner." She put one of the seeds in her mouth and fell into a deep sleep. She slept and slept, and the ogre's wife continued fanning her the whole time. When three days had gone by and she was still not awake, the ogre looked at her and said, "What a pity, but I believe that she must be dead."

The ogre went to the town and brought home a coffin made of gold. He put the girl in it and set it on the river. Very far away King Peacock was standing on the levee with his retinue, enjoying the cool breeze. He saw something bright and shiny floating on the river. He ordered his courtiers to see what it was. They took a skiff and could not believe their eyes. It was a coffin, and they brought it to the king. When he saw the pretty girl who seemed to be sleeping, he said, "Take her to my chambers." He was hoping that he would be able to wake her up. He moved her to a bed and rubbed her hands and face with cologne water, but to no avail. Then he opened her mouth to see what pretty teeth she had. He saw something red in her front teeth and tried to remove it with a golden pin. It was the seed, which fell on the floor. The girl awoke and said, "I am so glad to see you."

The king replied, "I am King Peacock, and I want to marry you." The girl said, "Yes," and there was such a wedding that they sent me to tell the story everywhere, everywhere.

THE BEAUTIFUL DAUGHTER

Robert Hamill Nassau (1835–1921) tells us in the preface to his memoir that in 1861 he sailed from New York City on a "little brig" named the "Owen Eagle" to the island of Corisco on the West Coast of Africa. For four years he lived on the island as "preacher, teacher, and itinerant to the adjacent mainland" (iv). For close to forty years he remained in Africa, living in other parts of the continent (Benita, Kangwe, Baraka, and Talaguga, among other places) and discovering that "the same customs and religion prevailed." Whenever he made new acquaintances, he steered the conversation to a study of the "native thought." "This has been the history of a thousand social chats,—in canoes by day, in camp and hut by night, and at all hours in my own house, whose public room was open at any hour of day or evening for any visitor, petitioner, or lounger, my attention to whose wants or wishes was rewarded by some confidence about their habits or doings" (vi). The Board of Foreign Missions sponsored him with funding to turn his voluminous notes into a book (1904).

Nassau's story about a beautiful girl offers a compelling example of how tales mix and mingle to produce new versions of themselves. In "The Beautiful Girl" the names are both African (Ogula) and European (Maria), and the motifs are drawn from native lore as well as from nonnative sources. The girl's beauty is not just superficially physical; it is also enhanced by her inner beauty—"gracefulness, amiability, humility." Note also that female evil seems to move across a generational divide, with both a mother and her grandmother-like accomplice, as natural-born killers.

THE BEAUTIFUL DAUGHTER

ONCE THERE WAS a beautiful woman. She was the daughter of a king and had married, and her name was Maria. She had a magic mirror with the power to speak, and she used it every day, particularly right before she was about to go out for a walk. She would take the mirror from its hiding place, look at it, and ask, "Mirror! Are there any other women as beautiful as I am?" And the mirror would reply, "Mistress! There are none."

She would do this every day, and with each passing day she became ever more jealous at the thought of having a rival.

Before long she gave birth to a daughter and became a mother. She began to realize that the child was very beautiful, even more beautiful than she was. The child grew in gracefulness, amiability, humility, and she was not at all aware of her own beauty.

When the girl was about twelve years old, the mother was afraid that her daughter might begin to realize how beautiful she was and would begin to compete with her, even if unintentionally. She told her daughter that she must never enter a certain room where she kept her cosmetics. The mother continued looking into her mirror and going out every day to put her beauty on display.

One day the daughter thought to herself, "Oh, I'm ever so tired of all these rules!" So she took the keys and opened the door to the forbidden room. She looked around but didn't see anything particularly interesting and went back out again, locking the door behind her. The next day the mother went into the same room and then went out for a walk. Once the mother had left, the girl thought to herself, "I will go back in and take a closer look at what's in there." This time she looked more carefully and saw a pretty little casket on the table. She opened it and found a mirror. There was something so strange about it that she decided to look more closely at it. While she was doing that, the mirror spoke to her and said these words: "Oh, my dear girl! No one is as beautiful as you!" The girl put the mirror back in its place and left the room, fastening the door shut. The next day when the mother went into the room before her walk, she asked the mirror the same question as always, "Is there anyone else as beautiful as I am?" The mirror replied, "Yes, mistress, there is another person fairer than you."

The mother left the room in a fit of anger, and suspecting that her daughter had been in the room, she said, "Daughter, did you go into that room?" The girl replied, "No, I didn't." The mother pressed her, "Yes, you did. Why else would my mirror tell me that there is another woman more beautiful than I am? And you are the only one who is even close to me in beauty."

For all these years the mother had kept the daughter in the palace, never allowing her to be seen in public, for she dreaded the idea of hearing anyone else praised for her beauty. The enraged woman sent for her father's guards and handed the girl over to them, issuing this order to them: "Go out into the forest and kill this girl."

They obeyed the orders and took the girl into the woods along with two big dogs. When they reached the forest, the guards said to her, "Your mother told us to kill you. But you are so good and so beautiful that we can't bring ourselves to do it. We are going to just let you go, and you can wander around in the forest and see what happens."

The girl left, and the guards killed the two dogs so that they could show the mother the blood on their swords. Once they did this, they returned to her and said, "We murdered the girl, and you can see her blood on our swords." The mother was satisfied.

Back in the forest the girl wandered around aimlessly until she happened to reach a house in what looked like a village. She went up the front steps and tried the door. It was unlocked, and so she entered. She could not see or hear anyone. But she noticed that the house was in disarray, and she began tidying up. After sweeping the floor and putting everything in order, she went upstairs and hid under one of the beds.

What she did not know was that the house belonged to some robbers who spent their days stealing. At night they would bring their plunder home. When they returned that evening, they were startled to find the house tidied up, with all their possessions arranged in neat piles. They were amazed and asked, "Who has been here and cleaned up the house so nicely?"

They prepared their dinner, ate, drank, and then went to sleep. But they did not clear the table or wash the dishes.

The next day they went out again to rob people. Once they had left, the girl, hungry and frightened, crawled out of her hiding place and then cooked a meal for herself. Then, as on the first day, she swept the floor and washed all the dishes. Then she prepared a meal for the men so that it would be ready for their return late in the afternoon. Once again she arranged everything neatly in the house and went back to her hiding place.

When the robbers returned that day and put away their haul, they were surprised to find the house was neat and even more surprised to find a meal on the table. And they started to wonder, "Who is doing all of this for us?"

First, they sat down to eat. Then they said, "Let's look around and figure out who is doing all this work for us." They searched everywhere but could not find anyone.

The next day the robbers armed themselves as usual before leaving, and they left the house in disorder, with all their loot scattered about.

After they left, the girl emerged from her hiding place and cooked, ate, washed up, swept, tidied up, and prepared the evening meal as she had done the night before.

When the robbers returned, they were even more astonished than before and exclaimed, "Who in the world is doing all of this? If it is a woman, we will take her in as a sister. She can manage the household and keep our things in order. No one will be allowed to marry her. If it turns out to be a man, he will have to join us in our handiwork."

The next day they were about to leave the house and carry on with their usual activities, but they decided to leave one man behind. He planned to stay there, hide, and figure out what was going on. They would finally figure out who had been keeping house for them.

After they left, the girl, who had no idea that one of the robbers was still there, emerged from her hiding place and set to work as usual. When she went outdoors to start the fire for cooking, the one who had stayed behind suddenly appeared. She was frightened and tried to run away, but he shouted after her, "Don't be afraid! Don't run away! Come back! Why are you afraid? You're not doing anything wrong, and you have only done good things for us. Come over here!" The girl came back and said, "I was afraid that you were going to kill me!"

The robber approached her and said, "What a beautiful girl you are! When did you get here, and who are you?" She told him her story. And once she had finished all the household chores, she sat down with the robber to wait for the others to return. When they arrived back at the house and saw the two, they said to him, "So you found her!" The robber said he had. His comrades looked at her and exclaimed, "Oh, what a beautiful girl!" To calm her down, they said to her, "Don't be alarmed! You are going to become our sister."

They took all of their plunder and asked her to take care of it and to be in charge of the house. That's how they lived for some time—the robbers stole, and the girl took care of them.

One day the wicked mother at the castle began to worry that the guards might not have obeyed the orders to kill her daughter and thought, "Maybe the child was not really killed." She had a servant who was a very old woman and was also devoted to her. She told her everything and asked, "Please go out and search through every town. If you find a girl who is very beautiful, it will be my daughter. You must kill her for me." The old woman replied, "Yes, my friend, I will do this for you." So she left and began searching everywhere.

The very first place she arrived turned out to be the robbers' house. No one was around, and so she entered the house and found the girl all alone. Because the girl was so beautiful, she knew right away that this must be her mistress's daughter. The girl offered her a chair and asked if she wanted anything. The old woman exclaimed, "Oh, what a nice-looking child you are! Who are you, and where is your mother?" The girl was not expecting anything bad to happen and told her story.

The old woman said to her, "Your hair looks a little messy. Come over here and let me fix it up for you." The girl let the old woman braid her hair. The old woman had hidden a long, sharp nail in her sleeve. When she finished doing the girl's hair, she plunged the nail deep into the girl's head, and the girl collapsed instantly, as if dead. Looking at the limp body, the old woman said to herself, "Good for me! I have now done my friend a big favor." And she went away, leaving the corpse lying on the ground. Before long she was at home with a full report to the mother about what she had done. The mother felt sure that her friend was not deceiving her.

When the robbers returned that day, they found the girl on the ground. They were deeply distressed and began to examine the body, trying to determine the cause of death, but they could not find any wounds. The body was not at all rigid, just limp. There was no perspiration on the head and neck. So they decided, "We can't possibly put this face that still looks alive into a grave." So they made a handsome casket, overlaid it with gold, and placed gold ornaments on the girl's clothes. They decided not to nail down the lid but made grooves that allowed the lid to slide so that you could open and close the casket. Fearful that the body might begin to decompose, they placed the coffin outdoors in the open air. And to keep the casket out of reach of animals, they hung it up in the air. Twice a day, once before they left and once when they returned, they would pull down the casket, remove its lid, and look at the fresh face of their "sister," who seemed very much alive.

One day while they were out at work, a man named Eserengila (Talebearer) happened to come upon their house. The town in which he lived had a chief named Ogula. When Eserengila arrived at the house, he could not find anyone around. But right away he caught sight of the golden box hanging in the air. "What a nice thing!" he exclaimed, and he rushed back to his master Ogula and said, "Come and see what a lovely thing I have found. You will want to bring it back home with you!" So Ogula went with him, and Eserengila brought down the gilded box from where it was hanging. They did not enter the house, and they had no idea what was going on in there. They hurried back to Ogula's house with the box, without looking at what was inside it, and placed it in a small room.

A few days later Ogula went back into the room to see what was in the box. He noticed that the top of the box was not nailed down and that you could slide it back. As soon as he figured that out, he opened it and saw a beautiful young woman in there. He was filled with wonder. She was apparently dead, but there was nothing about her that had the odor of death to it. And since she was not emaciated, he imagined that she had not died of some disease. He examined the body to try to figure out how she had died. But he found nothing and said out loud, "This beautiful girl! How in the world did she die?"

He put the lid back on the coffin and left the room, closing the door carefully behind him. Then he returned to look at the beautiful face of the corpse, and he let out a sigh and said, "Oh, I wish this beautiful creature were still alive. She would make such a nice playmate for my daughter, who is just about the same size." Again he went and shut the door carefully behind him. He told his daughter never to enter the room, and she agreed that she would not; but he himself continued to visit the girl every day.

A few days went by, and Ogula's daughter grew tired of seeing her father keep going into a room forbidden to her. One day, after he had left the house, she said to herself, "My father has told me I can't go into that room, but now I'm going to go in there and see what's in it." She entered and saw the gold-plated box and said, "Oh, what a nice box! I'm going to open it and see what is inside it."

She began to draw back the lid and saw a human head with beautiful hair that had golden ornaments woven into it. She slid back the lid completely and now saw the body of the young woman and exclaimed, "A beautiful girl! And she has such nice hair, and the ornaments are so lovely!"

She had no idea why the girl could not move and said, "I wish she would speak to me, and then we could become friends, because she is about the same size that I am." And so she greeted the stranger with the words, "Mbolo! Mbolo!" There was no answer, and she then said, "Why don't you answer me when I greet you, Mbolo?" She was so disappointed that she slid back the cover and left the room.

Something about the door aroused the suspicion of the girl's father when he returned home, and he asked her, "Did you go in that room?" She answered, "No! You told me not to go in there, and I did not." The next day Ogula went out again, and his daughter thought she would take another look at the beautiful face. She went into the room and drew back the lid, and once again she greeted the girl, "Mbolo!" There was no answer. Once again she grew irritated and said, "I am greeting you, and still you refuse to greet me!" And then she added, "May I play with you, touch your forehead, and feel your hair? Maybe you have lice, and I can pick them out of your hair?" She began touching the hair with her fingers and felt something hard. Looking more closely, she discovered that it was the head of a nail. Astonished, she said, "Oh, there is a nail in her head! I'm going to try to pull it out!"

As soon as she pulled out the nail, the girl sneezed, opened her eyes, looked around, sat up, and said, "Oh, I have been sleeping for such a long time." The other girl asked, "You were asleep?" And the girl replied, "Yes." Then Ogula's daughter greeted her, "Mbolo!" and the girl answered, "Ai, Mbolo!" and the other girl responded, "Ai!"

Then the beautiful girl asked, "Where I am? What kind of place is this?" The other girl answered, "Why, you are in my father's house." And the girl then asked, "But who brought me here? How did I get here?" Ogula's daughter told her the whole story about Eserengila and his discovery of the gold-plated casket. The two quickly became very fond of each other, and before long they were fast friends. They played and laughed and talked and hugged all afternoon long.

After a while the beautiful girl grew tired, and she said, "You had better put the nail back in and let me sleep a little longer." So she lay down in the box, and Ogula's daughter put the nail back in her head. Before they knew it, she was fast asleep again.

Ogula's daughter slid the lid back in place and left the room, closing the door carefully behind her. She had now lost all desire to leave the house and play with her friends. Her father began to take notice and urged her to visit her friends and play with them as she had done before. But she declined, making excuses and saying that she had no wish to do so. Her only interest was in that room with the gold-plated casket with the beautiful girl in it. Whenever her father went out, she would rush over to the door, go in the room, slide the lid down, and pull out the nail. Her friend would then sit up, and the two would play together and become fast friends again. Ogula's daughter, seeing that her friend needed sleep because she had not eaten, started bringing her food daily. And the girl grew strong, and she was happy and in good health.

This went on for many days without Ogula knowing anything about it.

But it happened one day, when the two girls were playing together, that they became so absorbed by their games and their conversation that Ogula's daughter did not realize that her father was about to return. Suddenly he appeared at the door and was surprised to see the two girls talking. The daughter was frightened when she saw her father. But he was not angry and calmed her down by saying, "Don't be afraid! How did you manage to bring this girl back to life? What did you do?"

The girl told her father all about what she had done, especially how she had removed the nail. Then Ogula sat down by the girl in the gilded box and asked her to tell him the story of her life. She left nothing out. Then he said, "Since your mother is the kind of person who sends people out to kill, I, as chief of this region, will investigate the matter tomorrow.

I will call together all the people living here, and there will be a gathering tomorrow morning. You must stay here, and you shall be my wife."

The next day everyone living in the area was summoned: the wicked mother, the guards, the old woman, and everyone else, except for the mysterious robbers. The entire matter was taken up, point by point, and near the end of the discussion, the beautiful girl, accompanied by Ogula's daughter, appeared at the gathering.

As soon as Maria saw her daughter enter, she gave a start, looked at the old woman, and shouted at her, "That girl is still alive! Not dead yet! I thought you killed her!" The old woman was astonished, but she insisted in turn, "Yes, I killed her. I kept my promise to you!"

The girl sat down, and Ogula asked her to tell her story to everyone present. She began by talking about the magic looking glass, the guards, the robbers' house, and so on, up to the stay at Ogula's house.

Everyone began shouting and denouncing and threatening the mother and the old woman. The two were frightened, and they ran away to a distant land, never to return.

The beautiful young woman was married to Ogula, and she in turn was very happy to have Ogula's daughter as her friend.

The robbers, back in their hideaway, heard nothing about the meeting, and they continued to grieve for their lost sister. They had no idea what had become of her. And so the story ends.

The above story is probably no more than 200 or 250 years old, the name "Maria" doubtless being derived from Portuguese occupants of the Congo country. [Note from collector of the tale.]

THE MIRROR OF MATSUYAMA

Filial piety is a virtue that trumps all else in this narrative, and even the stepmother is won over by the girl's devotion to her dead mother. The mystery of the mirror, with its ability to reproduce more than a reflection, is an attractive feature of the story, as an artifact that creates family conflict but also resolves it. Unlike most stories about beautiful girls in conflict with their mothers, this Japanese tale, published in English in 1912, values forbearance and forgiveness over ill will and retribution.

THE MIRROR OF MATSUYAMA

In ancient days there lived in a remote part of Japan a man and his wife, and they were blessed with a little girl, who was their pet and idol. On one occasion the man was called away on business in distant Kyoto. Before he went, he told his daughter that if she were good and dutiful to her mother, he would bring her back a present she would prize very highly. Then the good man took his departure, mother and daughter watching him go.

At last he returned to his home, and after his wife and child had taken off his large hat and sandals, he sat down on the white mats and opened a bamboo basket, watching the eager gaze of his little child. He took out a wonderful doll and a lacquer box of cakes and put them into her outstretched hands. Once more he dived into his basket and presented his wife with a metal mirror. Its convex surface shone brightly, while on its back there was a design of pine trees and storks.

The good man's wife had never seen a mirror before, and on gazing into it, she was under the impression that another woman was looking out at her as she gazed with growing wonder. Her husband explained the mystery and bade her take great care of the mirror.

Not long after this happy homecoming and distribution of presents, the woman became very ill. Just before she died, she called her little daughter to her side and said, "Dear child, when I am dead, take good care of your father. You will miss me when I have left you. But take this mirror, and when you feel most lonely, look into it and you will always see me." After saying these words, she passed away.

In due time the man married again, and his wife was not at all kind to her stepdaughter. But the little one, remembering her mother's words, would retire to a corner and eagerly look into the mirror, where it seemed to her that she saw her dear mother's face, not drawn in pain as she had seen it on her deathbed but young and beautiful.

One day this child's stepmother chanced to see her crouching in a corner over an object she could not quite see, murmuring to herself. This ignorant woman, who detested the child and believed that her stepdaughter detested her in return, fancied that the little one was performing some strange magical art—perhaps making an image and sticking pins into it. Full of these notions, the stepmother went to her husband and told him that his wicked child was doing her best to kill her by witchcraft.

After listening to this extraordinary recital, the master of the house went straight to his daughter's room. He took her by surprise, and as soon as the girl saw him, she slipped the mirror into her sleeve. For the first time her doting father grew angry, and he feared that there was, after all, truth in what his wife had told him. He repeated her tale forthwith.

When his daughter heard this unjust accusation, she was amazed at her father's words, and she told him that she loved him far too much ever to attempt or wish to kill his wife, who she knew was dear to him.

"What have you hidden up your sleeve?" asked her father, only half convinced and still much puzzled.

"The mirror that you gave my mother and that she on her deathbed gave to me. Every time I look into its shining surface, I see the face of my dear mother, young and beautiful. When my heart aches—and oh! it has ached so much lately—I take out the mirror, and mother's face, with its sweet, kind smile, brings me peace and helps me to bear harsh words and cross looks."

Then the man understood and loved his child the more for her filial piety. Even the girl's stepmother, when she knew what had really taken place, was ashamed and asked forgiveness. And the child, who believed she had seen her mother's face in the mirror, forgave, and trouble forever departed from the home.

THE GIRL AND THE DOG

Diedrich Westerman, the editor of the 1912 volume in which this story appeared, left for the Sudan in 1910, on a trip funded by the Prussian Board of Education. He studied the languages and cultures of the Shilluk peoples, an ethnic group of Southern Sudan (the third largest after the Dinka and the Nuer). Westerman produced an extensive anthropological study of the Shilluk and included rich folkloric resources. *Jwok,* as he explains, was the supreme being in their religion. In many ways, the story can be seen as a cautionary tale about parental recklessness, with the daughter as a victim of her mother's rash promise and a father's failure to protect his child. The hunters in the story become protectors and raise a child forced into isolation and servitude.

There once lived a woman, and she had no children. She went out into the bush one day and found a dog. "Oh, Jwok!" she cried out. "I want more than anything else to have a child! If you grant my wish, I will have the child marry this dog." Jwok granted her wish, and she bore a child that grew to be a beautiful girl. One day the child went into the bush and discovered the dog out there. It was a white dog, and it said to her, "Go to your mother and tell her that the dog is asking when you will be given to me in marriage."

The girl returned home and found her mother and told her what had happened. The mother listened to her entire story. The girl told her that she had found a dog in the bush and that he had told her, "Go to your mother and tell her that the dog wants to know when he finally will be able to marry."

The mother began to weep and told the girl's father about everything that had happened. The father said, "Take her to the dog as you promised." They found the dog lying down in the bush, and the girl was handed over to him.

The dog and the girl both departed and descended down into the ground. The dog was Jwok. They went into the house of the dog, and there were many trees around it. And the dog said, "You shall always eat with me; and you will not move from this enclosure." The other people in that place told the girl to stay in the center of the enclosure. The dog explained to the girl that all the others were slaves. Then the dog went away, leaving the girl behind. She had entered the grounds of the dog, a vast space, and this house was the house of Jwok.

One day the girl decided to run away, and when she jumped up in the air, the ground below her split. She escaped and ran off as fast as she could. When the dog saw her, he ran after her. The girl ran straight into a house that was in a river. It was a large house. The dog came too, and he stayed right by the house. There were seven people living in that house, all men, and there were no women living there. The men were hunters, and they lived on meat.

The girl hid herself in the house. When the men came home from the hunt and found that there was food on the table, they asked, "Who cooked this for us?" They were astonished and started searching the house. They found the girl, and they were overjoyed. They told her that she could stay with them and become their sister. And the girl decided to stay and told them about how she had been chased by a dog. "Where is he?" they asked. "He is in the ground below the house," she said. The men dug around the house, and once they found the dog, they took him and shot him. The dog died, and they tossed him into the bush.

Seven years passed by, and the girl said, "I want to go and see the bones of the dog." The men said, "Stay here, and don't go back." The girl replied that she was going to go, and the men went with her. The girl searched around, and when a bone injured her foot, she fell down dead. The men wept. Then they took her body and placed it on the waters. The girl was carried away by a current and brought back to her native country. Some fishermen found her and pulled her out of the water. They told the king about what they had found. The king hired an old woman to wash the girl with water. The woman discovered a bone in the dead girl's body. She pulled it out, and suddenly the girl sneezed and came back to life.

The king was told that the girl had sneezed and had come back to life. "Where did you come from?" he asked her. The girl replied, "I came here from a house down by the river." The king asked, "How did you get there?" She told him that her father had handed her over in marriage to a dog. But the dog had chased her, and she had fled to a house in the river. The king wept when she told her story, for he was the girl's father. Her mother soon appeared, and she wept as well. Then the couple bought some cows and sacrificed them. The three returned home together.

That is all—the story is finished.

THE UNNATURAL MOTHER AND THE GIRL WITH A STAR ON HER FOREHEAD

Henri-Alexandre Junod (1863–1934), the Swiss-born African missionary and anthropologist who collected this tale, was based in Limpopo Province, the northernmost province of South Africa. With another colleague, he codified the language of the Tsonga people. In 1912 he published *The Life of a South African Tribe,* which described local traditions and gathered together a number of folktales, among them the one included here. Junod was fascinated by folklore's cross-generational appeal and how "men, girls, youngsters, will sit quietly for hours, listening to an old woman who keeps them under the spell of her tale" (215). He noted that "The Unnatural Mother" may be a Bantu tale and that it had been told to him by a middle-aged woman named Martha, who heard it from her grandmother at a time when few missionaries were present in the region. The story contains what Junod believed to be "an extraordinary mixture of wholly incongruous elements" (265), among them the skin color of the mother. *Muhanu* was the term used to designate the "unnatural mother," and when Junod asked Martha directly, "Was she really a White woman?" Martha replied, "Yes."

THE UNNATURAL MOTHER AND THE GIRL WITH A STAR

Here is how the tale begins: Once upon a time there was a woman with a moon on her forehead. As a child, she lived with her parents, but one day her parents died. Her mother left her a large mirror. Once she was grown up, she married and went to live with her husband, taking the mirror with her. She liked to bathe, and after bathing she would arrange her curly hair, place the mirror on the table, and say to it, "My mother's mirror, is there anyone in the country more beautiful than I am?" The mirror would answer, "You are surpassed in beauty only by what is in heaven" (*ñwa nya ka tilo*). Then the woman felt very happy, removed the mirror from the table, and sat down, her mind thoroughly at peace. Not much later, she became pregnant. Before the child was born, her husband left for Mosapa and gave his wife the following strict instructions: "I am going to Mosapa to hunt elephants. If the child is stillborn, keep one of its bones for me." "Very well," the woman said, and the man left for the elephant hunt.

The woman remained at home with her servant, who stayed in the house until she was about to give birth. When she began to feel labor pains, she said to her servant, "Heat some water up for me. I would like to take a bath." The servant put water on the fire to heat. Then the woman took a bath, put the mirror on the table, combed her hair, and said to the mirror, "My mother's mirror, is there anyone in this country more beautiful than I am?" "You are surpassed in beauty only by what is in heaven," was the reply. Then the woman put the mirror away, spread some blankets on the floor, and gave birth to a daughter. The baby was born after sunset, but there was a bright light in the house when she was born. The villagers were terrified and said, "It looks as if the house is on fire!" The light was coming from a brilliant star shining on the baby's forehead.

The mother took good care of her little one and kept her in a nice bed. She bathed her and combed her hair as usual but forgot about her mirror. The child was growing and began to sit up. She could even stand now and walk a few steps. She toddled about in her mother's hut. The village folks were astonished and said, "What can it be that is burning in the chief's hut?" They did not know that a child had been born and was living there. Then the servant told them, "My mistress has a daughter!"

The child grew older and began taking walks outside the house, always holding her mother's hand. One day the mother took the mirror, bathed the child, and combed her hair. The little one's hair was even more lovely than the mother's because the star on her forehead sent out rays of light, like beads on her head. The mother gazed at her daughter and began to feel afraid of her. She asked her mirror, "My mother's mirror, is there anyone in the country more beautiful than I am?" The mirror answered, "Think carefully. I told you that your beauty is surpassed only by what is in heaven, and by that I meant the infant that was in your womb. You are surpassed in beauty only by your child." The woman took the mirror and broke it. She was angry about the words it had spoken. She picked up the pieces and threw them behind a box. Then she went to her hut, dressed the child, and put a hat on her. Next, she dressed herself and put on her own hat. She put a pretty umbrella into the child's hands, took her own, and they set out together.

The two went up a mountain where there was a high road along which many people passed. The mother said to the people there, "Look at me, and tell me if you think there is anyone more beautiful than I am?" They replied, "You are certainly very beautiful, Mother, but the child with you is more beautiful than you are." The woman began to feel unhappy and went home with the child. Each day she went to the mountain road and asked the same question, and the people replied, "You are beautiful, but you are not so beautiful as your child with a star on her forehead."

The child grew older and was about as tall as her mother, whose name was Nhwanene. One day, the mother found a small calabash, which she gave to her daughter to draw water, saying, "Don't go to the place where people generally go to draw water, but go to the spot where there is a high precipice." She said to herself, "The child will tumble over and die." But the girl did not go to the high precipice; she went to the place where everybody else went. When she reached home, her mother said, "Didn't you hear me when I told you to draw water at the spot where there is a high precipice?" The girl replied, "Mother, I went where you told me to go," for she was well aware that her mother wanted to kill her.

Nhwanene called her *kafirs,* or servants, and said to them, "If I told you to kill this girl, would you obey me? I am willing to give you a sack of money." They said, "Yes." Then she said, "Take the child and kill her. After you have killed her, cut off her little finger and cut out her heart and liver. Bring them back to me, so that I may know for sure that you have killed her."

The *kafirs* said to the young girl, "Let us be off!" They all went away together. When they came to a certain spot, they said to the girl, "Listen! Your mother told us to kill you. If we let you go, will you be able to run far away by yourself?" "Certainly," she said, "I can easily run away alone. Although I don't know the country, I will be able to find a home somewhere." "Will you be brave," they asked, "and let us cut off your little finger?" She held up her little finger and told them to cut it off. They did so. She stooped down, tore off a piece of her dress, and bandaged the stump. Then she ran away and bathed in the river and in the sea. Wherever she went, she bathed.

As for the *kafirs,* an antelope suddenly leaped out of the bush, and they hunted it down. Then they cut it up, took out the heart and liver, and brought them, along with the little finger, to their mistress. The woman thanked them heartily, saying, "You have done well, for my daughter was more beautiful than I am, and that was what haunted me. That is why I wandered about on the mountains, because she was more beautiful than I. Now I can be happy again!"

The child continued on her way and reached a large house belonging to white folks, the people of Yibane. She reached this place in the evening, after sunset, and went inside. It was the house of the chief, but it was quite empty. Everyone had left to go out and steal. Those people abducted men, locked them up, and then ate them. Yibane was their chief. It was for him that they kidnapped people.

When the robbers were returning home, they saw a bright light in Yibane's house and started running as fast as they could, crying out, "The house is on fire!" Yibane threw open the door and found the young girl seated on his bed. He said to her, "My daughter, where did you come from?" and he embraced her, adding, "Now I have indeed found something really beautiful!" Then he had second thoughts and said, "You are not my daughter. You will be my wife. When you grow up, you will marry me. I will give up all my evil ways and cast them away from me!" Accordingly he gave the order, "Go and find all the people you have imprisoned and set them free. Never again hunt men to kill and eat them." His people thanked him and said, "We will never again eat men now that we have such a beautiful princess!" Yibane said, "Go and bathe and come back clean, all of you, for I have found a lovely wife!" When the girl had grown to be about the height of his daughter Shihahanhlanga, Yibane ordered a wedding feast to be prepared. The people went into the marshes to gather sugar cane and to build a large mill to crush the cane. Yibane went out on this business with all his people, and the young girl remained alone, knowing that she was soon to be married.

Just then the little servant boy who used to play with her when she was quite young happened to pass by. The girl was at the window, and the servant saw her. He said to himself, "I have never seen anyone like this woman, although I have traveled through many lands." He never suspected that it was his former playmate. He ran back to the girl's mother and said, "I saw a girl with a star on her forehead, but she did not see me." The mother said, "Well! Take these beautiful slippers to her. Don't you think she would like to buy them?" The servant replied, "Give them to me. I will take them to her." He rushed off and reached the house on a day when Yibane was away, busy crushing sugar cane. He found the girl at home and offered to sell her the slippers: "How much do you want for them?" she asked. "Whatever you would like to give me," he replied. "They are very pretty. Wait a moment: I must just try them on."

The girl went into the house and put on the slippers. No sooner had she done so than she fainted and died. The boy ran home to the mother and told her that the girl was dead. "That is good," she said. "You certainly had the last word!" When Yibane returned home from the sugar mill, the girl did not come out to meet him. He opened the door and found her lying on the bed. He thought she was asleep and tried to awaken her but could not. Then he saw that she was lifeless. His people heard him weeping, turning everything topsy-turvy and saying, "I shall never be able to find a wife as beautiful as she! The best thing I can do is to live alone, for all my dreams turned on her!"

Yibane made arrangements for a coffin and lined it with cloth, putting some money into it. Then they carried the young girl off to bury her. But Yibane said, "She shall never be put into the ground. Place her on a tree and build a canopy over her, a large canopy of planks, stretching a long way around!" They had to use force to restrain him, for he wanted to kill himself. The people took some silken cloth and made a canopy over the coffin so that the heat would not harm it.

The chief of that country, Matlotlomane, had a son. This son went out hunting one day. He came to the spot and, looking up into the tree, said to his servant, "What in the world is that thing glittering up there?" He had caught sight of the golden nails used to shut the coffin tight. The servants said, "Let us run and see who can touch the tree first!" The chief's son reached it first, the servants later. He said to them, "Climb up the tree and bring the box down. Be careful not to let it fall."

Once the coffin was brought down, he unlocked it with a key attached to it and tried to open it up. He had hardly raised the lid when he saw a light inside. He quickly closed it up again and said to his servants, "Take it home." They all worked hard to lift it, for the box was heavy, and they arrived at their village after dark. The young man told the servants not to say a word to his father about what they had found: "Only tell him," he said, "that I am not feeling well." He gave them all the game he had killed and said, "Don't bring me any meat. You can eat all the game yourselves. No one may enter my room!"

The chief's son shut himself up in his room, lifted the girl out of the coffin, and put her on the bed. He sat down on the ground and began to weep, saying, "I have found my wife. How lovely she is, but, alas, she is dead!" He called his youngest brother, who lived in another room, and said to him, "Bring me some water; I want to bathe." But he used the water to bathe the young girl, thinking she might possibly revive. The parents were astonished to see a bright light in his room. They questioned the servants who had been hunting with him, but all they said was, "We don't know anything about it." Then the parents asked, "What is the matter with our son?" The servants replied, "We don't know; all he told us was that he had a headache."

Several days passed with the son eating nothing and drinking nothing. He would not let anyone enter his room. He placed the young girl on another bed and mourned and mourned and mourned her.

One day he put the girl on his own bed. It was early in the morning. His brother came in and found him washing the girl's face. The brother said, "Where did you manage to find so lovely a woman? I congratulate you." And while congratulating his brother, he shook the girl's leg and took off her slipper. Then he took off the other slipper, and the girl suddenly awoke and came to life again. The chief's son thanked his youngest brother and said, "You have acted with great wisdom! I thought you were but a little boy, and you have been wise enough to bring the beautiful girl back to life again!"

The chief's son took two shillings out of his purse and gave them to the boy. He himself would not leave the room. He refused to go and visit his mother. He wanted nothing more than to gaze at the young girl. He sent his brother to his mother to get some water to bathe the girl. There were many rooms in the house. Then he asked the young girl, "Do you think you could walk?" He took her by both hands, for her limbs were stiff, and he took her into one of the rooms, where there was a large bath. Then he plunged her into the water. After finishing her bath, they rejoiced, for they saw the star shining brightly on her forehead. The brother left, and he did not dare tell his mother what had happened, for all the servants had told him, "If you are asked any questions, you must hide the truth." All he did was ask for food for his brother, saying, "He is feeling a little better now."

The parents were very glad to know that their son was recovering. They slaughtered some chickens for him, thinking it was he alone who would eat all the meat. They didn't know about the girl who was soon well enough to eat. She put on weight and grew strong, and nobody knew anything about her.

When the elder brother saw that the girl was in good health, he sent the younger one out of the room, saying, "Now you had better return to our mother." The younger brother was annoyed at being turned out like that, so he went and told his parents everything. He said, "My brother is sheltering a girl, but she is not from this country. If you look at her, you will be so dazzled that you will have to turn your eyes away. But once you become accustomed to her face, you will not be able to take your eyes off her." His parents said, "We will go and see her." "Yes," he said, "but don't let him know that I told you! Go quietly, and when she is seated at the table, you will see her." The parents started to go to their son's room. They could see that it was lit up and asked the younger brother, "Are we seeing the light of lamps?" "No," he said, "the light is coming from a star on the girl's forehead." They entered the room while their son and the girl were sitting at the table. They greatly admired her beauty and were very happy. The mother embraced her, saying, "This is indeed a lovely girl!" The father was also much taken with her beauty and said, "This woman would suit me very well as a wife!" The mother rebuked him, saying, "I will leave with all my children if you take this woman as a wife! She is not for you! I am your wife! What you are thinking is sinful."

"That is true! I have sinned. My head was turned by her beauty!" he replied. They said to him, "Don't do anything like that again!"

A splendid feast was prepared for the son's wedding to the young girl. She was soon with child. Her husband said to her, "I am going to Mosapa to hunt elephants." His wife began to weep. "Oh," he said, "I will be back, but I can't forget the hunt." Time passed, and the woman became the mother of twins—a boy and a girl. She wrote a letter to her husband, at Mosapa, to tell him the news and sent it to him by a servant. This man passed by the former home of the girl with the star, the place where the mother was living. Everyone there was drinking, and they asked him to drink with them. After the servant had fallen asleep, the mother took the letter and read it. She saw that it was signed by "she who has a star on her forehead." "It is from her," she cried; "then she is still alive!" She tore up the letter, burnt it, took another piece of paper, and wrote, "Your wife has given birth to two monkeys," and she put the paper into the servant's pocket. The servant found the husband, who read that his wife had given birth to two monkeys. In reply he wrote, "Never mind! They are mine. Don't harm them. I will play with them when I get back."

The servant started the return journey, and once again he passed by the village of the girl's mother. There they made him drink once more, and the woman took the letter and wrote another one to replace it, which said, "Put out her eyes, cut off the nipples of her breasts, and place one child on her back, the other on her bosom. Make her walk through the bushes, be torn by thorns and pierced by spines, and so let her suffer!" They woke the servant and said to him, "Be off. The sun has already set." He arrived safely at his mistress's village and handed the letter to her father-in-law, who, when he had read it, burst into tears. The father and mother were afraid to give the letter to their daughter-in-law. They said, "Our son has gone mad. He insists that the children must be killed because they are twins! They could not make up their minds what to do. Finally they decided that they had to give the letter to their daughter-in-law, since it was from her husband, but they said to her, "As for us, we will not touch you or do you any harm. If our son wants to have this done, he must do it himself!" The wife said, "No, you must do it." She felt sure this letter had not come from her husband, and she said, "Go and do it." Then they put out her eyes, cut off the nipples of her breasts, tied one child in front of her, the other behind, and she set out from home.

The beautiful woman did not walk upright but crawled on her hands and knees. She reached the forest at sunset, covered in blood. Thunder came from the sky and spoke to her, saying, "My daughter, what are you searching for?" She replied, "I want nothing at all. They have put out my eyes; they have cut the nipples off my breasts and have driven me from home with one child tied on in front and one behind, and my flesh will soon be torn by thorns." The sky continued, "Don't be afraid, my daughter. Keep on walking, and when you come to the river, cross it without fear." When she reached the river, she found it was very wide. "My little ones might drown," she said but then said, "Never mind!" She threw herself into the water and swam across. Under the water she found a steamboat, and when she emerged from the river, she was traveling on the steamboat. Her eyes were back where they had been, and so were the nipples of her breasts. She sat down and saw some food that had been prepared but did not know where it had come from. Then she began to eat, and her children played around her.

Around this time her husband returned from Mosapa with elephant tusks. It was after sunset. He looked all around for his wife but could not find her anywhere. He made inquiries, and they told him everything. He did not make a fuss and just said, "Point me in the direction she went," and they showed him. He followed her and found little pieces of clothing torn off and strewn all along the way. He came to the forest and passed through it. He also reached the river but could not find his wife there. At last he found her, and by then the steamboat was gone. Once again he saw the star that lit up her face. He also saw her children; the girl had a star on her forehead like her mother, and the boy had a moon like his grandmother. He smiled on them and took them home without asking any questions. His parents were afraid he would be very angry with them, but nothing bothered him after what he had experienced.

THE HUNTER AND HIS SISTER

The collector of this Dagur tale traveled to Tengke Commune in Morin Dawaa in the 1980s, where he located a storyteller named Qiker, who told 120 stories in a matter of a couple of weeks. "Sayintana," the collector, tried hard to record precisely: "I've never dared to change even a little or polish the style. I did my best to retain the original style" (3).

The Dagur are one of many ethnic minorities living in China today. With a population of just over one hundred thousand, they live mainly in Inner Mongolia, and the language spoken by them belongs to the Mongolian language group of the Altaic language family. It has never been codified to form a written language.

The troublemakers in this tale are the first and second wives of the heroine's brother, who play a mysterious game with anklebones. Chinese folktales frequently place the source of hostility in a stepmother, second wife, or mother-in-law rather than in a biological mother, and it is something of a challenge to find stories directly representing mother-daughter conflict.

THE FAIREST OF THEM ALL

Long ago a famous hunter named Zhaosi lived with his beautiful younger sister, Changlihuakatuo. Zhaosi was fond of Changlihuakatuo and built a two-story house with a bedroom on the second floor near his own home for her. Whenever he returned from hunting, he divided with her whatever he brought back. This made the elder two of his three wives jealous. One day, when he had left to hunt, First Wife said, "Zhaosi is not fair to us. He only likes Changlihuakatuo. If it were not for Changlihuakatuo, we would get the fur and meat that he now shares with her." Second Wife said, "I've had the same thought for a long time. Let's kill her." Third Wife said, "I want no part of those plans."

First Wife and Second Wife took some gold and silver *galoha* to Changlihuakatuo's home and shouted, "Let down the ladder!" Changlihuakatuo looked out. Seeing her two sisters-in-law below, she let down the ladder. When they came into her room, the two wives said, "Changlihuakatuo, let's play with these anklebones. We'll throw them up in the air, catch them in our mouths, and then take them out through our navels." Changlihuakatuo said that she was not sure how to play this game and suggested that the two wives should play first. Each wife tossed an anklebone into the air and caught it in her mouth. Changlihuakatuo opened her mouth, and just as she was about to toss an anklebone in the air, First Wife threw an anklebone down her throat. Changlihuakatuo could not swallow it, nor could she breathe. She appeared to be dead. The two wives happily put her body on the bed in the room and cheerfully returned home.

When Zhaosi returned home that afternoon, he discovered that his sister was "dead." After three to four days had passed, during which he could neither sleep nor eat, Zhaosi had a carpenter build a three-tiered red coffin. At the bottom he put a coat made from marten and lynx pelts. Then he placed Changlihuakatuo in the middle, with clothing, along with gold and silver ornaments on top. He placed the coffin on a sled pulled by two deer and said to them, "When the iron chain pulling the sled breaks, you may leave the coffin." The deer nodded three times and left. After pulling the sled for many days, the chain broke at the stroke of midnight when they were passing the third home in a village. The sound of the breaking chain woke up an old, childless couple living in that house. They went outside and saw what they thought was a cabinet. They took it inside and opened it up. They were delighted to find precious gold and silver ornaments and a beautiful coat but even more delighted to find the girl. She did not look at all as if she were dead. Every day they propped her up into a sitting position on the *kang*, and at night they put her into a sleeping position.

A villager named Harandehan had a son named Harenide. One day the son's hunting falcon landed on the old couple's roof. When Harenide went inside the home to ask for permission to go up on the roof and get his falcon, he saw the beautiful Changlihuakatuo sitting on the *kang*. When he returned home, he did not rest until his father, through a matchmaker, persuaded the old couple to allow his son to marry their daughter. In fact, the couple did not want anyone to marry her. They only agreed because of the matchmaker's constant visits. They decided that on the wedding day they would report that their daughter had died halfway to the groom's home, and that would end the matter.

When the wedding day arrived, Changlihuakatuo was put on the bridal sedan, taken to the groom's home, and seated on the south *kang*. Her mother sat by her. After the wedding feast, it was the duty of the new daughter-in-law to rise and see off the departing guests, but Changlihuakatuo remained seated on the *kang*. Enraged by this rudeness, Harenide slapped Changlihuakatuo on the back, and she coughed up the anklebone. She drew a deep breath and said, "Oh, I've been sleeping for such a long time." Hearing her daughter speak, the mother said, "My daughter fell ill on the way here and has not eaten a thing all day. Please prepare a bowl of millet gruel for her." The food was prepared, and Changlihuakatuo ate two bowlfuls.

A second day of feasting took place the next day, and Changlihuakatuo's mother told the girl how they had found her. She added, "My name is Ertireken, and my husband's name is Atirekan." Changlihuakatuo said, "I'm Zhaosi's younger sister, and my name is Changlihuakatuo."

Later at his home, Atirekan thought, "My wife has been gone for several days now. Probably something terrible has happened because we sent a dead girl to the groom's home." Just then a cart drew up to his home, and his wife was in it. She told him about everything that had happened. They were both overjoyed to have such a beautiful daughter and such kindhearted and wealthy in-laws.

A year passed, and Changlihuakatuo gave birth to a son. One day she asked a neighbor girl to take care of her son while she attended a wedding. Before she left for the wedding, she taught the neighbor girl to sing this song:

Zhaosi's nephew, rockaby, rockaby!
Changlihuakatuo's son, rockaby, rockaby!
Harandehan's grandson, rockaby, rockaby!
Harenide's son, rockaby, rockaby!

Meanwhile, Zhaosi had set off in search of his sister, whom he was unable to forget. After searching for her for a long time and finding no trace of her, he happened to walk by the home of the neighbor girl and heard her singing. He entered the home. After talking with the girl, he understood everything that had happened to his sister. After a happy reunion with her, he asked her to visit his home. They then returned home together to deal with the wives.

Zhaosi ordered his wives to confess. Not much later, two carts arrived, one bearing Changlihuakatuo's foster parents, the other carrying his sister, husband, and child. The sight of Changlihuakatuo terrified the two older wives. The third went quietly away to prepare a meal. After they had eaten, Zhaosi called his three wives. He said to his sister, "Who tried to kill you?" "First and Second Wives. I did not see the Third Wife," she replied. Zhaosi asked his older wives how they wished to die. "I want to be pulled apart by four horses. I know what I have done is wrong," said First Wife. Second Wife said, "I am willing to commit suicide," and she walked behind the home and hanged herself. Zhaosi dealt with his first wife as she had requested, said good-bye to his sister and her husband, and invited the old couple to live with him as his foster parents. They lived happily together.

THE WITCH'S DAUGHTER

It is something of a challenge to locate Chinese heroines who belong to ATU 709, but in this story published in 1938, with its half-red and half-green peach and catatonic heroine, elements of the story we know as "Snow White" flash out at us. The elasticity of tropes becomes evident in the connections between the half-red, half-white apple of the Grimms' wicked queen and the peach with similar colors but also in the power of a human to transform into a witch. With its many impossible tasks and magical pursuits, the story is invested with a vital energy and élan that give us what must surely have been a crowd-pleaser in storytelling circles. The shocker of an ending to "The Witch's Daughter" makes it unique in the canon of tales about beautiful girls.

THE WITCH'S DAUGHTER

In the inner reaches of some remote mountains there was a small hut made of straw. An old man lived there with his three sons. Every day the father would go out to look for firewood, and one day he met an aged widow in the woods. She was wearing white clothes and seated at a square stone table playing chess. Since the old man was himself a faithful player, he stopped to observe the game.

"Will you play against me?" the widow asked.

"Certainly," said the old man, and when the widow asked about the stakes for the match, he suggested betting the wood he had gathered. The old woman said, "No, we can't play for wood, because I don't have any. But do you have children? And how many?"

When she learned that the old man had three sons, she was very pleased and said, "That's perfect, for I have three daughters. If you win, I will send them as brides for your three sons. But if I win, you must send me your boys to become my sons-in-law."

The old man stroked his beard for a while, but he finally agreed. He lost every game they played, and when the widow rose to leave, she said, pointing toward a dark valley, "My house is over there. You can send me your eldest son tomorrow, three days later the second, and, after another three days, the youngest."

The woman left, and the old man went back home without collecting any more wood. He let his sons know what had happened, and they were pleased when they heard his report.

The next day the man sent his eldest son to the house of the widow. Three days later he sent the second, and on the sixth day he sent the youngest.

The third son wandered through the woods for a while until he met an old hermit with a white beard who asked him where he was going. "I am going to the house of the widow who lives in the valley, and I am about to become her son-in-law. My two brothers are already there," the youngest son said.

The hermit sighed and said, "That widow is an old witch. She has only one daughter, and she uses her as a decoy for young men and then kills them. Your elder brother was eaten by a lion that waits by the outer gate of her house, and your second brother was devoured by the tiger stationed at the inner door. You have the good fortune of meeting me." Taking an iron pearl from his chest, he continued, "Throw this at the lion by the outer gate." After that he gave the third son an iron rod and said, "Give this to the tiger by the inner gate. Then cut off a branch from the cherry tree by the stream. When you reach the third door, push it open with the branch, and you will be able to enter safely."

The young man took the iron pearl and the iron rod and went into the cherry wood to cut off a branch. After thanking the hermit, he entered the valley where the witch lived. Soon he came upon a house that was as wide as it was tall. At the outer door he threw the iron pearl at the lion, who began to play with it. At the second door he threw the iron rod at the tiger, who also began to play with it. The third door was shut fast, but he gave it a shove with his cherry-tree branch. "Boom!" a thousand-pound block of iron dropped down, and the door opened. If he had opened it with his hands, he would surely have been crushed.

The witch was sitting down, sewing in her room, when she heard a loud noise at the door. She looked out and saw a young man come in, and she knew that it must be the third son of the old man. She wondered how he had managed to pass safely through all three doors. When he entered, she pretended to be very pleased and said, "You have arrived just in time. I have a bushel of linseed that I want you to sow over in that field before it rains. When you return, we will celebrate your wedding."

The young man looked outside, and sure enough the sky was full of dark clouds. It looked as if it was about to rain. He took the bushel of linseed and went out into the field, but the ground was so covered with weeds that he thought, "How can I possibly sow this field without a bullock and plough?" He tried to pull up a few weeds but then decided to lie down and go to sleep. When he woke up toward evening, he realized that a herd of swine had turned up the soil and pulled up all the weeds. So he sowed the linseed, thanked the swine for their help, and returned to the old woman.

When the woman saw him coming, she asked, "Have you finished sowing those seeds?" "Yes," said the young man. But the widow frowned. "You didn't bother looking at the sky?" she grumbled. "Why did you sow those seeds? All the clouds have vanished, and the moon is shining brightly. It's not going to rain, and the seeds won't sprout. You are going to have to pull them all out, and don't leave a single one in the ground. When you return, we will celebrate the wedding."

The youngest son bit his lip, took the empty measuring cup, and went out into the field to search for the seeds. For a long time he searched for the seeds but found little, and his back began to ache from bending down. He looked up at the moon in sorrow and then looked down to find thousands upon thousands of ants, which had appeared out of nowhere and were now dropping seeds into the measuring cup. In no time it was completely full, and the son returned to the widow after thanking the ants. When she saw him, she asked, "Do you have all the seeds?" "Yes," the son replied. "Good," and she nodded. "I am going to go to sleep now. Tomorrow I will have a new task for you."

The next morning the old witch told him, "I am going to hide. If you are able to find me, we will celebrate the wedding." And no sooner had she uttered those words than she was gone. The son searched high and low but could not find a trace of her. While he was looking, he heard a voice call out from the top of the house, "My mother has hidden in the garden. She turned herself into a half-red, half-green peach that is hanging on a tree against the wall. The green part is her back, the red her cheek. Bite her in the cheek, and she will turn back again."

The son looked up and saw a maiden in a sea-green dress, with rose-pink cheeks like the half-opened flower of a lotus. He knew she must be the witch's daughter, and blushing with confusion, he went quickly into the garden. Sure enough, there against the wall was a peach tree, and hanging on it was a half-green, half-red peach. He plucked it, bit the red side, and flung it onto a stone, whereupon the old woman stood before him, with a stream of blood running down her cheek. "Son-in-law! Son-in-law! You nearly crushed me to death," she said. But the young man answered, "How could I know you had turned into a peach?"

The old woman turned to go, saying as she was leaving, "Bring me a bed of white jade from the palace of the Dragon King, and we will celebrate the wedding."

While he was standing in the garden, his head bowed down, the daughter came to him and asked what was on his mind. "Your mother told me to bring her a bed of white jade from the palace of the Dragon King," he said. "But no mortal can pass through the sea to his kingdom."

The daughter consoled him, "That is really quite simple. I have a golden fork. If you draw a line across the sea with it, a path will open up, and you can go wherever you want."

The young man took the fork, walked over to the seashore, and drew a line. In a flash a path was formed through the waves, and it led straight to the palace of the Dragon King. When he arrived, he saw the king and told him that he was there to borrow a bed of white jade. "Certainly," the king said. "In the back palace there are many beds of white jade. Just choose the one you want."

The young man was very pleased, and after picking one of the beds of white jade, he returned to the widow. When she saw that he had been able to bring back the bed, she said to him, "In the west, on the mountain of the Monkey King, there is a big drum. Bring it back to me, and we will beat it at the wedding."

Just as the son was leaving, the daughter appeared and asked, "What task did my mother give you now?"

"I am supposed to steal a big drum from the mountain of the Monkey King," he said.

"I have heard that the Monkey King left for the Western Heaven and has not yet returned," the daughter said. "Beneath the mountain there is a lake of mud. If you roll around in the mud like the Monkey King, the little apes will think you are their ancestor and will take you to their homes. I will give you a needle, some lime, and some bean oil. You must take them all with you, and when danger threatens, throw the needle behind you first, then the lime, and finally the oil."

The son took the three things, went to the lake of mud beneath the mountain, and rolled about until his entire body, save for his eyes, was caked with mud. He ran quickly up the hill, and all the little apes came down from the trees and cried, "Grandfather, you have finally arrived!"

The little apes gathered round him and bore him off in a big chest. The son clapped his hands and said, "Your grandfather has come a long way and is very hungry. Quick, go into the peach orchard and bring me back some peaches." Off they ran, as fast as they could, into the peach orchard with baskets of all sizes. But the young man jumped down from the chest, grabbed the big drum that he saw hanging in a shelter, and ran away. He had not gone far when he realized that the monkeys were following him, screaming, "Big bad thief! You pretend to be our grandfather and then go and steal our big drum! Wait until we catch you!"

The son quickly took the needle out of his pocket and tossed it behind him. It turned into a mountain of needles. The little apes pricked their skin and scratched their eyes on it, but they continued to pursue him. Then he took out the lime and tossed it behind him, and it turned into a mountain of lime. The little apes with their torn skin and bleeding eyes stuck to the lime and suffered such terrible pain that some of them died, but they continued to pursue him. Then he tossed the bottle of bean oil, and when the oil poured out, the mountain became slippery. Whenever the little apes wanted to climb up, they slipped back down again. The son escaped and returned to the old woman before the sun set.

When the widow saw that he had brought back the big drum, she said to him, "It is still early in the day. Go into the garden and cut down two hair-bamboo sticks so that we can make a mosquito frame for you."

But the son thought, "What sorcery is there in the garden?"

He plucked up his courage and asked the daughter. "The gardener is a hairy man," she said. "He likes to flay men and eat their fingers. If you must cut down the bamboo, it will be dangerous."

The daughter took out a coat of coconut and wrapped it around his shoulders. Then she placed ten small bamboo reeds on his fingers and gave him a double-edged hatchet. "Be quick," she said, "and nothing will happen to you." The son ran into the garden, found the bamboo, and cut it down. But a dark, hairy man came out of the thicket, grabbed the coconut coat with one hand and pulled off the bamboo reeds with the other. Thinking that the coat was the skin and that the bamboo reeds were fingers, he began to eat them. In the meantime the son ran off.

When the old woman saw him coming, she asked, "Have you brought me the bamboo?"

"Yes," said the son.

"Good," said the widow, "but you have not eaten anything all day. Here are some noodles made from wheaten flour."

The son was really very hungry, and he went into the kitchen and took the cover off the pot in there. He grabbed the delicious white noodles with his hands and began to eat them, but soon he began to feel pain, terrible pain. The door opened, and in came the servant girl with a lamp. She saw him and said, "My mistress asks that you join her."

The son went up to the beautiful maiden, who told the servant to hoist the young man up on a beam, pull off his shoes, and beat his body with them. After a few blows, ten small snakes fell from his mouth and crawled around on the floor. The maiden untied the young man and said, "My mother is always trying to hurt you. She gave you snakes to eat instead of noodles. Go tell her that the wedding must take place now!"

The next evening the wedding really did take place. The drum of the Monkey King was beaten at the entrance to a room in which could be seen the bed of white jade from the palace of the Dragon King. A beautiful mosquito net had been made with the bamboo. Everything was fine and beautiful. But when the two went to bed, a river began flowing across the bed, right in between the husband and wife. The wife said, "This is just another one of my mother's tricks." She looked all around until she found a pitcher of water under the dressing table. There was a bit of wood floating in the water. She removed the wood and poured out the water, and all at once the river vanished.

The wife said to her husband, "We have to flee right away. My mother will continue to try to harm us." She took a torn umbrella and a rooster and handed them over to her husband, and the two fled in the middle of the night.

The moon was half full and lit up the road in the hills. The two had gone but a few miles when suddenly they heard a whirring sound above their heads. The wife took the umbrella and said, "My mother has sent a flying knife after us. If the knife senses blood, it will fall. But if you toss the rooster in the air, the knife will go after it and kill it."

The husband did as he was told, and the knife vanished into thin air. A little later the wife said, "The knife is sure to return. Chicken blood is sweet, and human blood tastes salty. My mother will know that she did not succeed in killing us. What are we going to do?"

The husband listened carefully, and before long he heard the whirring sound made by the flying knife. He began to weep and said, "I am going to die." But the wife refused to let that happen. "I'm the one who must die because I can come back to life again. After I die, you must take my body back home and buy a large lotus pail. You can put my body in it. In seven times seven days I will come back to life again."

When the wife finished speaking, she went outdoors, and the knife stopped whirring. The young man saw his bride lying on the ground, with eyes closed and her face as white as a pear blossom. The knife had plunged in her heart, and blood was pouring out of it. He wept bitter tears and carried her back to his home.

It was not yet light in the east when he arrived home. He told his father about everything that had happened, and the father began to weep when he heard that his two older sons had been killed by the witch. The son had brought back the pail with him. He covered up his wife's body and kept watch.

After forty-eight days he heard loud moans coming from the pail, as if someone was in great pain. Then he thought, "If I don't let her out now and wait another day, she may die again." And so he took the lid off the pail. Slowly his wife lifted up her head and said softly, "Why did you uncover me a day too soon? Now I see that it is not our destiny to be together." Then her head sank down slowly, and her eyes closed shut. She was dead forever.

NOURIE HADIG

Susie Hoogasian-Villa collected this tale, published in 1966, from Mrs. Akabi Mooradian, an Armenian immigrant living in Detroit, Michigan. "Nourie Hadig" has many of the standard-issue features (moon as the authority on beauty, recruitment of hit man, blood-stained shirt as evidence of murder, catatonic princess, and so on) found in versions of "The Beautiful Girl." But instead of discovering a house with seven dwarfs or a band of robbers, the heroine finds her way to a place filled with riches that serves as shelter for a sleeping prince. The "stone of patience," like many household objects in fairy tales, becomes an inanimate confidant that enables the heroine to tell her story out loud, even when she has sworn to tell no one her story. The embedded tale not only creates a *mise en abyme* effect but also reminds us of the power of storytelling as a path to liberation and social justice. (The gypsy slave, purchased with pieces of gold, does not have the chance to tell her own story in this narrative.) The heroine's name, Nourie Hadig, means "tiny bit of pomegranate," perhaps echoing the pomegranate seeds given to Persephone by Hades.

THERE WAS ONCE a rich man who had a very beautiful wife and a beautiful daughter known as Nourie Hadig. Every month when the moon appeared in the sky, the wife asked, "New moon, am I the most beautiful, or are you?" And every month the moon replied, "You are the most beautiful."

But when Nourie Hadig came to be fourteen years of age, she was so much more beautiful than her mother that the moon was forced to change her answer. One day when the mother asked the moon her constant question, the moon answered, "I am not the most beautiful, nor are you. The father and the mother's only child, Nourie Hadig, is the most beautiful of all." Nourie Hadig was ideally named because her skin was perfectly white and she had rosy cheeks. And if you have ever seen a pomegranate, you know that it has red pulpy seeds with a red skin that has a pure white lining.

The mother was very jealous—so jealous, in fact, that she fell sick and took to her bed. When Nourie Hadig returned from school that day, her mother refused to see her or speak to her. "My mother is very sick today," Nourie Hadig said to herself. When her father returned home, she told him that her mother was sick and refused to speak to her. The father went to see his wife and asked kindly, "What is the matter, wife? What ails you?"

"Something has happened that is so important that I must tell you immediately. Who is more necessary to you, your child or myself? You cannot have both of us."

"How can you speak in this way?" he asked her. "You are not a stepmother. How can you say such things about your own flesh and blood? How can I get rid of my own child?"

"I don't care what you do," the woman said. "You must get rid of her so that I will never see her again. Kill her and bring me her bloody shirt."

"She is your child as much as she is mine. But if you say I must kill her, then she will be killed," the father sadly answered. Then he went to his daughter and said, "Come, Nourie Hadig, we are going for a visit. Take some of your clothes and come with me."

The two of them went far away until finally it began to get dark. "You wait here while I go down to the brook to get some water for us to drink with our lunch," the father told his daughter.

Nourie Hadig waited and waited for her father to return, but he did not return. Not knowing what to do, she cried and walked through the woods trying to find shelter. At last she saw a light in the distance, and approaching it, she came upon a large house. "Perhaps these people will take me in tonight," she said to herself. But as she put her hand on the door, it opened by itself, and as she passed inside, the door closed behind her immediately. She tried opening it again, but it would not open.

She walked through the house and saw many treasures. One room was full of gold; another was full of silver; one was full of fur; one was full of bird feathers; one was full of chicken feathers; one was full of pearls; and one was full of rugs. She opened the door to another room and found a handsome youth sleeping. She called out to him, but he did not answer.

Suddenly she heard a voice tell her that she must look after this boy and prepare his food. She must place the food by his bedside and then leave; when she returned, the food would be gone. She was to do this for seven years, for the youth was under a spell for that length of time. Every day she cooked and took care of the boy. At the first new moon after Nourie Hadig had left home, her mother asked, "New moon, am I the most beautiful, or are you?"

"I am not the most beautiful, and neither are you," the new moon replied. "The father and mother's only child, Nourie Hadig, is the most beautiful of all."

"Oh, that means that my husband has not killed her after all," the wicked woman said to herself. She was so angry that she went to bed again and pretended to be sick. "What did you do to our beautiful child?" she asked her husband. "What ever did you do to her?"

"You told me to get rid of her. So I got rid of her. You asked me to bring you her bloody shirt, and I did," her husband answered.

"When I told you that, I was ill. I didn't know what I was saying," his wife said. "Now I am sorry about it and plan to turn you over to the authorities as the murderer of your own child."

"Wife, what are you saying? You were the one who told me what to do, and now you want to hand me over to the authorities?"

"You must tell me what you did with our child!" the wife cried. Although the husband did not want to tell his wife that he had not killed their daughter, he was compelled to do so to save himself. "I did not kill her, wife. I killed a bird instead and dipped Nourie Hadig's shirt in its blood."

"You must bring her back, or you know what will happen to you," the wife threatened.

"I left her in the forest, but I don't know what happened to her after that."

"Very well, then, I will find her," the wife said. She traveled to distant places but could not find Nourie Hadig. Every new moon she asked her question and was assured that Nourie Hadig was the most beautiful of all. So on she went, searching for her daughter.

One day when Nourie Hadig had been at the bewitched house for four years, she looked out the window and saw a group of gypsies camping nearby. "I am lonely up here. Can you send up a pretty girl of about my own age?" she called to them. When they agreed to do so, she ran to the golden room and took a handful of gold pieces. These she threw down to the gypsies, who, in turn, threw up the end of a rope to her. Then a girl started climbing at the other end of the rope and quickly reached her new mistress.

Nourie Hadig and the gypsy soon became good friends and decided to share the burden of taking care of the sleeping boy. One day one would serve him; and the next day the other would serve him. They continued in this way for three years. One warm summer day the gypsy was fanning the youth when he suddenly awoke. Since he believed that the gypsy had served him for the entire seven years, he said to her, "I am a prince, and you are to be my princess for having cared for me such a long time." The gypsy said, "If you say it, so shall it be."

Nourie Hadig, who had heard what was said by the two, felt very bitter. She had been in the house alone for four years before the gypsy came and had served three years with her friend, and yet the other girl was to marry the handsome prince. Neither girl told the prince the truth about the arrangement.

Everything was being prepared for the wedding, and the prince was making arrangements to go to town and buy the bridal dress. Before he left, however, he told Nourie Hadig, "You must have served me a little while at least. Tell me what you would like me to bring back for you."

"Bring me back a *saber dashee* [stone of patience]," Nourie Hadig answered.

"What else do you want?" he asked, surprised at the modest request.

"Your happiness."

The prince went into town and purchased the bridal gown, then went to a stonecutter and asked for a *saber dashee.*

"Who is this for?" the stonecutter asked.

"For my servant," the prince replied.

"This is a stone of patience," the stonecutter said. "If one has great troubles and tells it to this *saber dashee,* certain changes will occur. If one's troubles are great, so great that the *saber dashee* cannot bear the sorrow, it will swell and burst. If, on the other hand, one makes much of only slight grievances, the *saber dashee* will not swell, but the speaker will. And if there is no one there to save this person, he will burst. So listen outside your servant's door. Not everyone knows of the *saber dashee,* and your servant, who is a very unusual person, must have a valuable story to tell. Be ready to run in and save her from bursting if she is in danger of doing so."

When the prince reached home, he gave his betrothed the dress and gave Nourie Hadig the *saber dashee.* That night the prince listened outside Nourie Hadig's door. The beautiful girl placed the *saber dashee* before her and started telling her story: "*Saber dashee,*" she said, "I was the only child of a well-to-do family. My mother was very beautiful, but it was my misfortune to be even more beautiful than she. At every new moon my mother asked who was the most beautiful one in the world. And the new moon always answered that my mother was the most beautiful. One day my mother asked again, and the moon told her that Nourie Hadig was the most beautiful one in the whole world. My mother became very jealous and told my father to take me somewhere, to kill me and bring her my bloody shirt. My father could not do this, so he permitted me to go free." Nourie Hadig said, "Tell me, *saber dashee,* am I more patient, or are you?"

The *saber dashee* began to swell.

The girl continued. "When my father left me, I walked until I saw this house in the distance. I walked toward it, and when I touched the door, it opened magically by itself. Once I was inside, the door closed behind me and never opened again until seven years later. Inside I found a handsome youth. A voice told me to prepare his food and take care of him. I did this for four years, day after day, night after night, living alone in a strange place, with no one to hear my voice. *Saber dashee,* tell me, am I more patient, or are you?"

The *saber dashee* swelled a little more.

"One day a group of gypsies camped right beneath my window. As I had been lonely all these years, I bought a gypsy girl and pulled her up on a rope to the place where I was confined. Now, she and I took turns serving the young boy, who was under a magic spell. One day she cooked for him; and the next day I cooked for him. One day, three years later, while the gypsy was fanning him, the youth awoke and saw her. He thought that she had served him through all those years and took her as his betrothed. And the gypsy, whom I had bought and considered my friend, did not say one word to him about me. *Saber dashee,* tell me, am I more patient, or are you?"

The *saber dashee* swelled and swelled and swelled. The prince, meanwhile, had heard this most unusual story and rushed in to keep the girl from bursting. But just as he stepped into the room, it was the *saber dashee* that burst.

"Nourie Hadig," the prince said, "it is not my fault that I chose the gypsy for my wife instead of you. I didn't know the whole story. You are to be my wife, and the gypsy will be the servant."

"No, since you are betrothed to her and all the preparations for the wedding are made, you must marry the gypsy," Nourie Hadig said.

"That will not do. You must be my wife and her mistress." So Nourie Hadig and the prince were married.

Nourie Hadig's mother, in the meanwhile, had never stopped searching for her daughter. One day she again asked the new moon the question, "New moon, am I the most beautiful, or are you?"

"I am not the most beautiful, nor are you. The princess of Adana is the most beautiful of all," the new moon said. The mother knew immediately that Nourie Hadig was now married and living in Adana. So she had a very beautiful ring made, so beautiful and brilliant that no one could resist it. But she put a potion in the ring that would make the wearer sleep. When she had finished her work, she called an old witch who traveled on a broomstick. "Witch, if you will take this ring and give it to the princess of Adana as a gift from her devoted mother, I will grant you your heart's desire."

So the mother gave the ring to the witch, who set out for Adana immediately. The prince was not home when the witch arrived, and she was able to talk to Nourie Hadig and the gypsy alone. Said the witch, "Princess, this beautiful ring is a gift from your devoted mother. She was ill at the time you left home and said some angry words, but your father should not have paid attention to her since she was suffering from such pain." So she left the ring with Nourie Hadig and departed.

"My mother does not want me to be happy. Why should she send me such a beautiful ring?" Nourie Hadig asked the gypsy.

"What harm can a ring do?" the gypsy asked.

So Nourie Hadig slipped the ring on her finger. No sooner was it on her finger than she became unconscious. The gypsy put her in bed but could do nothing further.

Soon the prince came home and found his wife in a deep sleep. No matter how much they shook her, she would not awaken; yet she had a pleasant smile on her face, and anyone who looked at her could not believe that she was in a trance. She was breathing, yet she did not open her eyes. No one was successful in awakening her.

"Nourie Hadig, you took care of me all those long years," the prince said. "Now I will look after you. I will not let them bury you. You are always to lie here, and the gypsy will guard you by night while I guard you by day," he said. So the prince stayed with her by day, and the gypsy guarded her by night. Nourie Hadig did not open her eyes once in three years. Healer after healer came and went, but none could help the beautiful girl.

One day the prince brought another healer to see Nourie Hadig, and although he could not help her in the least, he did not want to say so. When he was alone with the enchanted girl, he noticed her beautiful ring. "She is wearing so many rings and necklaces that no one will notice if I take this ring to my wife," he said to himself. As he slipped the ring off her finger, she opened her eyes and sat up. The healer immediately returned the ring to her finger. "Aha! I have discovered the secret!"

The next day he exacted many promises of wealth from the prince for his wife's cure. "I will give you anything you want if you can cure my wife," the prince said.

The healer, the prince, and the gypsy went to the side of Nourie Hadig. "What are all those necklaces and ornaments? Is it fitting that a sick woman should wear such finery? Quick," the healer said to the gypsy, "remove them!" The gypsy removed all the jewelry except the ring. "Take that ring off too," the healer ordered.

"But that ring was sent to her by her mother, and it is a dear remembrance," the gypsy said.

"What did you say? When did her mother send her a ring?" asked the prince. Before the gypsy could answer him, the healer took the ring off Nourie Hadig's finger. The princess immediately sat up and began to talk. They were all very happy: the healer, the prince, the princess, and the gypsy, who was now a real friend of Nourie Hadig.

Meanwhile, during all these years, whenever the mother had asked the moon her eternal question, it had replied, "You are the most beautiful!" But when Nourie Hadig was well again, the moon said, "I am not the most beautiful, nor are you. The father and mother's only daughter, Nourie Hadig, the princess of Adana, is the most beautiful of all." The mother was so surprised and so angry that her daughter was alive that she died of rage then and there.

From the sky fell three apples: one for me, one for the storyteller, and one for the person who has entertained you.

BLANCA ROSA AND THE FORTY THIEVES

Well-known in Spanish-speaking lands, both in Europe and in the Americas, the story of Blanca Rosa, here from a collection published in 1967, seems to have some remote connection with the tale about forty thieves in *The Thousand and One Nights.* That it is intended more for adult audiences is suggested by both the gory details of the mock murder (with eyes and tongue served up on a platter) and the staging of the deaths of the prince's sisters as well as the repeated references to a naked heroine, who is stripped of her clothing on more than one occasion. Combining the sublime with the monstrous, the sacred and the profane, the story idealizes the figure of Blanca Rosa—her beauty is so overpowering that she is thought to be "the Virgin of Heaven." In 2012, Pablo Berger directed a silent film inspired by the Grimms' "Snow White" called *Blancanieves.* Set in 1920s Seville, it tells the story of a girl named Carmen who runs away with a troupe of dwarfs to become a bullfighter.

BLANCA ROSA AND THE FORTY THIEVES

A CERTAIN WIDOWER HAD a beautiful daughter called Blanca Rosa who was the living image of her mother. The mother, upon dying, had left the girl a little magic mirror and had said that if she ever wanted to see her mother again, all she had to do was take out her looking glass and it would give her what she desired. After some time, the widower married again, this time to a very envious woman. When the stepmother saw the daughter talking all day with the mirror, she took it away from her.

This lady considered herself the most beautiful woman in the world. She asked the mirror, "Who is the most lovely of all women?" The mirror answered, "Your daughter." As the little glass didn't flatter her with the right answer, she became furiously envious and ordered her daughter killed. The men who were supposed to do the job abandoned the girl, and a little old man helped her.

Meanwhile the stepmother asked the mirror once again who was the most beautiful woman in the world. "Your daughter, who is still alive," was the answer. In a rage, she called for the little old man who had helped the girl and sentenced him to death if he failed to bring her the tongue and the eyes of her daughter. Now the old fellow had a pet dog with blue eyes. Seeing that he couldn't defend the poor girl, he decided to kill the dog and convince the stepmother that he had followed orders. After this, he left Blanca Rosa to God's care in the forest. The stepmother was very pleased when he brought her the blue eyes and the tongue on a silver platter.

For a long while, the life of Blanca Rosa was sad and full of pain, until she came by chance upon the hideout of forty thieves. One day when she had perched high in the crown of a tree, she observed a band of men leaving the forest. The girl climbed down to the den from which they had emerged and was dazzled and amazed to see all manner of jewels and delicious dishes. The good food was what she most wished for, so she crept in and ate to her heart's content, returning afterward to the treetop and falling into a deep sleep.

When the thieves returned to their lair, they found everything strewn about and suspected that somebody had found them out. The leader, however, didn't think so but left a guard at the entrance just to make sure. When they had all gone off on their forays the next day, Blanca Rosa came down again. The guard saw her and was fascinated with such great beauty. He believed that she was a being descended from heaven and dashed off pell-mell to give the rest the news. But when they returned to the camp, nobody put much stock in what he said. After this, the chief ordered five men to stand guard to observe this strange apparition. All of them saw Blanca Rosa and reported the same news, believing that it was the Virgin of Heaven come to punish them. Meanwhile Blanca Rosa enjoyed her time in the hideout while the thieves were away. On their return, they found nobody.

The chief himself decided to stand guard, for he couldn't be convinced of all these goings-on. Great was his surprise when he saw Blanca Rosa descend from the tree. Never before had he seen such a beautiful woman. He begged her pardon, thinking that she was surely the mother of God, and called his companions to repent and adore her. But Blanca Rosa, full of anguish, protested that she was not the Virgin but just a poor orphan cast out of her stepmother's house. The only thing she wanted was shelter so as not to die of hunger in her solitude. The thieves refused to believe this and continued to worship her as the Virgin. They built her a throne of gold, dressed her in the most lovely clothes, and adorned her with the most precious jewels. From that day on, Blanca Rosa lived happy and content among her robber "relatives."

It was rumored in the city that there was in the forest a den of thieves who worshiped a beautiful woman. When the stepmother got wind of this, she refused to believe it and insisted that she was the only beautiful one in the world.

"Little mirror," she asked the charm, "by the power God has given you, tell me who is the most beautiful of all."

"Blanca Rosa is the most beautiful woman," answered the little glass.

In desperation, the stepmother sought out a sorceress and offered her a great sum of money if she would only kill the lovely stepdaughter. The old witch searched through the forest until she found the hideout and, with lies, cajoleries, and flatteries, was able to see Blanca Rosa. When the old charmer was sure it was the right girl, she pretended to be a poor woman who wished to show her gratitude for some gold that the girl had once given her. She handed the girl a basket of fruit, but Blanca Rosa told the old woman to keep it, for she already had a great deal.

"If you won't accept this bit of fruit," croaked the old lady, "at least let me touch your dress and run my hands over your silky hair." She stroked Blanca Rosa's head and jabbed her with a magic needle. Instantly the girl dropped into a deep, deep sleep. The old hag slipped out in a wink and went to the stepmother to tell her that her daughter would trouble her no longer.

When the thieves arrived at the forest lair, they found their precious queen sleeping. Since she didn't stir for many days, they believed her dead. After great weeping and many efforts to revive her, they resigned themselves to the task of the burial. Her outlaw friends placed her in a casket made of pure gold and silver, dressing her beautifully and adorning her with the most exquisite necklaces and pearls. They sealed her in against the least little drop of water and threw the casket into the sea.

Now there was in a certain city a prince who lived with his two old-maid sisters and was very fond of fishing. One day he was out in his boat pulling in some nets when he saw in the waves something that sparkled and shone over the waters. Anxious to get to the bottom of this mystery, he called some fishermen to help him land the beautiful floating casket. They loaded it into his boat, and he took it home, shutting himself in his room. The casket was riveted so tight that he couldn't open it until he brought his whole tool kit to the task. After seven days and seven nights of labor, he removed the lid and found the girl dressed in lovely garments and bedecked with jewels. He tenderly removed the body from the casket and placed it on his bed, where he stripped it of its clothing and took off the jewels one by one, puzzling over the mystery of this being. When he found nothing, it occurred to him to comb her silky hair. The comb got snarled on a little bump, which the prince removed with a pair of tweezers. Immediately the fair girl sprang back to life, and he realized that she had been bewitched all this time.

"Where are my thieves?" cried Blanca Rosa, seeing herself alone with a man she had never met and totally naked. To console the distraught girl, the prince began to tell her the tale of how he had found her floating on the waves, assuring her that he was a good person and that she had nothing to fear. She would not be calmed down and insisted on leaving, so the prince drove the needle back into her head and walked outside to consider what he could possibly do with the lovely maiden. Meanwhile the prince's two sisters were at their wits' end, trying to figure out what their brother was doing locked in his room day and night. He didn't even appear for meals. They began to keep watch through the keyhole. How great was their shock when they spied a golden casket and heaps of jewels!

The prince returned to his room after long thought and removed the needle once again from Blanca Rosa's head. He told her that he had not been able to find the forty thieves and asked her to remain in his house under his protection, as his wife. If she didn't wish to go into the street, she could remain in her room, and nobody would know the secret.

One fine morning when the prince decided to go fishing and left the sad and melancholy Blanca Rosa in her room, the two sisters were seized with curiosity and opened the door. They were indignant at seeing such a pretty girl seated on the bed. Immediately they stripped her of her fine clothing and necklaces and threw her naked into the street. Blanca Rosa frantically tried to hide and eventually arrived, breathless, at the house of an old cobbler. She was crying so bitterly that the old man took her in and hid her. The prince arrived home and found her room empty with the clothes strewn on the floor. Disconsolate, he wandered aimlessly in search of the lovely girl until someone told him about a beautiful young woman at the cobbler's house. Sure enough, he found Blanca Rosa there and took her joyfully back to his own place, where he began preparations for the wedding. As a punishment for his sisters, the prince sent for two wild horses and had the old maids bound to them head and foot. The bucking broncos tore them into a thousand pieces. Immediately after this, the wedding was celebrated with great pomp. The forty thieves attended at Blanca Rosa's request and brought the bride many marvelous gifts. She and the prince lived very happily for all the rest of their lives.

THE WONDER CHILD

Like versions of "The Beautiful Girl" from India, this Jewish-Egyptian story published in 1996 turns a precious jewel into the source of the girl's power and also of her vulnerability. Kohava is not just a "beautiful baby girl" but an accomplished musician who plays "beautiful melodies," a talented painter of "lovely pictures," and a devout reader of religious tales. Note that this story gives the beautiful girl "lustrous black hair" and skin "as smooth as the outside of a peach." Texture rather than color is emphasized in this tale, when it comes to skin.

THE WONDER CHILD

Long ago, there lived a rabbi and his wife who had no children. They prayed every day for a child of their own, but their prayers were never answered.

Now it is said that the sky opens at midnight on the night of Shavuoth, and any prayers or wishes made at that time come true. So one Shavuoth, the rabbi and his wife decided to stay awake, so that their prayers would be certain to reach God's ears.

To their amazement, at midnight the sky parted like the waters of the Red Sea, and for one instant the world was filled with the glory of heaven. And in that instant both the rabbi and his wife wished for a child. That night the rabbi's wife dreamed of a wonder child, a girl who would be born to them holding a precious jewel. In the dream the rabbi's wife was told that the child must keep the jewel with her at all times, for her soul was inside it. And if she ever lost that jewel, she would fall into a deep sleep from which she would not awaken until the jewel was returned.

The next morning, the rabbi's wife told her husband the dream, and he was much amazed. And, indeed, things occurred exactly as foretold, and nine months later a beautiful baby girl was born. In her right hand she held a precious jewel, which seemed to glow with a light of its own. The rabbi and his wife named their daughter Kohava, which means "star," and the rabbi set the jewel in a necklace for her to wear around her neck.

One day, when Kohava was only three years old, she picked up her mother's flute. She had never played a flute before, but the moment she put it to her lips, beautiful melodies poured forth. Not only could she play any musical instrument, but at a very young age, she taught herself to paint lovely pictures, to write the letters of the alphabet, and to read books. Her favorites were the books on her father's shelves that told stories of the ancient days when Abraham and Moses walked in the world.

As the years passed, Kohava grew into a beautiful girl. Her lustrous black hair shone in the sunlight. Her dark eyes sparkled like the dazzling jewel she wore around her neck. Her skin was as smooth as the outside of a peach, and her smile brought happiness to everyone who met her.

Now the rabbi and his wife realized that their daughter was truly a wonder child, as the dream had promised, and they gave thanks to God. But in their hearts was the fear that someday she might be separated from her necklace and lose her soul. That is why the rabbi and his wife watched carefully over Kohava and rarely let her leave home.

One day the rabbi and his wife learned that the queen was going to visit the bathhouse that very day and that she had invited all the women of the village to come there. Kohava asked her mother if she, too, could go, for she had never seen the queen. At first her mother was afraid, but at last she agreed to let her go.

When the two arrived at the bathhouse, the women looked at Kohava in amazement. "Where did she come from? Why, she is more beautiful than the queen!" they exclaimed.

When the queen heard this, she grew angry. "Who is this girl?" she asked her servants. They replied that Kohava was a Jewish girl of great beauty and that it was said that she could play any musical instrument set before her.

The queen demanded to see Kohava for herself. And when she realized that the girl's beauty did indeed outshine her own, she was filled with jealousy and with the sudden fear that her son, the prince, might see Kohava and fall in love with her. And that would be a terrible thing, for she wanted the prince to marry a princess, not a poor Jewish girl.

The queen had one of her servants bring forth a flute and commanded the girl to play it. At once Kohava played a melody so beautiful that it brought tears to everyone's eyes—everyone's, that is, except the queen's. Then the queen commanded that the girl play a violin and after that a harp. And from every instrument that Kohava touched, beautiful melodies poured forth. When the queen saw that Kohava truly had a great talent, she ordered, "This girl must return with me at once to my palace to serve as one of my royal musicians."

The rabbi's wife was heartsick at the thought of Kohava going off to live in the palace, yet she knew that they must obey the queen. But before Kohava left, her mother took her aside and whispered that she should never ever take off her necklace, nor should she tell anyone that it held her soul. Then the mother and daughter kissed good-bye, and Kohava rode off in the royal carriage with the queen.

Now the queen had no intention of letting Kohava be a musician, for in that way her son, the prince, might see her. Alas, as soon as they reached the palace, she shut Kohava in the dungeon and ordered that she be left to starve.

So it was that the confused girl found herself imprisoned and frightened for her very life. She would have died of hunger had not the prison guard, overwhelmed by her beauty and gentleness, brought her food in secret. In her dark cell, Kohava wept for her mother and father and prayed to be saved from the evil queen.

One day the queen went down to the dungeon to see for herself if Kohava was still alive. As she walked into the dark cell, she was surprised to see a glowing light. When she looked closer, she realized that the light was coming from the jewel Kohava wore around her neck and that the girl was, indeed, still alive.

"Give me that necklace!" the queen demanded. "I want it for myself." Kohava was terrified, for she remembered her mother's warning. But the queen, not waiting for Kohava to obey, pulled it off herself. And the moment she did, Kohava sank into a deep sleep.

The queen was delighted to see Kohava dead. "Ah, I'm rid of her for good," she cried. Then she ordered the prison guard to bury Kohava far away from the palace where no one could ever find her. But when the guard reached the woods far away from the palace, he saw that Kohava was still breathing, and he realized that she was only asleep. So he brought her to a hut he knew of in the forest and left her there. Day after day, Kohava slept a long, dreamless sleep, and no one except the guard knew she was there.

One afternoon, when the prince was out riding in the woods far away from the palace, he saw that very hut and decided to stop and rest there.

When the prince entered, he was astonished to find a sleeping girl, and he lost his heart to her the moment he saw her. The prince wanted to tell her of his love, but when he realized that she would not wake up, he was very sad. So the prince put a guard outside the hut to protect the sleeping beauty. Every day he came to visit her, and every day he shed tears because she would not awaken.

As the days passed, the queen noticed the sadness of her son, and one day she asked him what was wrong. He told his mother that he was in love with a beautiful young girl. "Is she a princess?" asked the queen.

"Surely," said the prince, "she is a princess."

"In that case," said the queen, "would you like to give her a gift to show your love?"

"Oh, yes," said the prince, "I would like that very much."

"Then I know just the gift for a beautiful princess," replied the queen. "It is something very special." And she brought forth the jewel that she had taken from Kohava. The prince took the necklace to the sleeping girl at once, and the moment he put it around her neck, she woke up.

"Who are you?" asked Kohava as she looked around the small hut. "And where am I?"

The prince told Kohava how he had found her and how she had awakened at the very moment he had placed the necklace around her neck.

Kohava looked at the jewel and remembered how the queen had snatched it from her. "Where did you get this?" she asked.

And so she learned that the one who had saved her was none other than the queen's son. And when the prince learned of his mother's evil deed, he realized that Kohava's life was in danger. He decided to leave the girl in the hut while he hurried back to the palace.

When he arrived, he went straight to the queen. "Mother, I have great news," he said. "I'd like to get married."

"I can see how much you love this princess," said the queen. "I will give orders for the wedding preparations to begin at once!"

Every servant worked night and day. The cooks prepared a magnificent feast, the gardeners cut huge bouquets of roses, and the maids polished the silver goblets until they shone. By the seventh day, everything was ready. All the people of the kingdom came. They gathered at the palace and whispered to one another, "Who is the bride?" For not even the queen had seen her. But when the bride arrived, she was wearing seven veils, and no one could tell who she was.

Among the thousands of guests were the rabbi and his wife, who had come hoping they might see their daughter, Kohava, from whom they had not heard since the day the queen had brought her to the palace.

At last the wedding vows were spoken, and the guests waited breathlessly as the prince lifted the veils, one by one. And as he lifted the seventh veil, everyone gasped at Kohava's great beauty—everyone, that is, except the rabbi and his wife, who could not believe their eyes, and the queen, who thought she was seeing a ghost. Screaming with terror, she ran from the palace as fast as she could—and never was seen again.

So it was that the prince and his new bride became the rulers of the kingdom, and Kohava was reunited with her father and mother. At the palace Kohava continued to play music and make people happy with her songs. And the love that Kohava and the prince had for each other grew deeper over the years, and they lived happily ever after.

THE JEALOUS MOTHER

Jilali El Koudia, like many folklorists and anthropologists before him, was worried that the stories told by the women in his family would one day disappear. He decided to collect tales told by members of his immediate family as well as by storytellers from various cities in Morocco. No purist, he quickly recognized that his informants tended to be "wordy" and "repetitive." By "rewriting, reconstructing the plots, and filling the gaps," he was able to create compact, "readable" narratives that still captured the spirit of the oral narratives. "The Jealous Mother," published in a collection of Moroccan tales in 2003, is unusual in providing a counter-narrative to the happily-ever-after of most "Snow White" tales, one that elevates a utopian social community over heterosexual love and marriage. *Fulana* is a designation for a woman whose name is not known, and an *attoush* is a covered carriage placed on a horse or camel.

THE JEALOUS MOTHER

There was once an extraordinarily beautiful woman, her beauty equal only to that of the moon itself. When she was married and got pregnant, she used to go out at night and address the moon. "O moon," she would say, "you and I are both beautiful, so beautiful that no one can compete with us."

The moon would answer her. "True, you and I are beautiful," it would reply, "but the one still in your womb is yet more beautiful. She will outshine us."

The mother started to worry about her future as the most beautiful woman on Earth. When the time approached for her to give birth, she called in a midwife she trusted. She asked her to bury the baby as soon as it was delivered and to replace it with a puppy dog. She gave her a lot of gold, and so the matter was settled.

The midwife produced a puppy and laid it beside the mother. She then took the baby girl away, but instead of burying her, she kept the girl secluded inside her house and took care of her.

The woman's husband came home. "Just look at what God has given us," she said. "A puppy dog!"

The man was stunned. Fearing public shame, he immediately threw the dog away.

The midwife raised the baby girl in secret until she grew to the age of ten. It was only then that some people in the neighborhood set eyes on her and started talking about an astonishingly beautiful girl. The midwife claimed it was her own daughter. She named her Lalla Khallalt El Khoudra. Whenever people mentioned a beautiful woman, they would say, "She is not as beautiful as Lalla." Soon her name was on everyone's lips. In time, rumors reached the ears of her real mother, and she began to suspect the midwife of treachery.

One day the mother approached the midwife. "Can you please send me your daughter?" she asked. "She can help me disentangle a ball of wool thread."

The old woman agreed and, in exchange for a handful of gold, sent her daughter.

When the real mother set eyes on the girl, her heart started beating with jealousy. She gave the girl a large ball of thread and asked her to stretch it until it was completely untied. Lalla walked on and on, day and night, until she found herself in a strange environment—the land of ghouls. When her mother guessed she had walked that far, she cut the thread. Now Lalla could not find her way back home.

Night had already fallen. Lalla started looking around for a shelter to spend the night. She soon realized she was in the midst of strange creatures that looked like the ghouls in tales she had heard from the old midwife. Scared of being eaten alive, she climbed onto a roof and hid herself among the thatch. It was not long before she discovered that her hiding place was the house of seven ghoul brothers, all bachelors. All they had was a slave who cooked for them.

Early in the morning the ghouls went out to hunt. The slave remained behind alone to prepare their food. All of a sudden she heard something up on the roof, and looking up, she saw a very beautiful face staring down at her. "If you're a human being," the slave exclaimed, "say so. But if you are a jinn, go away."

"I am a miserable human being," Lalla replied. "I'm dying of hunger and thirst. Please help me."

The slave now invited her down and gave her some food and water. But she warned her that the owners of the dwelling were seven dangerous ghouls; she advised her to stay out of sight, or else they would eat her up.

So Lalla went back to her hiding place. Every day, when the ghouls went out, the slave invited Lalla to join her and taught her how to cook. Lalla learned fast and was very useful to the slave.

As day followed upon day, the ghouls began to notice a difference in the cooking; it tasted better and better. A new flavor had been added to their food. They discussed this change among themselves and decided that the next day the youngest brother should stay behind and conceal himself to see what the slave was adding to the food.

The other six brothers left. The slave woke up and as usual called Lalla down from her hiding place. They started cooking together, but now Lalla was doing most of the work while the slave relaxed. The youngest ghoul waited for a while, but then he jumped out from his hiding place and surprised them both. Lalla was frightened and remained glued to the spot. But the ghoul spoke very softly to her, assuring her that she would not be harmed. To the contrary he gave her a warm and friendly welcome. As soon as his eyes looked at her, he fell in love and decided to marry her.

When his brothers returned, he met them at the door and told them what had happened. They all sat down and discussed the matter. They agreed to give the couple a great wedding ceremony the very next day.

With the presence of such a charming beauty, their life had been completely transformed into a paradise. They were all very happy.

From then on, the care and attention of all seven brothers were devoted to Lalla. She was the one who did the cooking, and the slave was now left neglected. Day after day she became more and more jealous. "Promise me," she said to Lalla one day, "that you will share everything with me." Lalla agreed and swore an oath on it.

Everything went according to plan. The slave slept most of the time, and Lalla did the housework. One day, while Lalla was preparing the food, she came upon a long bean. She ate half and nudged the slave to give her the other half, but the slave pretended to be sound asleep and did not wake up. After a while, she gave a yawn. "Weren't you nudging me a while ago," she asked Lalla, "or was I dreaming?"

"Yes," replied Lalla cheerfully, "I've half of a bean for you."

She reached for her head scarf and untied a knot where she had hidden the bean, but to her disappointment and horror she could not find it. The slave complained that she had broken her promise and reprimanded her.

In the evening the slave took her revenge. She poured water on the fire, so that when the time came to prepare the food for the ghouls, Lalla had no fire. Afraid that they would be angry, she begged the slave to help her find some fire. Time was running out, and soon the ghouls would be returning home. The slave told her to go out and borrow some fire from a neighbor.

So Lalla went out to the dwelling of an old ghoul named Uncle Yazit, who was notorious for his ferocity and cunning. But Lalla knew nothing about him. She knocked on his door and waited. He looked outside. "What do you want?" he asked. "Why are you crying?"

"Uncle . . ."

"Yazit. Uncle Yazit."

"Uncle Yazit, please give me some fire quickly."

"Oh, is that all you want? You can have as much as you want. But first, do you want me to pierce your stomach with a red-hot nail, or do you prefer to be marked on the forehead with a sharp knife?"

She stood there stunned, not knowing what to do. He yawned, and she could see his teeth arrayed like sharp knives.

"Make your mind up," he said in a tone of menace, "or I'll—."

She chose to be marked. He handed her the fire and then cut her forehead until blood started streaming down. She turned away and headed back home apace, with the blood dropping behind her and marking her path. Suddenly, a pigeon appeared and tried to dry her blood with its wings, but Lalla thought it was playing with her and shooed it away. "Oh, please, leave me alone now!" she cried. "I'm so miserable and don't feel like playing."

The next day Uncle Yazit followed the drops of blood until he found her door. He knocked. "Give me your finger," he said, "or I'll eat you."

She pushed her finger through the keyhole. He sucked some of her blood, then left.

And so every day Uncle Yazit visited Lalla and sucked some of her blood. Gradually, she started feeling weak and looking pale. Her deteriorating health affected her work and cooking. The ghoul brothers started to notice the change in both her behavior and the taste of her food. They wondered why she was looking so miserable and pensive all the time. Wasn't she happy? Did she miss her home? Weren't they kind enough to her? They always did their best to make her feel comfortable and to bring her everything she wished. So what was going wrong with her? They discussed the matter among themselves and agreed to leave the youngest behind to watch her. He concealed himself somewhere and kept an eye on her movements. In the evening he heard a knock at the door. Lalla went to answer it. Uncle Yazit had come on his usual visit, and she pushed her finger through the keyhole. He sucked her blood and left. Meanwhile, the youngest ghoul just watched from his hiding place and kept quiet. He could not confront Uncle Yazit on his own even if he wanted to.

He waited until his other brothers came back and told them what he had seen. They discussed the problem and made their plan. The next day they decided not to go hunting. Lalla and the slave were both surprised to see them staying home. They asked the ghouls what was wrong, but they simply answered that they were having a rest day. The house was very quiet.

The time came for Uncle Yazit's daily visit. When he asked Lalla for her finger, the youngest brother leaped to her side. "Tell him to go away," he whispered in her ear, "or he'll be destroyed."

"Your finger, or I'll eat you!" Yazit yelled.

Lalla answered as she was instructed. Yazit repeated his demand in a more threatening way, but still she dismissed him with harsh words. When his anger reached its peak, he forced open the door, and it gave way. He fell into a *metmoura,* the trap the brothers had dug during the night and covered with hay. Now they sprang from their corners and looked down at him. "Now, Uncle Yazit," they shouted in unison, "you're going to rise from that hole in smoke!"

Then they called out for Lalla. "How dare you allow a stranger to visit you during our absence?" they yelled at her angrily. "You've betrayed us!"

They threatened to send her after Yazit and meet the same fate. But she started weeping and told them the whole story.

They looked at the slave and saw her trembling. They dragged her by her hair and flung her down into the pit with Yazit. They piled wood over them and lit the fire. The smoke rose until nothing was left but black ashes.

Then they resumed their normal life, going out hunting every day while Lalla busied herself preparing their food.

Little by little Lalla recovered her health and serenity. Her complexion was rosy, and that brightened up the brothers' life like a magic candle. They enjoyed her charm, and all felt happy again. Every day they showered her with gold and silver. They all loved and worshiped her like a goddess who made them human. By now her room was piled high with precious presents.

One day a Jew, a wandering merchant, passed by the house, shouting, "Sweets! Clothes! Cosmetics! Everything you need!" When he heard a voice from inside the house, he stopped his donkey. He led his donkey over to the door and waited. Lalla came out, and he showed her his wares. She chose a few things and asked him for the price. He said he was exchanging his goods for wool, old copper, or silver utensils. She went in and filled a whole sack with silver and gold and gave it to him. He was amazed at her generosity and asked for her name. She said, "Lalla Khallalt El Khoudra," and then asked him, "Do you know a tribe called So-and-so?"

He said he was much traveled, because his trade took him everywhere. So naturally he knew that tribe only too well. "Please," she begged him, "if you go back to that tribe, ask for a woman called Fulana. She's my mother. Please give her my greetings and tell her I miss her so much."

The Jew promised and departed, still shouting, "Sweets! Clothes! Cosmetics! Everything you need!"

A few months later, his travels brought him to the tribe where Lalla's mother lived. An old but beautiful woman called out to him so she could buy a few things, and she paid him with a handful of wool. When he saw what she was offering him, he laughed at her. "Oh," he said, "you're not like Lalla Khallalt El Khoudra, who gave me a sack of gold and silver for half of what you have bought."

It was then he remembered the promise he had given Lalla. "Oh," he went on with a sigh, "her beauty surpasses that of the moon itself!"

He was about to ask the old woman if she knew a woman named Fulana, when the goods she bought fell from her hands to the ground. "Please," her mother said, "tell me more about her. I'm her mother."

The Jew was surprised. "She sends you her warmest greetings," he said. "She misses you so much."

"Tell me," the woman insisted, "how is she? Where is she living?"

"She lives in the country of ghouls. But she has become their queen. They worship her and serve her like slaves. They give her all the gold in the world. She is very happy, the richest and the most beautiful woman I've ever seen in my life."

"When will you see her again?"

"Very soon, for sure. Perhaps in a month or two."

The old woman asked him to wait. She went in her house and searched for a present to send her dear daughter. She wrapped a ring in a handkerchief and handed it to the Jew: "Please, give her this. Tell her it's a token from her mother, who loves her so much. Tell her to put it under her tongue when she is cooking to protect her against the evil eye."

The Jew promised to convey the message and went on his way.

Two months later the Jew found himself back in the country of ghouls. He remembered the message and went straight to Lalla's house. She was delighted to see him again. She chose a few goods and paid him with another sack of gold and silver. He told her he had seen her mother, who was very happy to hear about her. He then produced the present the mother had sent and repeated what the woman had advised her daughter to do with it. Lalla wept with joy and kissed the handkerchief in which the ring was stored. She sighed and said she would do as her mother suggested. Then the Jew left to carry on his business.

When Lalla sat down to prepare the meal for the brothers, she untied the handkerchief and put the ring under her tongue. A short while later, she fell into a swoon and remained in a coma, looking as still as death. When the ghouls returned home, they found her frozen to the spot. They shook her, but she remained motionless. They cried the whole night and ate nothing.

The next day they made her an *attoush,* a sort of couch of gold and silver and her best jewelry, and laid her down in it. They called their camels and asked each of them one by one, "How long can you carry Lalla?"

"One year," one said.

"Ten years," another said.

"As long as I live," said a third with the name Naala (or Shoe).

So the ghouls fixed the *attoush* firmly on the back of the third she-camel. "Do not stop for anyone," they told the camel. "Roam the world. Remember your secret name is Naala. Respond only to this name."

The she-camel agreed and departed.

Naala traveled very far, from one place to another, stopping only to eat and drink and never allowing anyone to come close to her. She crossed deserts, valleys, rivers, and jungles. She saw all sorts of nations until she reached a territory that was ruled by a famous, rich sultan. When his soldiers saw a she-camel carrying something shiny, they informed him and then chased the camel everywhere. But their efforts were in vain. The sultan consulted all his magicians, who were helpless in the face of this phenomenon.

As the sultan was riding toward his palace, he heard an old woman laughing. He stopped his horse. "Why are you laughing, old woman?" he asked.

"All your soldiers and magicians can't catch a she-camel as old as I am!"

"Do you mean you can catch her?"

"Old as I am, I will bring her to you."

"Listen, woman! If you do, I'll make you rich forever. If not, I'll kill you. Now go!"

They all ridiculed the old woman and considered her as good as dead anyway. Some said she had nothing to lose. She started running in the direction of the she-camel. Suddenly, she lost one of her shoes and started yelling, "My shoe! Shoe! Shoe!" The she-camel heard her and stopped. She kneeled down and waited for the old woman.

Everyone stood there astonished, including the sultan who now believed she had some supernatural powers. The she-camel was then brought into the palace. When the *attoush* was carefully searched, they discovered inside the corpse of a sleeping beauty. The sultan asked his physicians to examine the body thoroughly. They noticed a strange ring stuck under her tongue. When they removed it, the beautiful woman uttered a scream like a newborn baby and started breathing. Gradually, she regained consciousness and opened her eyes. The sultan was struck by her extraordinary beauty and decided to marry her.

Naala the she-camel was taken inside the palace and taken care of. The slaves took Lalla away and gave her a good bath. The following day the sultan took her for his wife.

Days went by, but Lalla never forgot the seven ghoul brothers. Every day she went out and addressed her camel. "How are your feet?" she would ask. "Did you have a good rest?"

When the she-camel's feet had healed and she was ready for another journey, Lalla made her preparations secretly.

One very early morning the sultan had to go to the court for an urgent meeting. Lalla waited for a little while, then slipped away from her room. She took the *attoush,* fixed it on the camel's back, and settled herself in it. "Now don't answer anyone at all," she whispered to the camel.

They fled from the palace. When the soldiers saw her running like a shadow, they informed the sultan. He ordered them to chase her. They did their best, but it was impossible to catch up with her. They gave up and returned to the palace empty-handed. The she-camel went farther and farther without stopping, through deserts, valleys, rivers, and jungles, until she finally reached the territory of the ghouls.

The seven brothers were still in mourning, keeping themselves shut up inside their house. Then all of a sudden, as the camel approached, Lalla let out a loud cry. When they heard her, they sprang to their feet and went out to find the camel standing at their doorstep with the shiny *attoush.* Lalla looked out at them with a smile and waved her hands. They were all very happy. They welcomed her and made a great feast in her honor. Their dwelling became a paradise once again. They all gathered around her. "Now," they said, "never answer the door for anyone! Never go out! We cannot afford losing you again!"

BIBLIOGRAPHY

CREDITS

BIBLIOGRAPHY

INTRODUCTION

Abate, Michelle Ann. "'You Must Kill Her': The Fact and Fantasy of Filicide in 'Snow White.'" *Marvels & Tales* 26 (2012): 178–203.

Ames, Janet. "Snow White Revisited." *Ladies Home Journal*, August 1993, 92.

Anderson, Graham. *Fairytale in the Ancient World.* London: Routledge, 2000.

Bacchilega, Christina. "Cracking the Mirror: Three Revisions of 'Snow White.'" *boundary 2*, 16 (1988): 1–25.

———. "Fairy-Tale Adaptations and Economies of Desire." In *The Cambridge Companion to Fairy Tales*, edited by Maria Tatar, 79–96. Cambridge: Cambridge University Press, 2015.

———. *Fairy Tales Transformed? Twenty-First-Century Adaptations and the Politics of Wonder.* Detroit: Wayne State University Press, 2013.

———. *Postmodern Fairy Tales: Gender and Narrative Strategies.* Philadelphia: University of Pennsylvania Press, 1997.

Barzilai, Shuli. "Reading 'Snow White': The Mother's Story." *Signs* 15 (1990): 515–34.

Behlmer, Richard. "They Called It 'Disney's Folly': *Snow White and the Seven Dwarfs* (1937)." In *America's Favorite Movies: Behind the Scenes*, 40–60. New York: Frederick Ungar, 1982.

Bettelheim, Bruno. *The Uses of Enchantment: The Meaning and Importance of Fairy Tales.* New York: Vintage Books, 1976.

Bolte, Johannes, and Georg Polívka. "Sneewittchen." In *Anmerkungen zu den Kinder- und Hausmärchen der Brüder Grimm*, vol. 1, 450–64. Leipzig: Dieterich'sche Buchhandlung, 1913.

Bottigheimer, Ruth B. *Grimms' Bad Girls and Bold Boys: The Moral and Social Vision of the Tales.* New Haven, CT: Yale University Press, 1987.

Brewer, Derek. *Symbolic Stories: Traditional Narratives of the Family Drama in English Literature.* Cambridge, UK: D. S. Brewer, 1980.

Brusatin, Manlio. *History of Colors.* Boulder, CO: Shambhala, 1991.

Byatt, A. S. "Ice, Snow, Glass." In *Mirror, Mirror on the Wall: Women Writers Explore Their Favorite Fairy Tales,* edited by Kate Bernheimer, 64–84. New York: Anchor, 1998.

Canepa, Nancy, ed. *Teaching Fairy Tales.* Detroit: Wayne State University Press, 2019.

Chainani, Soman. "Sadeian Tragedy: The Politics of Content Revision in Angela Carter's 'Snow Child.'" *Marvels & Tales* 17 (2003): 212–35.

Cohen, Betsy. *The Snow White Syndrome: All about Envy.* New York: Macmillan, 1996.

Da Silva, Francisco Vaz. "Red as Blood, White as Snow, Black as Crow: Chromatic Symbolism of Womanhood in Fairy Tales." *Marvels & Tales* 21 (2007): 240–52.

Edwards, Carol. "The Fairy Tale 'Snow White.'" In *Making Connections across the Curriculum: Reading for Analysis,* 579–646. New York: St. Martin's, 1986.

Ellis, John M. *One Fairy Tale Too Many: The Brothers Grimm and Their Tales.* Chicago: University of Chicago Press, 1983.

Finlay, Victoria. *Color: A Natural History of the Palette.* New York: Random House, 2002.

Gilbert, Sandra M., and Susan Gubar. *The Madwoman in the Attic: The Woman Writer and the Nineteenth-Century Literary Imagination.* New Haven, CT: Yale University Press, 1979.

Girardot, N. J. "Initiation and Meaning in the Tale of Snow White and the Seven Dwarfs." *Journal of American Folklore* 90 (1977): 274–300.

———. "Response to Jones: 'Scholarship Is Never Just the Sum of All Its Variants.'" *Journal of American Folklore* 92 (1979): 73–76.

Goldenberg, David. "Racism, Color Symbolism, and Color Prejudice." In *The Origins of Racism in the West,* edited by Miriam Eliav-Feldon, Benjamin Isaac, and Joseph Ziegler, 88–108. Cambridge: Cambridge University Press, 2009.

Holliss, Richard, and Brian Sibley. *Walt Disney's "Snow White and the Seven Dwarfs" and the Making of the Classic Film.* New York: Simon and Schuster, 1987.

Hurley, Dorothy L. "Seeing White: Children of Color and the Disney Fairy Tale Princess." *Journal of Negro Education* 74 (2005): 221–32.

Jones, Christina A., and Jennifer Schacker, eds. *Marvelous Transformations: An Anthology of Fairy Tales and Contemporary Critical Perspectives.* Peterborough, ON: Broadview, 2013.

Jones, Steven Swann. *The New Comparative Method: Structural and Symbolic Analysis of the Allomotifs of "Snow White."* Helsinki: Academia Scientiarum Fennica, 1990.

———. "The Pitfalls of Snow White Scholarship." *Journal of American Folklore* 92 (1979): 69–73.

———. "The Structure of 'Snow White.'" In *Fairy Tales and Society: Illusion, Allusion, and Paradigm,* edited by Ruth B. Bottigheimer, 165–86. Philadelphia: University of Pennsylvania Press, 1986.

Joosen, Vanessa. "Disenchanting the Fairy Tale: Retellings of 'Snow White' between Magic and Realism." *Marvels & Tales* 21 (2007): 228–39.

———. "Feminist Criticism and the Fairy Tale: The Emancipation of 'Snow White' in Fairy-Tale Criticism and Fairy-Tale Retellings." *New Review of Children's Literature and Librarianship* 10 (2004): 5–14.

Kaufman, J. B. *Snow White and the Seven Dwarfs: The Art and Creation of Walt Disney's Animated Film.* San Francisco: Walt Disney Classic Museum, 2013.

Lüthi, Max. *The European Folktale: Form and Nature.* Bloomington: Indiana University Press, 1986.

Mollet, Tracey. "'With a Smile and a Song . . .': Walt Disney and the Birth of the American Fairy Tale." *Marvels & Tales* 27 (2013): 109–24.

Naithani, Sadhana. *The Story-Time of the British Empire: Colonial and Postcolonial Folkloristics.* Jackson, MS: University Press of Mississippi, 2010.

Newell, William Wells. *Games and Songs of American Children.* New York: Harper & Brothers, 1884.

Ricoeur, Paul. *The Symbolism of Evil.* Translated by Emerson Buchanan. New York: Harper and Row, 1967.

Ruf, Theodor. *Die Schöne aus dem Glassarg.* Würzburg: Königshausen and Neumann, 1995.

Scarry, Elaine. *On Beauty and Being Just.* Princeton, NJ: Princeton University Press, 2001.

Schanoes, Veronica L. "Book as Mirror, Mirror as Book: The Significance of the Looking-Glass in Contemporary Revisions of Fairy Tales." *Journal of the Fantastic in the Arts* 20 (2009): 5–23.

Schickel, Richard. *The Disney Version: The Life, Times, Art, and Commerce of Walt Disney.* New York: Simon and Schuster, 1968.

Schmidt, Sigrid. "*Snow White* in Africa." *Fabula* 49 (2008): 268–87.

Schmiesing, Ann. "Blackness in the Grimms' Fairy Tales." *Marvels & Tales* 30 (2016): 210–33.

Stephens, John, and Robyn McCallum. "Utopia, Dystopia, and Cultural Controversy in 'Ever After' and 'The Grimm Brothers' Snow White.'" *Marvels & Tales* 16 (2002): 201–13.

Tautz, Birgit. "A Fairy Tale Reality? Elfriede Jelinek's Snow White, Sleeping Beauty, and the Mythologization of Contemporary Society." *Women in German Yearbook* 24 (2008): 165–84.

Teverson, Andrew. *The Fairy Tale World.* London: Routledge, 2019.

Tolkien, J. R. R. "On Fairy Stories." In *The Tolkien Reader,* 2–84. New York: Ballantine, 1966.

Uther, Hans-Jörg. *The Types of International Folktales.* 3 vols. Helsinki: Suomalainen Tiedeakatemia, Academia Scientiarium Fennica, 2004.

Warner, Marina. *From the Beast to the Blonde: On Fairy Tales and Their Tellers.* London: Chatto and Windus, 1994.

———. *Once upon a Time: A Short History of Fairy Tale.* Oxford: Oxford University Press, 2016.

Whitley, David. *The Idea of Nature in Disney Animation from "Snow White" to "Wall-E."* Farnham, UK: Ashgate, 2008.

Zipes, Jack. *Breaking the Magic Spell: Radical Theories of Folk and Fairy Tales.* Austin: University of Texas Press, 1979.

———. *Don't Bet on the Prince: Contemporary Feminist Fairy Tales in North America and England.* New York: Routledge, 1989.

———. *The Enchanted Screen: The Unknown History of Fairy-Tale Films.* New York: Routledge, 2011.

RETELLINGS

Anholt, Laurence. *Snow White and the Seven Aliens.* Illustrated by Arthur Robins. New York: Orchard Books, 2002.

Barthelme, Donald. *Snow White.* New York: Atheneum, 1978.

BIBLIOGRAPHY

Bedford, Jacey. "Mirror, Mirror." In *Rotten Relations*, edited by Denise Little, 120–43. New York: DAW, 2004.

Block, Francesca Lia. *The Rose and the Beast: Fairy Tales Retold*. New York: Joanna Cotler Books, 2000.

Blumlein, Michael. "Snow in Dirt." In *Black Swan, White Raven*, edited by Ellen Datlow and Terri Windling, 21–55. New York: Avon, 1997.

Burkert, Nancy E., illus. *Snow-White and the Seven Dwarfs: A Tale from the Brothers Grimm*. Vancouver: Douglas and McIntyre, 1987.

Carter, Angela. "The Snow Child." In *The Bloody Chamber and Other Stories*, 91–92. New York: Penguin, 1979.

Coover, Robert. "The Dead Queen." *Quarterly Review of Literature* 8 (1973): 304–13.

Crone, Joni. "No White and the Seven Big Brothers." In *Rapunzel's Revenge: Fairytales for Feminists*, 50–56. Dublin: Attic, 1985.

Dahl, Roald. "Snow White and the Seven Dwarfs." In *Revolting Rhymes*, 11–17. New York: Knopf, 1982.

Doman, Regina. *Black as Night: A Fairy Tale Retold*. Bathgate, ND: Bethlehem Books, 2004.

Donoghue, Emma. "The Tale of the Apple." In *Kissing the Witch: Old Tales in New Skins*, 43–58. New York: HarperCollins, 1997.

French, Fiona. *Snow White in New York*. Oxford: Oxford University Press, 1986.

Gaiman, Neil. "Snow, Glass, Apples." In *Smoke and Mirrors*, 325–39. New York: Harper Perennial, 2001.

Galloway, Priscilla. "A Taste for Beauty." In *Truly Grimm Tales*, 97–106. Toronto: Lester, 1995.

Geras, Adèle. *Pictures of the Night*. London: Red Fox, 2002.

Gould, Steven. "The Session." In *The Armless Maiden and Other Tales for Childhood's Survivors*, edited by Terri Windling, 87–93. New York: Tor, 1995.

Hessel, Franz. "The Seventh Dwarf." In *Spells of Enchantment*, edited by Jack Zipes, 613–14. New York: Viking, 1991.

Hirsch, Connie. "Mirror on the Wall." *Science Fiction Age* 3 (March 1993): 59–61.

Hyman, Trina Schart, illus. *Snow White*. Translated by Paul Heins. Boston: Little, Brown, 1974.

Keillor, Garrison. "My Stepmother, Myself." *Atlantic*, March 1982.

Lee, Tanith. “Red as Blood.” In *Red as Blood, or Tales from the Sisters Grimmer,* 18–27. New York: DAW Books, 1983.

———. “Snow Drop.” In *Snow White, Blood Red,* edited by Ellen Datlow and Terri Windling, 105–29. New York: William Morrow, 1993.

———. *White as Snow.* New York: Tor Books, 2000.

Lynn, Tracy. *Snow.* New York: Simon Pulse, 2003.

Maher, Mary. “Hi, Ho, It’s Off to Strike We Go.” In *Rapunzel’s Revenge: Fairytales for Feminists,* 31–35. Dublin: Attic, 1985.

Murphy, Pat. “The True Story.” In *Black Swan, White Raven,* edited by Ellen Datlow and Terri Windling, 277–87. New York: Avon, 1997.

Neuhaus, Niele. *Snow White Must Die.* Translated by Steven T. Murray. London: Macmillan, 2013.

Poole, Josephine, and Angela Barrett, illus. *Snow White.* New York: Knopf, 1991.

Sexton, Anne. “Snow White and the Seven Dwarfs.” In *Transformations,* 3–9. Boston: Houghton Mifflin, 1971.

Sheerin, Róisin. “Snow White.” In *Cinderella on the Ball: Fairytales for Feminists,* 48–51. Dublin: Attic, 1991.

Stone, Kay. “Three Transformations of Snow White.” In *The Brothers Grimm and Folktale,* edited by James M. McGlathery, 52–65. Urbana: University of Illinois Press, 1991.

Vos, Gail de, and Anna E. Altmann. “Snow White.” In *New Tales for Old: Folktales as Literary Fictions for Young Adults,* 325–82. Englewood, CO: Libraries Unlimited, 1999.

Walker, Barbara G. “Snow Night.” In *Feminist Fairy Tales,* 19–25. San Francisco: HarperCollins, 1996.

Wenzel, David, and Douglas Wheeler. “Little Snow White.” In *Fairy Tales of the Brothers Grimm.* New York: Nantier, Beall and Minostchine, 1995.

Yolen, Jane. “Snow in Summer.” In *Black Heart, Ivory Bones,* edited by Ellen Datlow and Terri Windling, 90–96. New York: Avon, 2000.

———. *Snow in Winter.* New York: Puffin, 2011.

FILMS

Blancanieves. Directed by Pablo Berger. 2012.

Coal Black and de Sebben Dwarfs. Directed by Robert Clampett. 1943.

BIBLIOGRAPHY

Faerie Tale Theatre: Snow White and the Seven Dwarfs. Produced by Shelley Duvall. 1983.

Grimm's Snow White. Directed by Rachel Lee Goldenberg. 2012.

Happily N'Ever After. Directed by Paul J. Bolger and Yvette Kaplan. 2006.

Happily N'Ever After 2. Directed by Steven E. Gordon and Boyd Kirkland. 2009.

Little Snow White (The Legend of the Snow Child). Written by T. O. Eltonhead. 1914.

Mirror Mirror. Directed by Tarsem Singh. 2012.

Snow White. Directed by J. Searle Dawley. 1916.

Snow-White. Directed by Dave Fleischer. 1933.

Snow White and the Huntsman. Directed by Rupert Sanders. 2012.

Snow White and the Seven Dwarfs. Directed by David Hand. Walt Disney Productions, 1937.

Snow White and the Seven Perverts. Directed by Marcus Parker-Rhodes. 1973.

Snow White and the Three Stooges. Directed by Walter Lang. 1961.

Snow White: A Tale of Terror. Directed by Michael Cohn. 1997.

Snow White: The Fairest of Them All. Directed by Caroline Thompson. 2001.

Sydney White. Directed by Joe Nussbaum. 2007.

White as Snow. Directed by Anne Fontaine. 2019.

Willa: An American Snow White. Directed by Tom Davenport. 1997.

Credits

STORY CREDITS

"Little Snow White"

Source: Jacob Grimm and Wilhelm Grimm, "Sneewittchen," in *Kinder- und Hausmärchen,* 7th ed., vol. 1, 269–78 (1857; repr., Stuttgart: Reclam, 1984).

TRANSLATED BY MARIA TATAR.

"The Young Slave"

Source: Giambattista Basile, *The Pentamerone,* trans. Benedetto Croce (London: John Lane, The Bodley Head, 1925), 248–52. Originally written in the Neapolitan dialect and published in Naples in 1634 and 1636 by Ottavio Beltrano.

EDITED BY MARIA TATAR.

"The Death of the Seven Dwarfs"

Source: Ernst Ludwig Rochholz, *Schweizersagen aus dem Aargau,* vol. 1 (Aargau: H. R. Sauerländer, 1856), 312.

TRANSLATED BY MARIA TATAR.

"Maroula and the Mother of Eros"

Source: Bernhard Schmidt, ed., *Griechische Märchen, Sagen und Volkslieder* (Leipzig: Teubner, 1877), 110–12.

TRANSLATED BY MARIA TATAR.

"The Enchanted Stockings"

Source: Paul Sébillot, *Contes Populaires de la Haute-Bretagne* (Paris: G. Charpentier, 1880), 146–50.

TRANSLATED BY MARIA TATAR.

"Princess Aubergine"

Source: F. A. Steel and R. C. Temple, eds., *Wide-Awake Stories: A Collection of Tales Told by Little Children, between Sunset and Sunrise, in the Panjab and Kashmir* (Bombay: Education Society's Press, 1884), 79–88.

CREDITS

"Snow-White-Fire-Red"

Source: Thomas Frederick Crane, ed., *Italian Popular Tales* (Boston: Riverside, 1885), 72–76.

EDITED BY MARIA TATAR.

"The Magic Slippers"

Source: Henriqueta Monteiro, trans., *Tales of Old Lusitania from the Folk-Lore of Portugal* (London: Swan Sonnenschein, 1888), 136–43.

EDITED BY MARIA TATAR.

"The World's Most Beautiful Woman"

Source: W. Henry Jones and Lajos Kropf, ed. and trans., *The Folk-Tales of the Magyars* (London: Elliot Stock, 1889), 163–81.

EDITED BY MARIA TATAR.

"Silver-tree and Gold-tree"

Source: Joseph Jacobs, *Celtic Fairy Tales* (London: David Nutt, 1892), 88–92.

"King Peacock"

Source: Alcée Fortier, *Louisiana Folktales, in French Dialect and English Translation* (Boston: Houghton, Mifflin, 1895), 57–61.

"The Beautiful Daughter"

Source: Rev. Robert Hamill Nassau, *Fetichism* [*sic*] *in West Africa: Forty Years' Observation of Native Customs and Superstitions* (New York: Young People's Missionary Movement, 1904).

"The Mirror of Matsuyama"

Source: F. Hadland Davis, *Myths and Legends of Japan* (London: George G. Harrap, 1912), 196–98.

"The Girl and the Dog"

Source: Diedrich Westermann, *The Shilluk People: Their Language and Folklore* (Berlin: Dietrich Reimer, 1912), 205–10.

"The Unnatural Mother and the Girl with a Star on Her Forehead"

Source: Henri-Alexandre Junod, *The Life of a South African Tribe*, vol. 2 (New Hyde Park, NY: University Books, 1962), 266–69.

"The Hunter and His Sister"

Source: Kevin Stuart, Li Xuewei, and Shelear, eds., *China's Dagur Minority: Society, Shamanism, and Folklore* (Philadelphia: University of Pennsylvania, Department of Asian and Middle Eastern Studies, 1994), 136–38.

REPRINTED BY PERMISSION OF THE UNIVERSITY OF PENNSYLVANIA.

CREDITS

"The Witch's Daughter"
Source: Wolfram Eberhard, ed., *Chinese Fairy Tales and Folk Tales* (New York: Dutton, 1938), 38–49.
EDITED BY MARIA TATAR.

"Nourie Hadig"
Source: Susie Hoogasian-Villa, ed., *100 Armenian Tales and Their Folkloristic Relevance* (Detroit: Wayne State University Press, 1966), 84–91.
REPRINTED BY PERMISSION OF WAYNE STATE UNIVERSITY PRESS.

"Blanca Rosa and the Forty Thieves"
Source: Yolando Pino-Saavedra, ed., and Rockwell Gray, trans. *Folktales of Chile* (Chicago: University of Chicago Press, 1967), 145–49.
REPRINTED BY PERMISSION OF UNIVERSITY OF CHICAGO PRESS.

"The Wonder Child"
Source: Howard Schwartz and Barbara Rush, eds., *The Wonder Child* (New York: HarperCollins Children's Books, 1996), 1–7.
REPRINTED BY PERMISSION OF HOWARD SCHWARTZ.

"The Jealous Mother"
Source: Jilali El Koudia, ed., *Moroccan Folktales,* trans. Jilali El Koudia and Roger Allen (Syracuse, NY: Syracuse University Press, 2003), 53–63.
REPRINTED BY PERMISSION OF SYRACUSE UNIVERSITY PRESS.

ILLUSTRATION CREDITS

1. *Grimms Märchenschatz.* Illus. G. Tenggren. Berlin: Hermann Klemm, 1923. Image courtesy of Houghton Library, Harvard.
2. *Grimms Märchenschatz.* Illus. G. Tenggren. Berlin: Hermann Klemm, 1923. Image courtesy of Houghton Library, Harvard.
3. *The Red Fairy Book.* Ed. Andrew Lang. Illus. H. J. Ford and Lancelot Speed. London: Longmans, Green, 1890. Image courtesy of Houghton Library, Harvard.
4. *Kinder- und Hausmärchen gesammelt durch die Brüder Grimm.* Illus. Ludwig Emil Grimm. Berlin: G. Reimer, 1825. Image courtesy of Houghton Library, Harvard.
5. *Household Stories from the Collection of the Brothers Grimm.* Trans. Lucy Crane. Illus. Walter Crane. London: Macmillan, 1882. Image courtesy of Houghton Library, Harvard.
6. *Hansel and Gretel and Other Stories.* Illus. Kay Nielsen. London: Hodder and Stoughton, 1923. Image courtesy of Houghton Library, Harvard.

7. *European Folk and Fairy Tales.* Illus. John Dickson Batten. New York: Putnam, 1916. Image courtesy of Art Gallery of New South Wales.
8. *Told Again: Old Tales Told Again.* By Walter de la Mare. Illus. A(lice). H(elena). Watson. New York: Knopf, 1927. Reproduced from the author's collection.
9. *Grimm's Märchen.* Illus. Heinrich Lefler. Vienna: Munk, 1905. Reproduced from the author's collection.
10. Image courtesy of the Art Renewal Center.
11. *The Fairy Book: The Best Popular Fairy Stories.* Ed. Dinah Maria Mulock. Illus. Warwick Goble. London: Macmillan, 1913. Reproduced from the author's collection.
12. *A Treasury of Fairy Tales.* Ed. Michael Foss. London: Michael O'Mara Books. p. 131. Reproduced from the author's collection.
13. *Märchen-Strauß für Kind und Haus.* Berlin: Georg Stilke, 1882. Image courtesy of Houghton Library, Harvard.
14. *Fairy Tales.* Ed. Harry Golding. Illus. Margaret W. Tarrant. London: Ward, Lock, 1915. Reproduced from the author's collection.
15. Fine Arts Museum of San Francisco / Wikimedia Commons.
16. *The Anne Anderson Fairy Tales Book.* London: T. Nelson, 1923. Reproduced from the author's collection.
17. *Schneewittchen: Ein Märchen in Zwölf Bildern.* Illus. Lothar Meggendorfer. Stuttgart: Weise, 1910. childrenslibrary.org/Wikimedia Commons.
18. *A Child's Book of Stories.* Ed. Penrhyn W. Coussens. Illus. Jessie Willcox Smith. New York: Duffield, 1911. Reproduced from the author's collection.
19. *Hundert Illustrationen aus zwei Jahrhunderten zu Märchen der Brüder Grimm.* By Heinz Wegehaupt. Hanau: Verlag Werner Dausien. p. 24. Reproduced from the author's collection.
20. *Hundert Illustrationen aus zwei Jahrhunderten zu Märchen der Brüder Grimm.* By Heinz Wegehaupt. Hanau: Verlag Werner Dausien. p. 103. Reproduced from the author's collection.
21. The Queen / Witch, voiced by Lucille La Verne, in *Snow White and the Seven Dwarfs* (1937), directed by David Hand, © RKO Radio Pictures. Image provided by Photofest.
22. Kristen Stewart in *Snow White and the Huntsman* (2012), directed by Rupert Sanders, © Universal Pictures. Image provided by Photofest.
23. *Kinder- und Hausmärchen.* Illus. Hermann Vogel. Munich: Braun und Schneider, 1894. Reproduced from the author's collection.
24. © Mary Evans Picture Library / Peter & Dawn Cope Collection / age fotostock.

25. *The Fairy Tales of the Brothers Grimm.* Trans. Mrs. Edgar Lucas. Illus. Arthur Rackham. London: Constable, 1909. Image courtesy of Houghton Library, Harvard.
26. *My Book of Favourite Fairy Tales.* Illus. Jennie Harbour. London: Raphael Tuck and Sons, 1921. Reproduced from the author's collection.
27. *Folk Tales from Grimm.* Ed. Ethelyn Abbott. Illus. Dorothy Dulin. Chicago: A Flanagan, 1913. Reproduced from the author's collection.
28. *Fünfzig Kinder- und Hausmärchen.* Illus. Thekla Brauer. Leipzig: O. Spamer, 1900. Reproduced from the author's collection.
29. *Snow White and the Seven Dwarfs: A Fairy Tale Play Based on the Story of the Brothers Grimm.* By Jessie Braham White. Illus. Charles B. Falls. New York: Dodd, Mead, 1913. Reproduced from the author's collection.